NOSTOS

VOYAGE OF THE HEART'S RETURN

a novel by

DESPINA LALA-CRIST

translated from the Greek by
Robert Crist

*To my dear Dr. Macaluso,
with the great pleasure
of meeting him,*

Despina Lala Crist

Feb, '02

Seaburn Publishing Group
P.O. Box 2085
LI, City NY 11102

First published in the Greek language by Kedros
Translated by Robert Crist

Cover designed by Antonio Russo
Photo by Ray Henry

ISBN 1-885778-93-7

Printed in the United States of America

www.seaburn.com

ALSO BY THE AUTHOR

CHIILDREN'S STORIES
Mia Margarita *[A Daisy]*. *Athens: Kedros, 1980.*
Kapnos kai Vlacheies *[Smoking and Nonsense]*. *Athens: Kedros, 1981.*
H Istoria tis Tranoupolis kai ton Trelopoulaion *[The Story of a Great Town and Its Crazy Citizens]*. *Athens: Kastaniotis, 1984.*

YOUTH/ADULT NOVEL
Enas Mikros Theos Perissepse *[A Youthful, Superflous God]*. *Athens: Kedros, 1999.*

CRITICISM
Sto Kaleidoskopio tou Giorgo Heimona *[In the Kaleidoscope of Giorgos Heimonas]*.
Athens: Kastaniotis, 1984.

SHORT STORIES
Pairno Ampariza kai Vgaino *[Ready or Not, Here I Come]*. *Athens: SynchroniEpochi, 1981.*

NOVELS
Nostos. *Athens: Kedros, 1992.*
Ta Apomeinaria tou Theou *[The Remnants of God]*. *Athens: Kastaniotis, 1997.*

Dedicated to the memory of those
Who handed down to me the blessing
of this testament of anguish and passion
for life—my mother, father, brother, and
my aunt, the nun, Xeni . . .

PART ONE

"The fury of time has marked my flesh," the old woman groaned. "The terrors of time have torn my soul. Stormy years have swept me to this barren place. Nothing is real—neither life nor death. I'm exhausted, Maryo.* Close to a century on this earth, I haven't learned how to live—only how to live on!"

Maryo felt her mother's heartache. She shared the anguish of the aged woman who was lying tensely in bed.

"Life is merciless!" the old woman moaned. "My body is worthless. My senses are wrecked. My finger tips are torn by the roughness of the world. Bitter decades have numbed my tongue. Nothing is welcome to my eyes. My sight is filled with monstrous images.

"I can't endure anything I hear. My ears battered by waves of terror. And memory offers no comfort, Maryo. There is a heavy curtain covering the past. Whatever shows through its worn gaps is distorted, unreal. Help me, Maryo! I see nothing but horrors. I can't grasp the past or understand what is to come!"

The old woman was shuddering, and Maryo tried to soothe her, tucking pillows under her back.

"Look at me!" the old woman sighed. "Is this a human body? I am all twisted and shrunk! See how my belly has collapsed. My thighs have withered, and my legs are sticks. My spine is bent, my buttocks have shriveled! Sometimes, I could swear that I have grown a tail!"

"There, there, mother! Mother, dear!" Maryo soothed, but the voice burst out once more.

"If only my soul would let me rest! The soul, daughter, is a savage thing that lies in wait. Insidiously, relentlessly, it strikes!"

Maryo caressed her gently. She stroked her pure white hair, as the old woman plunged on.

"A long life of trials, Maryo, is filled with violations. I broke all the rules. The commandments that were given and the commandments I made, I broke them all. Trespasses, my daughter, enrich while they impoverish

*For explanations of various names and terms, see Glossary.

life. My acts poured into me and infected me down to my guts; they rotted my life. My life! An awful journey of endless torment. Time! Raging time and nothing but the fears it brought."

The old woman's eyes gaped in terror.

"From the beginning I was surrounded by things I feared. And my fears were justified!

"My greatest fear was God. 'God loves us all,' my sister, the nun, told me. To me God was my terror; stealthily, fiercely, he pursued me. And I fled off the track to avoid his fierce eye. I got away! I left him behind, far behind, but then came the other fears, the worldly ones. They, too, tormented my soul. They ravaged my body. The fear of war and rape. The fear of birth and death. The fear of people and loneliness. But the most savage of all fears is the one I am living now. The fear of bitter memories."

In tears Maryo caressed the thin white hair. She was shaken by her mother's anguish and by her own incapacity to bring relief. *If only I could transform my mother's memories!* she thought, caressing gently.

The old woman continued to mumble laments. She recalled event after event She trembled before an endless painful spectacle, but finally Maryo administered the drug of forgetfulness, and the two of them, mother and daughter, fell into deep sleep.

Maryo heard the postman's bell from the street in front of her house. Her heart filled with yearning. The sweetness of expectation filled her, overflowed, choked her. How long it's been since I've heard from him— oh, how long! *she thought. She jumped to her feet and dashed down the marble staircase. Her soles did not touch the stairs; her toes just brushed the surface and her body flew through the air. Her nightgown and hair fluttered behind her as she flew out through the doorway.*

The postman was waiting for her. His uniform was sparkling white and his smile gleamed against his smooth black skin. His eyes smiled as did his voice with the rich accent of southern blacks, the tone smooth, a jazz melody.

He extended the letter and she reached out with both hands. She stretched and stretched to take the envelope as she watched the children who were clamoring at the side of the white van. It was the van of the Good Humor man, the ice cream vendor, and the children were piping their requests. Her children were among them. Small children, very small.

"Vanilla! Strawberry! Chocolate!" they sang.

The letter fell heavily into her hands; with bent back and straining arms she dragged her feet toward the steps. The steps loomed before her eyes, a height she despaired to climb.

Maryo crawled, she wormed her body up each stair, mounting with clinging arms and legs. Struggling, she kicked at her nightgown, which was entangled around her legs. Perspiring, she labored upward. Midway on the stairway she stopped. Her feet dangling, with trembling fingers she tore the wrapping off the small package. Inside were layers of transparent plastic with cells like a beehive, and there she found his words. Within the cells were all the words. Small, round, chocolate-covered. With the thumb and forefinger of her right hand, Maryo extracted each one. With deep emotion and nostalgia she took them and popped them into her mouth.

She was jolted awake. Her mother's moaning clashed with her feelings. The sweetness in her mouth faded; it gave way to bitterness.

"What is it, mana? What can I do?" Her voice trembled. "This could be the end!" The thought flashed sharply as the old woman screamed.

"Maryo-o-o-o-o-o-o-o!" The room shook. "Maryo-o-o-o-o-o!"

"I'm here, mana! What is it?"

The old woman's eyes opened wide; with enormous effort she raised herself on her elbows.

"Maryo, save me. Death will never take me."

Shaken, Maryo soothed her quietly.

"Don't say such a thing, mother. No one's life goes on forever."

"I know very well what I'm saying!" The old woman's voice intensified. "Death will not come to me. I know it in my bones. How can I make you understand? I can't die. The mind—that, my child, keeps me alive. My mind refuses to give the command. The command to die. My mind is enraged. It needs to know before it commands the soul to leave the body.... so I can die, rest, and find peace.... Help me, Maryo! Help me I beg of you!"

"But what can I do, mana?"

"Satisfy my mind! Help me know, kori mou!"

"To know? Know what? Calm yourself, mana."

The old woman's disturbance intensified. She braced herself, sat up unsteadily, and looked deep into her daughter's eyes. Abruptly she revived. Suddenly her body regained its powers. She seized her daughter by the shoulders and gazed a long time weighing her mettle and the strength of her spirit. Slowly, deliberately, she commanded:

"Go back, Maryo! Travel back in time. Return to the beginning. See and understand. When you have understood it all, come back and tell me the secret."

"What secret, mana? What secret?"

"The secret of my life. What did I experience? Did I live or dream? Was it real or only a moment's nightmare?"

She leaned very close to Maryo, brought her lips to her ear, and cried: "Did I live? Why did I live? Why did I exist at all?"

Stunned, Maryo stared at her mother.

"And what about me? Do I live? Why do I live?" Burning hot, the words seared her mind.

"Return!" her mother insisted. "Take the ship of time. Travel back through the years, kori mou, and bring me the secret." Maryo's mother whispered calmly now; she sank back on the mattress and fell silent.

"You're late!" The man glared at Maryo.

"Late? What do you mean?" she protested.

"The ship has gone," he declared. He handed her an envelope.

"Everything is here. Tickets, passport, foreign currency, addresses. Everything you need. But the vessel has weighed anchor. It has left! It is gone!" he shouted hysterically.

She gazed toward the open sea. The ship under way was a huge, white, misty silhouette. With slow stateliness it was traversing the harbor. A channel of foam marked its path, and a thin line of smoke. The sun bent low and blushed, ready to touch the water.

"The ship makes a stop at the warehouse," a porter threw in as he passed nearby.

"Where is the warehouse?" she was about to ask but didn't have time.

"On the east side of the harbor-or-or-or-or!" someone shouted.

"So, you see, I wasn't la...," she said, breaking off.

She didn't want to say that word. She hated words that freeze time. Words like *yesterday. . . today . . . before . . . after* break life into fragments.

"I will board at the warehouse," she said with determination. "I will take that ship for the voyage back."

With the envelope clenched in her fist, she began to run, but she was blocked at once. The walkway, the wide passageway leading to the warehouse, was clogged with porters.

"Pardon me, pardon me. Let me through."

She gently made her way along, touching backs and shoulders. She felt hard muscular flesh baked by the sun, drenched in sweat, glued to the bone. The porters' arms were sinewy, bony extensions of the carts they were pushing. Their tanned heads were crowned with neatly combed and oiled hair. Dozens of porters packed the road, and Maryo was struck by their sameness. They all seemed to be cut from the same cloth, and Maryo moved among them choked by the stench of their sweat and their breath, sour with cheap wine drunk on empty stomachs. Hastening to pass the crowd of workmen, Maryo jumped onto a cart. The porter did not object, and she hopped from cart to cart on one side or the other and thus made her way forward, arms stretched out left and right to maintain her balance. She had dropped the envelope on the first cart, but she hurried on toward her destination. Now the road turned and suddenly grew steep.

Maryo watched the men strain. The veins on their necks stood out as they labored up the incline. Muscles bulged and large beads of sweat formed on their faces and bare chests, gleaming like tears before they broke and rolled off.

At the top of the rise Maryo hopped off the cart and took the first turn. It was a narrow alley, a dead end that descended into the area behind the warehouse. Now she could hear the shouts of the stevedores who were loading the ship's hold.

"Lower away-y-y-y-y-y! You, there, lower away-y-y-y-y-y-y!"

She breathed a sigh of relief, for the ship was still being readied for the voyage.

"I will make it aboard after all!" she assured herself.

She hastened to find the rear entrance to the warehouse. Extremely high, the wall cast a dense shadow over the whole area. Maryo felt along its surface with both hands, probing for the hollow that would mark the doorway.

The wall was crudely constructed. Some areas were built of brick and others of large, irregular stones. Portions of the surface were of sheet metal or cement, which solidly resisted the pounding of her fists.

She searched, she desperately searched, to find the opening.

The stevedores were still at work.

"Lift her u-u-u-u-u-p! Let her do-o-o-o-wn! Sto-o-o-o-o-p!" they thundered.

Maryo rushed back and forth pounding frantically on the wall that blocked her way to the ship. She feared that any moment the loading would be completed, that the workers' shouts would abruptly cease, the ship would sound a departing blast, and she would still face that awful wall. Her arms ached as she dragged her palms over the rough surface. Her fingertips blistered and bled. Tears of frustration filled her eyes, but her right hand finally struck a symmetrical hollow. She sighed with relief. It was a door frame, though it was narrower than usual, reaching to just a couple of inches above her head.

"The door—at last!" she smiled and began to shove, but the panel did not budge.

She took a run and hit the surface as powerfully as she could with her shoulders. She threw her body against it and beat on it with her fists. The blows fell heavily as sledgehammers; the door began to loosen and to grate with each stroke. Now there was a crack of around an inch at the edge of the panel, which was a worn plywood board fastened to the bricks with rusty nails.

"A good thing they didn't use sheet metal like they have in shipyards," Maryo thought as her last stroke detached the board, which slammed to the floor in a cloud of dust. She stepped across, lifted the panel and pushed in back into position. All the nails slid neatly into their grooves.

The warehouse was enormous. A single dim bulb, spotted with fly droppings, was the sole lighting. Through the wide, open doors in the wall opposite her, Maryo saw the vast white hull of the vessel. She remained still for a moment, her eyes adjusting to the semi-darkness. The warehouse was full of containers, massive wooden cases stacked in rows almost touching the ceiling. At the end of the aisle stretching before her, Maryo saw a figure.

It was a handsome young fellow with curly black hair and a thick sheaf of papers under his arm.

"He must be the dock foreman, who will help me go aboard," thought Maryo, moving in his direction. Then she paused, observing him closely. A pencil stub just showed in the thick hair by his left ear. The man raised his right hand, took the pencil, licked the point, and made an X on the boxes loaded by the stevedores. Then he leafed through his papers, checked off the items, and replaced the pencil behind his left ear. Maryo was stunned. The automatic movement of the right hand sticking the pencil behind the left ear pierced her memory. Looking at that young man, she reached inside herself to a precise spot amidst millions of stored images.

Her mother was leading her by the hand. She was a little girl, a very young child, with a white ribbon in her hair, and they were moving through a large grocery store in Athens. Uncle Giorgis was in charge of the storeroom. Moving to and fro between rows of sacks, large burlap sacks of supplies, he was holding a batch of papers and a pencil. Uncle Giorgis would lick the pencil point, make a small X on his papers, and stick the pencil behind his left ear. He would put hard candies in Maryo's pocket and give her two big chocolate bars, one for her and one for her brother.

"Uncle dear. . ." Her voice was low and hesitant. She was surprised by her childlike voice and by the strong feelings awakened within her. She felt again that deep love she had for her uncle. When he visited their home, her heart would glow with love.

Not long after the December demonstrations, when government soldiers fired on the crowd, he showed up in disguise. In the kitchen her mother was cooking—many dishes as they were prepared in the old country, and the house was filled with sweet aromas redolent with memory and nostalgia. Her brother and she were out in the street, waiting on the corner for the arrival of her uncle, whose swinging stride marked the step of the partisan fighter he was. They were waiting to meet him outside so they could run home and announce his arrival to their mother and to Uncle Giorgis's sister, who always inquired, "Has the 'kid' showed up?" His sister always called him the 'kid.' That day they waited a long while, returned sadly thinking he might not appear, and entered the house to find Uncle Giorgis settled in the best chair. His hair was blond now, his mustache bronze.

"The dye did something weird there," he said laughing.

He kept repeating that phrase, "something weird," roaring with laughter as his sister punched him lightly on the shoulder, saying, "Good thing mother is dead. Think how she would worry if she saw you now."

Oh, how much Maryo loved her uncle, who would give her and her brother a big hug, exactly as he did now, laughing. "Maria, Maraki, Maryo! Which beautiful name should I choose?" he asked again after so many years.

Maryo felt herself blush. "Just choose your favorite name, Uncle dear. It's all the same to me," she said.

As she gazed at him, she could see her father bringing the red wine to the table. He brought the wine in their large pitcher, sat down, and tapped with his agile fingers on the bottom of a pan. Her father drummed rhythmically, beaming with pleasure, and her mother, her figure erect and her long black hair gathered in a bun, came and went from the kitchen bringing the food. Her uncle baptized himself with wine; he poured wine on his hair. Good lord, he drenched his hair with wine and bellowed with laughter as they all sang in hushed voices. They sang prohibited partisan songs. It was dark outside, the windows shut, the door barred, and they sang.

"Softer, softer," they giggled.

They laughed again and again, and Maryo grew tired, became drowsy, and dozed in her chair. She felt her father's strong arms lift her and carry her to her bed as she wriggled in refusal, on the verge of tears, not wanting to sleep yet, but being drawn down helplessly into slumber, while at a distance they continued their songs and their talk of childhood, of the old country, endless tales of the old country of Asia Minor. And then to wake up in the morning and find they were all gone! Her heart felt empty because she had not stayed up till the end of the party. Why could she not have stayed awake till the very end? How could she have missed even a moment?

A sweet pain pierced her bosom and she wondered: where had all those childhood images been stored? Where had they lodged, retaining all the colors, the touch of things, the smells and that feeling of longing, heartache, and love?

"What brings you here?" she heard her uncle ask. "Where are you going?"

"I'm traveling back through time," she answered in a voice that was hers, her present voice.

"I knew it the moment I saw you!" he said. He gazed with yearning at the ship. "I'd like to come, too. I want so much to come along!" He sighed. "But I can't. It's impossible! It's too late now!"

The crane whined bitterly above their heads, and the loading net dropped at their feet.

"Well, now," he said, "off you go!"

He helped her step into the net. The sack of the net tightened under her arms, and Maryo stood gripping the cable. Uncle Giorgis whistled, and with a jerk the boom began its slow ascent. From up high she surveyed the panorama, the vast spread of the sea and the sun sinking on the horizon. As she looked down at her uncle far below, a thought suddenly popped into her mind. She bent over and urgently called:

"Uncle, dear, we heard that you were killed. We were told you were hit by gunfire in the mountains of Crete."

Uncle Giorgis laughed. The sound echoed hollowly on the apron of the dock. The voice had a powerful yet dying sound; it seemed to be dripping blood.

"Yes, Maria, Maraki, Maryo. You heard right. Look. Look here."

He jerked his shirt from beneath his belt and lifted it up. The flap of skin over his belly, stuck to his shirt, was also lifted. Snakes and eels, his guts sprang out of their warm coils. They sprang out; tangled and steaming they spilled onto the dock. They wriggled on the tiles; they wriggled furiously and spasmodically, and Maryo shuddered, trembled and closed her eyes. Never had she seen live black guts spill from bowels and flip like fish on the bottom of a wind-tossed boat.

She kept her eyes shut tight, but the voice, the words, and the images pierced her eyelids. She could see; she could see everything. She heard; she could hear everything.

Her uncle was shouting: "One of our own men-n-n-n-n-n machined gunn-n-n-n-n-ned me by mista-a-a-a-a-ke."

The dock was filled with ricocheting consonants and vowels. Maryo, bent beneath the weight of the syllables, grew heavy and collapsed into the net, her eyes still on her uncle. Suddenly she realized he was beginning to shrink. He was shrinking before her very eyes. That tall man was shrinking! He shrank to a minuscule spot, a spot of blood that dried and blackened at the center of the dock.

It got dark. Abruptly it was dark, black as pitch. Someone must have switched off the warehouse light, or had it burned out? Maryo hovered in the midst of emptiness. The boom continued to rise then jerked to a halt. She was suspended between the sky and the deep black ocean. Then there was a sudden grating turn and an even more sudden drop. A slight spasm, an abrupt movement, and the boom began to lower her into the depths of the hold. She had time to glimpse a flash of light. There was a flash somewhere in the distance the moment she was swallowed by the hold. The image shattered and its fragments dissolved in the darkness that boiled in the ship's belly.

A storm broke and lasted nine days and nine nights. The ship kept going on and off course. It zigzagged steadily toward its destination. God flashed in the sky. He tore his chaos with lightning and thunder. Mountains of water buffeted the ship. The roar could have awakened the dead, but Maryo lay motionless, uninvolved, as if she did not exist.

On the ninth day the swells fell calm and nudged the ship to the shore. The vessel entered the harbor and docked at the island of Chios.

Barbaric fury had battered these shores. There was a great upheaval on the continent opposite the island. Suffering throngs had come to the island. In anguish, they crowded the beaches, the squares, the side streets. The bitter smell of gall spread through the air.

Maryo's spirit was stricken. Her soul tore and bled before that throng. She felt intense pain. Her body ached from the pain of her people's expulsion from their homeland. It was as if she herself were a refugee. Her eyes were opened to the horrors of their fate, and she felt the shame of it penetrate her body. It was useless to tell herself repeatedly that all this was in the past, that this was the purge of 1922, which took place long before her birth. The refugees flooded into the port. Boats arrived packed with human bodies, bundles, and misery. Maryo lost heart; she regretted having come. She tried to turn away from all that agony. *Anyway*, she thought, *I could never find my mother's family*, but that instant she caught sight of Aunt Malama. She was seated at the end of the mole on a bundle of clothes, weeping because she could not find her mother.

"Your mother will be coming," Maryo shouted to her from a distance, pushing her way through the crowd toward her aunt. "Yes, here she is now!" she cried.

She felt a surge of unexpected joy, for her Grandmother Sgourafenia was coming toward her, pulled along by Maryo's father! It was Asimakis! He was as yet a youth the age of Maryo's own son, or even younger. An infantry volunteer, he was wearing a uniform including tunic, knickers, and leggings. His boots seemed too large and heavy for his slim feet. He tramped heavily toward Malama, drawing his mother along, who kept chanting,

"Kyrie, eleison. . . Kyrie eleison. . . Lord have mercy on us."

"Giagia! Giagia!" Maryo pitched her voice above the murmur of the crowd. "Don't be afraid, giagia, your time has not come. You are safe. Nothing will happen to you—nothing worse than what you feel this moment."

She strove to reach them. There was something she wanted to tell them, something she wanted to offer, but above all she wanted to reach her father. She stretched her arms, pushing nearer and nearer, and her fingertips almost touched him, but she just missed, blocked by two soldiers who were hurrying along the mole. Yet he was near enough for her to hear his breathing, which was quick and heavy as he now took the two of them, his mother and sister, in tow, and led them along, the bundle of clothing tossed over his shoulder.

Maryo stopped to watch them as they pressed their way through the crowd. They approached the large vessel anchored by the mole, and Maryo observed them carefully mount the gangplank, locate a place on the deck, arrange their possessions and find a spot to stand by the rail. Lighting a cigarette, Asimakis gazed down across the chaotic waterfront, and Maryo waved with both hands. She waved anxiously, calling,

"God be with you, father-er-er-er! God be with you-ou-ou-ou-ou-ou-ou!"

The syllables were scattered in the hullabaloo, but she continued to call. The water by the mole churned; and, saddened, Maryo heard the ship give a parting signal on its fog-horn. The ship sailed from Chios, bound for

Piraeus. "I wish they would hear me; I wish they would see me!" Maryo said to herself again and again.

Thick fog drifted in from the pelagos, swallowing the ship and filling the harbor. Maryo hurried. It was time to find her mother and her family. They were not on the mole. Where could she find them? She let her feelings guide her. Leaving the port, she turned from street to street and began to run. She found herself on the beach west of the town. She proceeded slowly as her feet sank into the sand and her body grew heavy. The sun was setting; she feared that darkness would close in before she found her mother.

She caught sight of the group in the distance—it was a black mass sunk in the sand. They reminded her of a very old photograph, and she was surprised she could recognize them. Perhaps she knew them from the agitation in her heart, which threatened to explode from its rapid, powerful throbbing. Trembling, she was moved to tears and wanted to shout, "I've come, mana—I've come!" Her legs were sinking almost to the knees in the fine, deep sand as she struggled toward them. They were all there on the beach; one would think that they were waiting for her. First she made out the figure of her mother. She was seated on the sand, a girl in her early twenties. Her dark gaze scrutinized the surrounding area, and her back was tensed in anger. Around her were her sisters and brothers, the ones that had survived. Her two younger brothers were there: Liapis, around fifteen, and Nikolos, twenty, in uniform, standing in leaden silence. Garoufalo, too, who was around twenty-five, slumped on the shore, her cheeks streaked with tears and black circles under her swollen eyes. The elder brother, Constantis, had thrown himself down, his face plunged into the sand, which greedily swallowed him. It almost covered his broken, half-naked body. Sleeping at his feet was Giannakos, his father, Maryo's grandfather. He slept like a small child, his hands pressed between his thighs, while Maryo's giagia, Despinyo, was on her feet scanning the coastline opposite.

Giagia was right in the middle of the group. Her feet were planted solidly and her gaze raked the distant shore. Her angry thin body threw off sparks, as her vision penetrated her ravaged homeland. She was seeking her cherished boy, her first-born son, Antonios.

Her fingers were tongs, black tongs that probed the rubble of the village. Her eyes pierced walls, penetrated storerooms, sought obscure lanes. Despinyo was searching. Breathless, frenzied, she was searching. She was barefooted. The soles of her feet were blistered and cut, but she ran; she had no time to lose. She ran up and down the village, in and out of the fields.

"I will find him, I will find him!" Despinyo vowed. "I will find my first born! "

Immersed in the search, she was oblivious to the pleas of the children there on the beach.

"Let's go, mana! Let's go! We've been here three days. Please, let's go to the convent."

Despinyo's feet were planted in the sand as her whole spirit frantically scoured the opposite shore. She searched in the churches, she checked the school, she bent under the bridge between the upper and the lower village. She combed their fields, the cabin at Pounda, and even the shed at Pyrgi, but her boy was not to be found—the newlywed lad, her sweet son Antonios, whom they called "Zacharenio." Breathless, Despinyo halted. She couldn't bear to take the road to Smyrni, but take it she must. She shut her eyes and went on. Black was the darkness before her eyes and in her soul when she came upon the procession. It was a bleak line of men, a ragged file that dragged itself along, weary and bowed, toward Smyrni. Near the ravine, an hour's walk from the village and not far from the city, Despinyo saw and recognized the men. They were the strong young men of the village, all with eyes cast down upon that black road, and she, trembling, took each one of them by the chin, lifted his head and looked him in the eyes. She sadly hugged her sister's eldest son, the mute, Nikolos. She saw Tsortsis, the school teacher, and Father Vagelis." Thrice-damned priest!" she whispered to him. "Your neck is still swollen from the scratches of revenge you earned!" Yet she could find some forgiveness for him in her heart and passed swiftly along the line, taking each man by the chin, gazing into every face. Then there, in the midst of those broken souls....

Southwind roared, northwind whistled, her body trembled, her heart shattered. A horrible shadow, the figure of her boy. Her shy boy, her first son Antonios, naked. Naked, with open palms he shielded his shame. Çer newly wed boy hid his shame and dragged along, alone in the midst of many. His whole being was smothered in a blanket of fear.

Like the figure of fear itself, he walked with head bowed. His mother took him roughly by the chin and lifted his head, but he perceived nothing. He only felt for an instant a hot blast of air across his cheeks and eyes. Her breast heaving, his mother cried out, "Antoni, yeh mou, take heart! Death demands spirit just as life does. Look death in the eye. My beloved son, live your death!"

But for her son all was lost. Terror had obliterated life and death. He was oblivious to his mother's presence. Her touch did not exist for him; her tear drops did not touch his cheeks. He did not feel her voice in his soul, nor did he feel the bullets that riddled his body. Thus totally cancelled his body was tossed along with the other bodies into the ravine near Smyrni. Throughout the area the Turks, the victors, were ravaging their prisoners.

Hearing the executioners' gunfire, Despinyo slumped to the sand. The shots shattered her ears, her body, her mind, her heart. Planted upright on the sands of Chios beach, three days erect and without food, three days deaf to all sounds—with the sound of that gunfire, she crumbled and released a piercing scream, "Antoni-i-i-i-i-i, child of my womb, flesh of my flesh!"

Constantis sank deeper in the sand, and Giannakos rose, the voice of his son echoing in his ears.

"He came to me in my sleep. My son came to me in my sleep," his words emerged with sobs. "My brave boy was crying and telling me again and again, 'Forgive me, father, for not obeying you.' That was what Antonios said."

Giannakos fell, his body broken, beside Despinyo. Garoufalo instantly broke into a lament and the brothers sprang to their feet. Their eyes flashed fire toward the mainland and their muscles strained in rage. Panagiota, Maryo's mother, stood up. Her vision alone was clear.

"Hurry, everyone! We must prepare to leave."

Like a sharp blade her voice sliced through the air and touched Maryo. Swiftly Panagiota spread a blanket by her mother's side.

"Antonis is gone," she said. "We must save mother."

The sons gently lifted Despinyo onto the blanket.

"Father," Panagiota continued, "this is no time for tears. We will mourn later. On your feet! You, too, Garoufalo! We are going to the convent."

A dark procession, they slowly dragged themselves forward and merged with the darkness. They were going to Aghia Skepi where they were expected by the eldest daughter, the nun Maria, whose name in the Lord was Theochtisti.

"She will relieve their great pain for a time," Maryo whispered.

It was Maria's nature to replace bitterness with sweetness. She was the blessed daughter, a gift from the deity. With both hands Maryo pushed time forward, far forward, and her children appeared before her. *My two blessings*, she thought, choked by nostalgia, and a wild yearning for her own time and her own children.

"My children," she breathed. "My children, my milk-white doves."

Darkness seemed to fall with bitter heaviness. Maryo could see nothing in the blackness. No light glimmered, not a single star. Only darkness, a thick blackness, blanketed the sea, and silence. Only the breathing of the sea could be heard, and grains of coarse black sand pricked Maryo the length of her body. The figure of Constantis was a narrow ridge in the sand; by his side, Maryo rested her hand on his shoulder.

Constantis was the second son, her mother's brother, who was around thirty. He was serving in the infantry, and during the panic of the retreat he arrived in the village to help his family. As a volunteer he had come from a land below the equator to defend his homeland. He had lived many years in Brazil, and at the small local Greek ouzeri word reached him that Greece was at war. Someone said that the Greek troops had reached Ankara, and Constantis feared he would not have time to join the cause. Thus, he rushed from the ouzeri to the harbor and took the first ship for the homeland.

So, he fought. He served in the depths of Anatolia, and when the awful time of retreat arrived he rushed to his home village of Alatsata with his heart in his mouth.

"Quickly, everyone!" he warned his family and the other villagers. "We've got to get out of here right now! A nightmare is coming!"

Constantis screamed till he was hoarse but no one listened.

Maryo felt her hand sinking with her uncle's shoulder as his form slipped deeper into the sand. He sank deeper and deeper and she felt his great pain. What anguish she felt for Uncle Constantis! Perhaps even greater pain than she felt for Uncle Antonios, who lost his life. Her soul ached for Constantis even more than for his mother, Giagia Despinyo, whose guts were corroded by the pain of her son's loss. *With time death appears unreal*, she thought. *It's just another human event shrouded in mystery. Its pain subsides.* Keen as a razor the memory of her brother slashed through her mind in refutation. *Yet it is covered*, the thought continued, *the pain of death is covered by the movement of life. Death comes to seem unreal. Sin, however—that is real. Nothing can cover that over. It leaves a deep wound in the human soul.*

She leaned down to her uncle.

"Constanti-i-i-i-i!" she whispered, "I want us to return. I want us both to go back. I want to see what you did which cost you so dearly. I want to witness your acts before you arrived in Chios. For every act is performed in common. All acts are shared human experience. And sin is passed on from generation to generation. Guilt enters us and demands absolution."

Now it was a caique that bore Maryo back through the week preceding her arrival in Chios. She set foot on the shores of Asia Minor at the peak of the catastrophe. It was the height of the purge; it was the summit of fear. The moment she arrived at Chesme, she was plunged into despair. *These hours were allotted to the people of this generation. Why should I, too, live through them?* she wondered. Tears of self-pity came into her eyes. She was ashamed of her thoughts. *We share all human experiences. I must see these things from up close and live these feelings of shame and despair. From up close I will touch the degradation of the triumphant and the defeated. Human actions are degraded in time of war—despicable the hero, wretched the victim.*

It was 1922. Ragged and harried, the Greeks were leaving the sacred soil behind. On horseback the Turks were bringing the Great Father of their nation into being. The Great Reformer ravaged and flayed people alive. *The Fathers—the Patriarchs of the Nations—their icons are built on blood*, Maryo thought, wiping away tears of rage with the back of her hand.

Maryo's father, a clean shaven lad, was an infantry volunteer. The handsomest young soldier in the midst of this troubled crowd at Chesme harbor, he was seeking his mother. Maryo's father had thick black hair, a head of curls like her brother's. His face was round and in the center was a little smile. It was a mischievous, gratuitous little smile, which led nowhere at all. It popped onto his face at the most inopportune moments and defied all his efforts to suppress it. When it disappeared, it fled of its own accord and left his countenance completely transformed. His eyes would narrow and a remote thoughtful expression would be etched on his face, that, too, leading nowhere at all.

At the age of eighty, Maryo's father struggled for months with illness and slipped into a coma. Maryo protested:"Not yet, father, not yet!" She gripped him by the shoulders. "Your time hasn't come; the doctor gives you another month at least."

Maryo shook her father and when he came to, he came to with that little smile on his face.

"Maryo! Maryo! Can you imagine it?" His eyes were filled with sparklers. "I was in the victory parade at Smyrni. Our captain led the ranks. He was so tall! Mounted on his mare, his head would touch our ceiling. I was just behind him with Manolios Koutsoubesis and Mitros Lebesis on either side of me.

"What did it feel like, Maryo? I can't describe it. Never had I thought I could be so happy. My chest was bursting with pride. What joy, Maryo!

What joy! The regimental band was right behind us playing a march...".

"Sometimes army bands are awful," said Maryo's husband, who knew about music. "All too often they're really bad!" he insisted, but Maryo was enthralled by this band.

The band was playing and the captain, back erect and head high, rode ahead, his company behind him, and in that company was Maryo's father, his gun on his shoulder and by his side two friends, Manolios and Mitros, and that little smile was on his face, the band blasting with pride, the drums pounding, and Maryo was the first to see a small black steel sphere no larger than a pear drop from the balcony of a two-story house, with a brief flash, a slight flash that dissolved in the sunset, the small explosion lost in the sound of the march. Maryo saw the captain's right arm separate from his shoulder, together with the sleeve and insignia, the lifeless arm falling to the asphalt on one side of the horse, and the captain without his right arm losing balance and falling on the other side, suddenly toppling lop-sided from his saddle and falling to the left side. Maryo saw him and heard when he landed, his high heavy boots and his slim long sword striking the asphalt, a tinny sound absorbed and lost in the percussion. Everything was silenced by the cheerful march played by the band which wasn't worthless, no, it wasn't worthless at all. They were playing joyously, sonorously and rhythmically, and the face of the young volunteer was instantly transformed, the little smile vanished and the face became that of a fierce soldier.

Her father was dashing, racing with his rifle held ready, and behind him Manolios and Mitros were sprinting to the two-story house. Their boots stained the white-washed stairway and made the flowerpots shake with their blooming stems on the steps' edge. The whole house shook. The men advanced, crouched and tense, kicked in the red wooden door, slammed it to the floor, pounded across it in their heavy boots, and with rage preceding their rifle barrels, leaped forward, aimed, and riddled the man's body with shots. They rushed to the other rooms and with blasts more rapid than the firing of thoughts hurled the bodies of the young women to the floor, and the older woman curled up under the kitchen table, fell head-downward, blood everywhere. . . blood. . . blood. . .

The sparklers faded from the old man's eyes. His mischievous smile faded and his soul darkened at the hour of death.

"Why? Why did he make us murderers? How could that fighter in the house have been so stupid? His three daughters were at home; his wife was right there in the kitchen. What possessed him to throw a grenade from his living room window?"

The old man sank into thought.

"His wife was cooking," he said after some time. "She was baking cheese pastry. The aroma of melted cheese was everywhere. The balcony was full of honeysuckle. The scent of blooming honeysuckle filled our nostrils, together with the aroma of cheese. Then came the stench. The stench of flowing blood. Red, scarlet, and the stink of Mitros Lebesis's puke. And mine. My stomach was empty and I retched bile."

He fell silent. When he spoke again one would think his speech was coming from somewhere down deep inside where it had been lost within him, within distant time, and his voice emerged slowly, with great effort.

"Where was that scene? Where was it hidden for so many years? Yet everything appeared before my eyes as if it was yesterday. Now. As if it was now. I see it all again. The girls are panting, terror in their eyes. And their lithe bodies! Those youthful bodies, how they snapped! How they broke and crumbled to the floor!"

He began to weep in agony.

Embracing her father, Maryo strove to comfort him. "Don't be afraid, father. Don't..."

She spoke softly, gently, to prevent his soul's further hurt at this weak, vulnerable hour of its departure. He continued to sob, lamenting, "I sinned. . . I sinned mortally."

"No, father, no!" she told him. "God does not keep an individual reckoning of such sins."

The old man hung on her words. What a blessing to him his daughter was! He knew it and trusted her implicitly.

"How can that be, kori mou? What is done about those sins?"

"Such sins are charged to all of us. That is what always happens in war. God does not go to where war is going on. He cannot endure the sight. That is why such awful things take place. But he does assign guilt. He charges all of us."

The old man searched Maryo's eyes. For a moment he was uncertain, but then the mischievous smile flashed on his face. He thought of the time which remained, and it seemed terribly short. He shouldn't waste a moment. He believed what his daughter said. The smile disappeared and was replaced by a thoughtful look.

Maryo never found out whether those last moments of thought led anywhere. Her father fell into a final coma and Maryo understood that nature had a way, better than hers, of bringing peace to the human soul.

How do the cells of memory work? Maryo wondered. *Since the cells die, how can their images be transmitted to the new cells? And how does each cell in itself function?* Memory's cells do not function the same for everyone. She had met many people with blank cells who saw only the present, which swiftly fell away into Lethe, darkness, forgetfulness. "Nothing remains of the past," they would state indifferently. "So what does it matter? Everything disappears—it is history." For Maryo nothing passed away. Time was bound to actions whose images remained, awakening feelings. Everything persisted within her, both that which she had experienced and that which her family had experienced. Everything was alive within her. *The cells of my memory are a sponge saturated with feelings. Wherever you touch me, I drip with sadness and love*, she thought painfully.

Maryo observed her father at Chesme, a smooth-faced youth amidst the chaotic crowd of refugees. *How could it be that he would not remember this!* she thought. He was looking for his mother. As a volunteer he had come from France when he heard of the war in Asia Minor. He had dropped everything. With only his clothes on his back he had embarked for Pireus, signed up for infantry service, and engaged in the fighting up to the battle of Aphion Karachisar. He was decorated for bravery, and then the retreat began. When he arrived at Smyrni, he stopped not a moment. He rushed to the village but found the house deserted. Only a few had remained in the village.

"Run!" he shouted. "Run for your lives!" he yelled as he raced off on his search.

Now, in Chesme, he asked a neighbor woman if she had seen his mother.

"Yes, my son," she told him. "She has gone to Agrilia. She is heading for Chios on Tsoumakos's caique.

He swiftly mounted a stray horse, and Maryo managed to seat herself behind him, holding on around his waist. How slim his waist was! It was like her son's, and that was the way she would hold onto her son from the back seat of the motorcycle, her heart overflowing with tenderness. She would rest her head on her son's back, just as she did now with her father. The taste of love is so sweet! So soothing to the body and mind! "Let that be the final taste of my last hour," she prayed. "The taste of love."

In Agrilia, the poisons of fear and hate drifted through the air. All faces held the same expression: eyes terrified, astonished. Bodies lay collapsed in the sand, possessions were strewn along the shore. In the streets, in the fields, everywhere, were corpses of animals.

Carcasses of horses, donkeys, mules, sheep and goats spread the stench of death. Blackening, bloated bodies were left by the animals' owners to avoid confiscation by the victor. Frightened stray dogs and cats scurried far from the grasp of passersby. There were carts everywhere carrying the possessions of a lifetime and of generations. Household things were piled on the sand, waiting to be transported to the Greek island of Chios.

The spectacle of the purge was horrifying. Maryo dismounted as her father went off to find his mother. She made her way into the frantic crowd. Most of the refugees were from her mother's village.

Suddenly a cart attracted her attention. It was small, neat, and painted bright red; the belongings it carried were brand new. Amidst this horrendous moil, that cart was a pleasant sight. The little horse was lively and stepped with spirit, as if he did not sense the inferno surrounding him. The lad who walked holding the cart's reins also appeared cheerful. Antonios, Giannakos's first son, was transporting his possessions with vigorous step. This strapping youth stood out in the crowd, and Maryo smiled. She was delighted to find that her uncle was so fearless. It was as if he were going on an holiday excursion.

Antonios was a newlywed. Not a month had passed since his joyful hour and the bliss had stayed with him. Delight was etched all over his face. The moment that Maryo encountered him, he had decided to take his little horse as well as the cart along with all their possessions across to Chios. "Whatever Tsoumakos asks," Antonios told himself, "I'll pay— provided my fine little horse comes along."

The thought of what lay in store for Antonios struck the smile from Maryo's lips. Her heart trembled for this lad who was hurrying toward his death. Now he was approaching the caique to talk to the skipper, but as he crossed the mole his bride rushed to him, throwing her arms around his neck and bursting into tears.

"They stole all our things!" she sobbed. "I went to say good-bye to mother. I was only away a moment, but everything was gone when I returned!"

Philio trembled, holding onto her husband with a tight embrace. Antonios was stunned. Electrified by the news, his body went rigid. He did not bend his head, though Philio was hanging on his neck. He remained stiff, unresponsive to her appeal. Motionless, he stared in the direction of the empty spot to which he had been hauling their possessions all morning. He had piled them neatly at a place on the beach where they would not be wet by the surf. That spot was empty now. Antonios's body remained motionless but his expression changed.

Despinyo, his mother, bit her lip. Her heart sank when she saw the change in Antonios's face. The joy of marriage which had been engraved on his features was beginning to fade. Despinyo knew that when a joy is blighted, it may never revive. She felt a shadow on her heart, and she rushed to her son.

"It doesn't matter, Antoni! Really it doesn't! Mere belongings can be replaced! What matters is that you are all right!" she urged so intensely that Philio was galvanized. It was not the words but the tone of voice that made her aware of the danger, and Philio tightened her embrace around her husband's neck so as to bring his perspired cheek down to touch her face. But Antonios did not bend. He did not heed his mother's words. He did not listen to her dark fears, nor feel the anguish of Philio, who was standing on the tips of her toes to touch his cheek. The only thing he felt was the sensation of being a refugee once more, as they had been six years before. Now it was happening all over again! Everything was going back to zero, to the very beginning, as if he were nothing. His father guessed his thoughts. Eyes flashing with anger and fear, he gripped his son's arm, pulled his pouch from his pocket and shook it before Antonios's blank gaze.

"Look here, Antonio! It's full of sovereigns, and this gold is all yours! Yours for all your effort, for all your sweat! All yours, Antoni! Antoni-i-i-i-i-i!"

The older man's voice broke.

The youth's unblinking gaze was completely blank. His sight seemed no longer to function. His eyes were turned back to the first purge, in 1916, when they were refugees in Thessaloniki. Refugees—miserable refugees! He would never be so again! His spirit would never be dragged to the ground!

Violently breaking Philio's embrace, Antonios threw the things off the cart right and left onto the sand. A rug flew into the water, and Philio lunged to grab it. Antonios's mother blocked her impetuous son but he pushed her aside and mounted the cart. She grabbed the horse's reins but the lad raised the whip and brought it down sharply on the horse's rump. The animal reared; Giannakos just managed to pull his wife to the side and they both fell onto the sand. The horse plunged forward. Antonios, stiffly erect, did not look back; he kept bringing down the whip, and the horse, wild-eyed and confused, dragged the cart between animal carcasses, piles of goods, and clusters of refugees. Maryo raced after the cart and just managed to pull herself onto its bed.

Only thirty days before, Antonios had mounted that cart as a bridegroom. In the village they had celebrated his wedding three days and three nights. At night they had feasted and swilled wine, firing festive shotgun blasts into the air. During the day they had transferred the articles of the bride's dowry to the home of the newlyweds, a sparkling-white two-story house near the entrance to the village. Philio's brothers were busy indeed moving rugs, embroideries, curtains, ornamented mirrors for the sitting room, hutches, and dining room furniture, all the things needful for the household. Antonios surveyed the hoard of things from his wife's dowry: the cooking utensils and supplies, mattresses, beds, chests. The cornucopia of goods made him self-conscious but he was deeply pleased. He wanted to touch each thing as the men in Philio's family brought load after load, and the women, including his mother and his Aunt Margi, readied the house, swept and tidied up, babbling words of praise for the sweet bride. The men popped tidbits into their mouths, washed them down with wine and laughed in celebration of the marriage, kidding the smiling Antonios with playful shoves and knowing winks. How delightful it was! And finally the great moment arrived, the blessed hour when he lay down by Philio's side. His hands came alive; they took on a life of their own. His fingertips trembled as they touched the girl. Both of them trembled, and his heart threatened to burst under this magic spell. With the yearning embrace, Philio's body steamed, Antonios's stretched in ecstasy, and then she froze; she shrank beneath his weight. As he lay back to rest by her side, Antonios felt Philio crying. Was it pain or modesty? he wondered in dismay.

Now he was standing in the cart whipping the horse, which, unused to rough handling, plunged in nervous frenzy. In the back of the cart, Maryo held on tight to the sides and braced herself as the wheels bounced over ruts and stones. She was tossed from one side to the other, and her heart beat in anguish. She dragged herself across the bed of the cart to sit by the driver. She was furious, furious with the young man's actions. "He is in such a hurry to go to death!" she kept intensely repeating. "What drives him to it, anyhow?" She was surprised by her lack of pity for this uncle. The only thing she felt was anger. She was infuriated by people who rush to die, as if life were so abundant they could afford to curtail it. She kept trying to reach the young man's side so she might discover why he was hastening toward his end. Her mouth filled with the acid taste of death. Full of bitterness and nostalgia, she was seized by a deep yearning to see her brother.

Finally she scrambled onto the front seat of the cart. Beside her, the standing Antonios was bringing the whistling whip down on the horse's flanks. She grabbed him so forcefully by the shirtsleeve that he lost his balance, was thrown sideways, and dropped onto the seat. Maryo, aroused by mixed feelings, shouted very close to his ear.

"Why? Why have you chosen to die? Don't you realize the pain you will cause?"

Antonios awkwardly slumped on the seat, let the whip slip from his fingers and the reins loose on his thighs. Feeling the change, the horse ceased to gallop. It fell into a slow trot along the road to Alatsata. Maryo continued to shout and push at her uncle for attention. He calmly turned and gazed upon her. She was electrified. *Does he see and hear me?* she wondered. *I think he does!* she realized with amazement.

Antonios smiled at her: a small smile, a wee, bitter smile. She was struck dumb. Her legs trembling, she strove to speak out again, but her voice remained trapped in her throat. Within the vacuum of space and time, Antonios saw and heard her. She had to speak; she had to grasp this unique opportunity. She swallowed dryly, took her heart in her hands, put it back in place, and spoke. Her voice emerged, words took form.

"Uncle, I must learn why you are going to your death. What is forcing you? What power does death hold over you?"

The air was paroxysmal with raging waves of sound, as the voice of Antonios was heard hollowly. "What concern is it of yours!"

As if regretting the harshness of his tone, he lowered his head and went on more quietly. "Why does a choice of mine matter to you?"

"It does; it does!" Maryo insisted. "There is another Antonios." Her mouth filled with bitterness. "There is an Antonios of the third generation."

The horse was now walking at a very easy pace, as if they were merely taking a drive in the countryside. They had left the main road and were traveling through an olive orchard to the rear of the village.

"What other Antonios?" asked her uncle with interest.

"Our Antonis—another sweet Antonios." She paused. "He, too, is headed for death," she said very quietly.

As she looked far into the distance, beyond the fields, she saw her Antonis. She discerned him in her town, in her time. He was pale, terribly pale. His eyes were a wounded crimson. He was revving his motorcycle on the track, the spiral track in the Circles of Hell. His mother, her hair tangled, covered with ashes, her heart in agony, was gripping the fence around the death track and shouting his name:

"Antoni-i-i-i, stop—come out! Come out, Antoni-i-i-i-i!" she passionately begged.

His brother and sisters, confused and terrified, simply cried, "Antoni-i-i-i-i! "

Antonis heard and saw nothing. Insulated in his black helmet, leather uniform, and high boots, he was like Charon seeking his likeness. A thin black figure withdrawn in his own world, he engaged the gears and shot up the spiral track.

The image of the city dissolved, and time turned back. Maryo again found herself by her uncle's side. Moving in the opposite direction, refugees with bundles of belongings were trudging toward Agrilia.

"I've got to know! I've got to understand why you're heading toward death. Why are you opening the way? Each person's new path becomes a road for others who are yet to come. Generations will follow the road which you etch," she whispered softly. "Why have you shut out everyone who loves you so much? Why have you shut them out of your heart?"

Antonios began to sob.

"I didn't shut them out of my heart; I sealed them deep inside. They are all inside me. They are deep within me hauling me this way and that, as they please. I can't stand it any longer!"

He sobbed uncontrollably, and Maryo tenderly patted his back. "Hush, now—hush. . .," she whispered.

"I am tormented by the love I feel for them. In vain I struggle against the dismay they make me feel. Their words don't touch me, their acts don't nourish me, their lives don't enrich mine."

Family members undermine one another, Maryo thought. *They wound and destroy one another.... Those closest to us are the only ones who fight without rules. They always hit below the belt. Everyone who knows you intimately, wounds you.*

Uncle Antonios's eyes were fixed on Maryo. Never had she seen such sadness in the gaze of a mortal. She was deeply shaken.

"I want to entrust you with another secret. I have kept it absolutely to myself," he said quietly.

Maryo continued to pat his back, nodding her head encouragingly. He was wondering whether he should confide such a great secret, and she understood. She realized what his secret was because it was hers also. Antonios had a wound, an incurable wound.

"I have a wound," he told her falteringly. "I have an open wound that bleeds and throbs in pain. No one has ever touched that wound to relieve it. They only make it worse. Each day it opens more deeply. Look here. . ."

He parted his shirt on the side of his heart. Maryo saw the deep scarlet hemorrhaging wound under his transparent skin. She recognized it as the human wound of loneliness, the first mark made by God when he withdrew his presence. The other deeper, connected, wound was made by Adam when he distanced himself from his partner. In the course of time the wound deepened and reached the soul.

"All of my insides are infected," Antonios sobbed.

That wound of loneliness becomes the magnet of death, Maryo realized, and her soul searched for the other Antonis. *What immense loneliness drove him to the Circles of Hell, shooting heroine?*

She shut her eyes but saw his cycle cut like a wedge into the metal ribs of the gigantic cylinder and slam his body against its ridged steel sides, which rent his suit, ripped through his flesh into his guts, smashing and slicing those human insides, those tender parts of the youth. She could not bear the sight; she could not endure the view of his lacerated flesh and shredded veins.

When she opened her eyes, she again found herself by the troubled flood of refugees. She was surrounded by downhearted folk. A scene drew her attention: a young soldier was slumped on a pile of bundles. He seemed totally exhausted. Lying awkwardly on his side, he dozed fitfully. A donkey came and stood nearby. From time to time the soldier opened his eyes and glanced indifferently at the animal; then he suddenly sat up and looked closely. The little beast had an erection, and the young man laughed. A moment later, without a thought, he abruptly stood up, drew his bayonet with his right hand, fell upon the animal and with a single stroke, in one swift motion, cut off its nature, severing it completely. He wiped the blade on his uniform trousers and sat down once more on the bundles. He continued to gaze in the animal's direction. Then he focused on the bloody thing that had fallen onto the powdery soil and on the creature that without its nature was thrashing and snorting in convulsions, shaking in a sustained fit. Again the soldier laughed.

Maryo grew pale. Her breath was cut off. Trembling, she could not control her breathing, which became shallow panting. Choked and asphyxiated, she could neither protest nor flee the spectacle. Like a camera lens, her eyes registered a spectrum of details, sending them all to be patterned on the roll of memory. There each detail was enlarged. *What kind of nature was it?* she wondered. *What kind of human nature severed the donkey's nature?* Her body vomited the image. She bent over and threw up, and at that moment another soldier appeared.

On his face he had an awkward little smile. He swung his rifle down from his shoulder and put the mouth of the barrel in the animal's ear.

He pulled the trigger.

The streets of Alatsata were empty. There were fires everywhere. The villagers had set fire to what they could not carry with them, and acrid smoke hung in the air. The moment the cart entered the village, Antonios realized the gravity of his error. No one was to be seen. The lanes were deserted, the houses empty and locked. Its head lowered, the horse avoided the fires and headed straight for home. At the garden gate, the animal stopped. Antonis jumped down and entered the house. It was empty and dark. At once he went back out, for a moment put his arms around his horse's neck, removed the reins and, slapping the animal on the rump, watched it trot off into the fields.

Maryo sat on the garden wall watching her young uncle. His face was pasty, whiter than his shirt. *How pale abandonment looks*. The thought carried her away into memory. She came and stood in her own time and again she saw. *White sheets, white clouds, white sea foam and flecks of white in his hair. But whiter still the whiteness of his last moments.* She bowed her head to the side of her heart and mourned once the brother she had just lost and missed so much.

Antonios shut the door of the house and closed the garden gate. He put the key in his pocket and took the road to the church of Aghios Panteleimonas. Inside the church he fell on his knees before the icon of the saint. He refused to speak to the villagers he found gathered there; he couldn't open his mouth. The townspeople had gathered to select a committee to negotiate with the Turks. Father Vagelis was there, Tsortsis the teacher, Kanelios—the doctor in the lower village—and Nikolios Galanis, who ran the large coffee house on the square. All of them were heads of families who still felt humiliated by the first refugee exodus. They refused to endure the humiliation of a second expulsion. They had come to the church for protection against the first rabid onslaught of attackers. Afterwards the committee would emerge from their asylum carrying a white flag; they would declare their submission. They simply had to remain in their homes, in their fields, on the soil they had plowed generation after generation, pouring their sweat into that soft, fertile earth of theirs. There they would remain. Everything had to turn out all right.

Maryo did not enter the church. She could not bear to see the faces of those people whose fate she knew. Their doom was terrible. The less she knew of them, the better for her memories. She decided to walk through the village, since she was eager to see where her mother and father were born and grew up. She wanted to see their home village before it was taken by the Turks. As she approached her grandparents' house at dusk, Constantis came running from the opposite direction and leaped over the wall into the front yard. Storm-tossed, with red eyes, Constantis was searching for his brother Antonios.

For two days they had been moving all their household possessions to the harbor Agrilia, the point of departure for the shores of Chios. They would go to the convent of Aghia Skepi to stay for a few days. Aunt Agni was Mother Superior, and their sister Maria—the nun Theochtisti—was also there. The whole family would be put up at the convent. Constantis and Antonios would go ahead to Athens to find work and a place to live, and later the others would join them. That was what had been decided.

It took two days to transfer their possessions to the port, and each time Tsoumakos's caique tied up at the dock Constantis reminded the captain that all their things would be loaded aboard before they crossed to Chios. Finally, when Constantis had made his last trip from the village, he arrived at the beach to find his folks writhing in the sand, filled with fear for Antonios's life. When Constantis learned what had taken place, he was furious. He felt like punching his old man. He grabbed him by the shoulders and shook him.

"How could you have let him do it? You might as well have shot him dead right then and there and be done with it! Then at least we could have buried him ourselves!"

He mounted his horse and headed for the village, shouting over his shoulder to his younger brother Nikolos: "Don't wait for me! Get out of here! Do you hear me, Nikolos? Take them to safety in Chios!"

Constantis was a soldier. He had returned from Brazil to volunteer for the infantry. He had arrived at the village from the front lines knowing what the Greeks had done in Turkish villages and what would be the consequences in Alatsata. Now he was searching for his brother in houses, barns, and sheds, avoiding the church. "Whoever went for asylum in the church," he thought, "will be trapped like a rat." Crouching to conceal himself, he raced from yard to yard. He combed sheds and stables, even chicken coops, but he had a gut feeling he would not find Antonios. Something inside him told him that his brother was lost forever. Now hoofbeats were thundering though the village streets. It was the Tsetes! *It's too late to help him! Too late!* The words pounded in his brain. *It's not like the time I found him naked behind the wall!* That time they had gone together to a back lane in Smyrni. It had all begun with dancing.

Constantis danced. He danced the hasapiko; he dipped and whirled as no other villager could. The villagers jammed the coffee house, lining the walls, sitting on tables, filling window ledges and doorways to watch the young man dance. He liberated his body, defied gravity, slapped the floor that could not hold him down, flew into the air. Constantis danced, and with him danced the hearts and desires of all his friends, who clapped to the tempo. After the dance, they pounded him on the back, hung on his shoulders, pinched his cheeks. They yearned to steal something he had, to absorb the fire of life which he possessed in such abundance.

It was then a fellow from Smyrni came up and whispered something in Constantis's ear that turned him on. He had worked the whole week like a dog, and each night at bedtime his mind had gone to the district to which the Smyrniot had referred. He burned to go there with Antonios and continually spoke of it, but his older brother was shy. Sunday arrived, and right after church he saddled the horse for himself and the mule for Antonios.

"Well, are you with me or not?" he shouted.

Without word the other mounted the mule.

"Take care, you guys!" the Smyrniot joshed as they brought their mounts to the stable.

Antonios modestly lowered his eyes and Constantis laughed. Reaching the back lanes, Antonios stayed at the first house, but Constantis went from one house to another. What he wanted above all was variety. Antonios stayed with that *hanoumissa*—that "harem girl" whose eyes brimmed with sensuality and whose body flamed with desire. Her words were sweet; her voice honey. Her breath was like a Turkish bath with aromatic steaming waters. The sweet thing stroked his thighs and set him trembling like lemon blossoms in a spring breeze.

"Come, my luscious stallion. Come, my pasha. Strip! Let me see your body! Show me your manhood!"

She deftly peeled off his clothes, and Antonios stood, head lowered, his hands in front of him. The lovely girl caressed him and spoke ever so softly. "Would you like to romp with me, my colt?"

The youth nodded his head.

"I'll strip too," she cooed.

Her silk sheath slipping to the floor, she stood completely naked before him.

Antonios shivered. He shuddered like the newborn colt he saw born in the fields, dripping with the waters of its mother's womb, slowly raising itself on spindly legs, then standing and walking, slowly gathering strength. Antonios's body felt like that; for the first time he felt his flesh so strong and ripe for a woman, and here was this luscious girl whispering to him to come and play. "Yes! Yes!" his heart clamored, and she gestured toward a rug by the opposite wall. Their game would begin by jumping to that rug. She went first but didn't make it. Antonios grinned, leaped, soared, aimed his feet toward the center of the rug, landed, and it sank beneath his weight. The rug slipped through the wide mouth of trap door and sent its victim plummeting to the floor below, as the opening shut above his head. Antonios heard the door slam , a heavy piece of furniture moved on top of it. Looking around, he found himself in a dark cellar. He was naked in a strange place, his clothes and money pouch in the room above. He crawled through a window to the yard and hid by a wall, waiting for sundown. As darkness closed in, Constantis found him there. He instantly grabbed his brother by the arm and thus naked dragged him to the woman's door and broke it down. He punched the two pimps within, gathered Antonios's clothing without his money pouch, and swore he would return to Smyrni and slit the throat of the charmer who had shamed his brother.

Antonios was ashamed for Constantis. He was ashamed of his cruel fists, of the men's blood-smeared faces; he was even ashamed for the sake of the beautiful *hanoumissa.* He didn't want to see her again; he only wanted to get out of there, to get back home, for none of that business was any way for a fellow to behave. All the way back to the village, Constantis laughed with relish, recounting his adventures of the day, everything he had done to the women he had been with.

Now Constantis was looking behind walls and within stables, but he knew all too well he would never see his brother again. *If he went to the church, he's a dead man*, he thought angrily.

"Yes, he is at the Aghios Panteleimonas church!" Maryo shouted.

Constantis cautiously approached. The Turks' horses were in the churchyard. Constantis heard screaming and wailing. Again the Tsetes had made their first attack against the local church. Crouching with the instinct of a wild animal, Constantis withdrew and made for his father's house on the outskirts of the village.

Maryo was frightened. She was frightened by the dust and thunder of the attacking horses' hooves and by the war cries of the Tsetes fighters. They sounded like the howling of wild beasts scenting their prey. This was the crowning of the festival, their day of martial glory. It would be set down in the history books. The slaughter would be praised; they would be decorated for valor, and they were ready! Their sabers were whirling high above their heads, but something even more terrifying stunned Maryo. Focusing on the horsemen one by one, she saw it: the Tsetes coming down on the village had their flies open, their organs bared. Their sex was exposed, and they all had erections! The sight of so many heroes in one place made Mayro tremble, and she tried to recall whether she had ever read in history books of warriors' genitals standing like flag poles above the lands they were conquering.

As the attackers approached, Constantis slid over a wall and, crouching, slipped into the fields. He trusted that the descending dusk, thickened by dust and smoke, would conceal him. Maryo followed. She ran as fast as she could but could not catch up. In a pasture not far from the house, she realized that the horsemen had caught sight of them. They spied the crouched figure of a fleeing man and spurred their horses in that direction. Three of them got wind of their quarry, and that was what they desired: loose wild game, not bodies caged in church.

They attacked with savage yelps. As they closed in, their sabers whistled high in the air as if they were sharpening them for the slaughter. Constantis managed to throw himself into a low shed. In the far corner, he made ready. Maryo rushed in behind him. They were both winded, fearful that their souls would melt from sheer terror. Constantis gripped a rusty sickle in his right hand. Pressed flat against the wall in a niche beside the doorless entrance, he held the sickle high and ready to strike. On the other side of the doorway, Maryo was also flat against the wall, a half-wall of sharp stones that pierced her back as her eyes pierced the darkness surrounding the shed. In that darkness loomed the black figures of the Turkish fighters and their horses circling the shed. The Tsetes were exuberant; they reveled in the panic that filled their youthful prey hidden within. Their spirits soared as their steeds reared by the shed, and they screamed curses and obscenities the infidel. One young fighter, unable to restrain himself any longer, crouched with saber extended and threw himself across the threshold. The sickle descended, sliced the air, and fell with enormous heft upon the inclined spine of the crouched Tsete; it rent bone, passed through the neck and severed the head. The head rolled, and the body buckled in a heap, thrashing, and jerking in hysterical search of its head, which tumbled at Maryo's feet. She was trembling and shuddering, unable to lift her hands to wipe away the blood that sprayed her. Eyes dilated by terror, she watched Constantis stride over the body and lunge through the doorway, seizing the fighter who was prepared to enter to join the festival of butchery. He had dismounted and taken two steps toward the doorway but had time neither to raise his sword nor glimpse his attacker as the sickle repeatedly hacked the backbone, mincing the neck, leaving it all but severed. The head danced spasmodically on the trunk, which slumped in the doorway. Enthralled,

Maryo beheld her uncle seize the third, as yet mounted, horseman, whose dumbfounded gaze had just encountered the gory spectacle of his comrade's body in death-throbs on the ground, and who fearfully jerked the horse's reins to flee. Its neck twisted by the reins, the animal reared high in anger, pitching the rider backward as Constantis seized him and hauled him. The Turk was too stunned to use his saber, or was paralyzed by the pulling, and Constantis flung him to the ground. He hacked him again and again with the now dull sickle, bludgeoned and rent him with the heavy blade, sending up a shower of blood that sprayed the attacker, till the fallen one lay motionless, yet Constantis continued the onslaught. Maryo stared at the face of the slaughterer. It was beyond recognition—a primitive face, savage and furious in triumph, the soul etched in a brutal, ecstatic grimace.

Maryo fell to her knees. "Forgive us," she sobbed, "O Lord! Forgive us!"

Three days and three nights, Constantis lay with his body sunk in the sands of Chios beach. He buried his body and denied its needs. His body obeyed; it suppressed its functions and sank into silence. In that silence the man prayed for forgiveness; in that silence he cleansed his soul of the joy it felt that moment of slaughter. Late the fourth day he lifted his head, and with great difficulty, his revived limbs. He crawled to the sea, threw himself in, bathed in the salty water, and set off naked and barefooted to the monastery of Aghios Minas. Late that night in the small hours, he arrived. The prior of the monastery absolved him from sin: "In battle, killing is not held to be a sin," he claimed.

Constantis could not comprehend such absolution. He remained at the monastery and joined the order, yet forever the sin, sealed deep within him, remained and tormented him.

Panagiota, Maryo's mother, got word of these events from her Aunt Marigi.

"Despinyo-o-o-o-o! Mori Despinyo-o-o-o-o!" Aunt Marigi yelled from the courtyard of the Aghia Skepi convent. "You poor thing, Despinyo! The Tsetes have taken Alatsata with their jewels hanging from their pantaloons! And they had nuts tha-a-a-t big, mori!

Pitch darkness fell over Panagiota's face. Constantis's bloodstained sickle was in her grip and she was lopping off jewels. She seized them with disgust in her left hand, calculated with her right, and in a single stroke severed them and tossed them into the road.

With glee she watched the Turks' expressions as the sickle fell and mutilated their sex. She savored their terrified grimaces as they pled for death instead of mutilated loins. She shoved the severed things under their noses and discarded them with a contemptuous fling. She sped from one Tsete to another, hacking with rabid fury. When the Tsetes were disposed of, she found other males and resumed her cutting, heaping their jewels in lanes, yards, hallways, kitchens, bedrooms, closets, shelves, till there was nowhere to stand or walk, and then she raced away. She dashed off, fleeing and escaping those heaps of manliness, and then she vomited, again and again.

Exhausted, Panagiota opened her eyes to find Maria standing over her, smiling. Her face was a bright summer noon, her head covered by the black mantle of a nun. Maria, her beloved Maria, was not Theochisti to her!

"You will get well. I know you will," she whispered. "Last night in my sleep I saw the Archangel Gabriel riding away from the convent, and no one was with him." She stroked her sister's hair and kissed her cheek. "For forty days you have worried us so much! I've never seen such a fever." She sat down at her bedside, gave her blessed water to drink, opened her breviary, and read a healing prayer. Panagiota felt her body reviving. The fever was subsiding. She had time to think, *I am with Maria, I am with Maria!* before she slipped into serene, restful sleep.

"I was so scared, mother," Maryo whispered. "I was wondering how you would survive to bear me. I too have been in agony for forty days."

At Aghia Skepi convent, high in the hills at the center of the island, Maryo rested. Her soul managed to nestle deep within her, and, hidden there, it remained immaculate. The turmoil which it had seen did not touch it. Now, here at the convent, Maryo nurtured her spirit. *The nucleus of life is a person's soul*, she mused. *The soul must remain whole.* With infinite care she had borne her soul through two evils, those of war and of refugee life. Now she was nurturing her soul on cosmic visions, the splendor of time, and the beauty of the world. Here in this peaceful place, when her mother had completely recovered and the family was setting off for Athens, Maryo again recalled her aged mother's command. She desired the secret of her life. Was what she lived the dream of a moment or a mad endless nightmare? *My image of her life is as yet unclear*, Maryo thought. *I must go back to the very beginning.*

PART TWO

"Cu-cu-roo-cu! Cu-cu-cu-roo!"

Maryo awoke in the farmhouse storeroom. The soprano hen had stepped into the barnyard delighted that it was morning and had burst into song. In the stable the donkey listened with bewilderment and then he too sounded his song. His nasal bass voice caught the goat's attention. She stopped chewing, then looked up, moved her head left and right, and hesitantly joined the chorus. Irritated by the hen, the rooster flapped down from their perch and pursued her. But she, lithe and small, escaped him and resumed her singing at a distance.

Maryo awoke in the midst of that festal morning choral. It was very early, a bright, clear day, and she felt rested, cheerful, buoyant. She sprang from her mattress and took a sprightly step into the yard. It was the beginning of the century. Her mother was as yet unborn, but Maryo was here at her house, in her yard, enjoying the greenery and animals on her place. She had made great efforts to reach this place at this moment. When the family had set off for Pireus, she had immediately departed from Aghia Skepi convent. She left in September, 1922, and with great exertion arrived at her mother's village of Alatsata after midnight one day in the Spring of 1900.

It was pitch-black everywhere; at the village square only a small lantern was lighted. Maryo could see only the shadowy forms of rows of two-story houses, and between them the lanes were like the open mouths of sleeping monsters. She took the road leading to the upper village. Before long she found herself walking in the densest darkness. Sight being useless, she placed her trust in her feet and hands. She slowly drew her feet over the cobblestones and traced walls and the sides of houses with her hands. She was lost in the maze of narrow lanes, and she searched desperately to return again to the right lane. Exhausted when she arrived, she dragged herself into the yard and around the house till she finally reached the door to the storeroom. With relief she opened the small wooden door, felt her way to an open area by the wall, and barely had time to make a soft mattress of hay.

Her body no longer ached; it had reached a point beyond pain. Lying on her improvised bed, she didn't have the strength to undress, or even to remove her shoes. Sleep came at one fell swoop and swept her to the land of dreams.

Now it was morning of a day fresh and new as her soul. The barnyard animals shied away when they saw her. She extended her arms to embrace the world. Dashing across the yard, she stopped before the steps of the house. There were eight bright white-washed steps, on the side of each step a pot with blooming flowers. Maryo flew up the stairs and stepped onto the verandah. She was deeply moved. She wanted to bound into the air as she had in childhood when words could not express the joy she felt. She felt like hopping and shouting with joy. Here she was already at the house, on the very *moudi* her mother had so often spoken of.

"It took three weeks to lay the floor of the *moudi*," her mother proudly recalled. "My mother told me how marble pieces were brought from the famous Smyrni quarry. They broke them into little chips with sledgehammers, laid the colorful chips in cement, and polished the surface with a big grinder. Our *moudi* looked like a mosaic floor! It glowed!"

The house was shaped like a gamma. Along the moudi on the long side of the gamma there were three high doors, painted gray and topped with fanlights. The first door was the door to their living room, furnished with a mirror from Smyrni, a buffet, a dining table and six chairs. The two older boys slept in the living room. Adjacent was the room where the three sisters slept. It was filled with pallets and bedding, and on one wall were the icons of the whole family's namesake saints. On the other wall there were several pegs where clothes were hung. The third room, which formed the short side of the gamma, was their kitchen. It was large, roomy, full of pots and pans that gleamed above the cooking fire in the corner, opposite which was grandfather and grandmother's wooden-framed double bed.

Everything was exactly as Maryo's mother had described it, except for the sweet smell exuded by the wooden floor, which she discovered now. Her mother had never mentioned that.

Slowly, ceremoniously, the sun rose on the horizon of the fields which stretched into the distance across the road from the house.

"Time to get up!" shouted Maryo, who was anxious to see the family.

First to rise was Grandfather Giannakos, her mother's father. Not yet forty, he was a powerfully built man. He reminded Maryo very much of her first cousin at that age. But this Giannakos had a very large mustache that completely covered his mouth. He was wearing Cretan knickers. Many years later, in a sweet moment of weakness, when his daughter Panagiota was being married to Asimakis, he was persuaded to shave his mustache and exchange his knickers for trousers. When the old man saw himself in the mirror he cried like a baby.

"It's not me any more," he cried.

He refused to attend the wedding and did not leave his room until the mustache had once more become a bush. He never removed his knickers again and was buried in them when his time came.

Grandfather Giannakos walked through the yard to the outhouse and then entered the stable to lead out the sheep, the goat and her kids. In the barnyard the animals waited by the open gate, cocking their ears for the sound of the shepherd's bell from the lane above. As soon as the shepherd turned the corner, they followed him. In the evening, upon the shepherd's return, the animals made their own way to the stable.

Grandfather fed the donkey, the mule, and the horses. As he was feeding the chickens, the aroma of coffee filled the yard. Carrying a tray with two large cups of coffee, Despinyo appeared on the moudi. How young grandmother was! A young woman hardly thirty! Slim and tall, with a rounded pregnant belly.

"You're going to have a girl!" Maryo shouted to her.

"Come, dear, your coffee is served," she called to Giannakos, setting the tray on a ledge.

Smiling, he bounded up the stairs to the verandah. Honey-sweet were the honey-colored eyes of Maryo's grandmother, and Maryo was delighted by her comely shape. Despinyo and Giannakos sat by the edge of the verandah, and Maryo sat down between them.

"Who could have guessed that I would meet you this way?" she told them tenderly.

Throwing her arms around their shoulders, she looked closely at her grandmother's face and saw that it had been scarred by smallpox.

"Marry that scar-face—never!" Giannakos declared when the match was proposed.

"You hair-brained oaf," his father snapped. "Don't you see her face pretty as the moon? Who sees any scars?"

"I do! I do, for sure!" the son blurted.

He was a handsome lad, then, in his prime, barely thirty, and Despinyo, the proposed bride, was twenty.

"Well, you knuckle-head—if you see the scars, you'd better see her farmland as well," his father insisted. "The field at Pyrgi alone is worth a cart-full of sovereigns."

During the following week, however, Giannakos would hear nothing on the subject. His old man kept cursing him, reiterating that his word was his bond.

"You'll marry her, all right, Giannako, and dance a jig besides. I gave my word—I'll never take it back."

Every evening Giannakos drank raki at the coffee house. Saturday had already arrived, and the next day, that Sunday, the engagement would be celebrated. Giannakos went especially early to the square to drink with his friend Vagelis of the Christofakis clan. He drank and drank that evening; he drank till he was soused. He climbed on his mule to return to his home in the upper village, but the mule, he was to swear, went his own way, carrying him along the road to the lower village and the home of Chroustallo. Chroustallo was the most gorgeous young thing in the village, but she was the daughter of Anestis Dimolas, the laziest villager of them all, who had plunged his family up to their neck in poverty, as Giannakos's old man put it.

The mule came to a stop outside her house, and since the house was low, Giannakos, on the mule's back, was very close to her window. He was never to recall pounding on the shutters, but he would always recall Chroustallo throwing them open as if she had been awaiting his arrival. She flung open the shutters, leaned out, grabbed him by his shirt, and began to plead.

"Take me away, Giannako! Take me away, light of my eyes! Tomorrow they will marry me to Kostyo the barber, that widower with four brats!"

"I've come for you, Chroustallo, my sweet," Giannakos warbled, lifting her onto the mule.

Past midnight, outside the village on the Smyrni road, having been informed by Vagelis, Giannakos's old man waited with Sideris, his brother.

"You lame-brain—what do you think you're doing?" barked the old man.

He gave him a cuff which struck both his thigh and the mule's rump. The animal almost threw both Giannakos and his Chroustallo to the ground.

"You, Sideri—take the girl back to her home! This lout is going to church for the engagement ceremony."

The girl began to sob.

"Now that you've made me a laughingstock, how can I go home? The whole village will point their fingers at me!"

"One peep out of anyone, and they'll have me to contend with!" said

Sideris.

That was enough. Not one villager spoke a word in public concerning the incident. So, in the end, Giannakos was engaged to Despinyo, and they were married. It was ten years now, a new child born each year, and he loved her more and more as time passed.

With her belly bulging, Despinyo approached Giannakos.

"Come, kale, would you like to feel our little angel kick!"

Maryo, too, stood near Despinyo and touched her grandmother's belly, feeling the restless child turning and thumping inside her.

"It's my mother, my mother!" she felt like shouting in joy.

The door of the first bedroom opened and the second-born child emerged with sleep-filled eyes. It was Constantis and he was eight years old. Behind him came the first-born, Antonios, a tall, slim boy with a fleeting smile.

From the other bedroom appeared the twins, Aggerou, followed by Maria. Maryo beamed with delight seeing all these aunts and uncles at this age. Garoufalo, her aunt who was to be a teacher, was the fifth child. Born handicapped, she crawled haltingly across the verandah. Fixing her vague gaze on her mother, she took refuge in her skirts, and Despinyo absent mindedly stroked the child's hair. The expected child was their seventh. Ten months before they had lost Sideris, their youngest offspring. For days he had cried in pain, unable to urinate. The cure-all prescribed by the village doctor and the herbs given by the medicine woman had done no good. On the night of the fourth day Sideris's death plunged them into grief, but now they were joyfully awaiting their seventh child.

Giannakos touched his wife's belly. He spread his large hand across its swollen curve. Both Despinyo and Giannakos smiled contentedly.

"Could it be, kale, that God has sent Sideris back to us?" Giannakos wondered.

"Yes," Despinyo replied, "he has restored his little soul to us."

In a quiet embrace they gazed upon their offspring; the moudi was crowded with little faces and was fragrant with the light perspiration of children's bodies.

It was Sunday morning. The sun had risen an arm's length above the horizon, the animals had been fed, and the family was preparing to go to church. Dressed in their best, the children gathered one by one on the verandah. Maryo smiled, admiring the picture before her. So many children and all so familiar to her! She knew every event that would shape their lives. How extraordinary, how strange, how troubling that knowledge was, but it was also delightful. Here in this time and place she was filled with tenderness. What a rare opportunity it was to be here this Sunday morning! A thought suddenly struck her. Would it be possible, looking at these children, for one to foresee their futures? Could one foresee their fates by looking at their faces and physiques? Surprised by the notion, Maryo got out her camera. She would capture all the children's emotions, gestures, and expressions on film, and at her leisure she would examine the preserved images. She snapped pictures, emulating the experts' skills. She wished to follow their example no matter how much effort it took. From the verandah wall she shot the children's heads from above and their faces in close-ups. Lying on the mosaic surface she caught an upward angle. She snapped smiles and tears, anger and cheerful talk. She got every posture and mood and then began her careful analysis.

Maryo was shaken. From the photographs the children's fate was clear: the images foretold the future. Antonios with that shy smile, full of goodness. It was clear that one day he would be slaughtered like a lamb. Constantis projected from the photograph with iron biceps. His long powerful arms seemed to shoot from his torso. His chest swelled, and that sharp horizontal slash above his chin was not a smile: it was a hard determined declaration. Aggerou flaunted her slim form, vanity in every gesture. Maria was a glowing spirit. Despinyo claimed that after the aching contractions and screaming pain that had given birth to Aggerou, Maria was born with the greatest ease. The mother maintained that the room was filled with light when the second twin was born. Now Maria was seven years old and still radiant. Garoufalo was slow in emerging from the uterus. Three days Despinyo forced herself to work in the fields, feeling only slight contractions. At the end of the third day, Garoufalo emerged, a placid child, light as a feather. When she passed two years of age, they realized that her legs were slow in developing. *But*, Maryo thought, *her dark eyes sparkle. Her face shows she'll become a teacher and write poetry as well.*

Musing, Maryo thought of her children and wondered whether she could discern their fate. She hastened to examine various photographs but affection carried her away into a myriad of memories which came and went as their faces changed and their bodies grew. Finally, Maryo understood with relief that she could see nothing of her children's fate. It seemed that she knew nothing of their present, past, and future. Only the fate of her ancestors appeared clear to her in the photographs.

But now it was Sunday and the Alatsata church bell was already pealing. The family hurried down the stairs, shut the garden gate, and took the lane to the church of Aghios Panteleimonas. He, the saint who is merciful to all, was the patron of the upper village.

In a wide lane just below the church Minas Archontoulis caught up with them. "Giannako, you and your missus are invited to our home tonight. We are celebrating the engagement."

"Blest be the hour to come, my Minas. Who is to be engaged?"

"I'm giving my Kalliopo," answered Minas with a serene smile.

"Our blessings! And who are you giving her to?"

"I'm giving her to your brother Sideris!"

Lowering his head, Minas was barely audible.

Gianakos's jaw dropped; he seemed about to speak but remained silent. Beside him Despinyo was holding Garoufalo in her arms, and she shifted the child's position. Giannakos took the child, held her close and tried to smile, but he could not appear complacent. He pitied Kalliopo. How could such a lass be matched with Sideris, the most shiftless, violent lout in the village? The truth was the truth, though it was about his own flesh and blood. Sideris was no man for a young woman like her. The idea rankled in Giannakos's mind as turned toward the church. He paused.

"Who was the go-between?" he asked irritably.

"Last night he came to us himself."

"Was he soused?" asked Despinyo.

"Tsk." Minas clicked his tongue negatively but hesitantly. "Well, he may have taken a drop."

"How many drops?" Giannakos persisted, shifting the child's position.

"Only a few. He was steady on his feet," Sideris's future father-in-law affirmed. "He knocked on our door a bit on the late side. We were already in bed."

Sideris pounded the door with both fists. "Mina Archontouli! Mina Archontouli!" he shouted in the darkness.

He hammered on the door and shoved with both hands. It remained solidly barred. Minas and his spouse had just fallen asleep, and they were slow to awaken. Sideris was in a state, and he pounded on both the door and the shutters with his iron fists. The couple was jolted awake. Louloudio, Minas's wife, jerked bolt upright and lighted a lamp; Minas trembled, realizing who was outside his door.

"What do you want, Sideri?" Minas asked in his gentlest voice. "What could bring you here at the witching hour?"

"Open up, Mina Archontouli; I'm here to talk to you man to man!"

"Just a moment," Minas replied.

He fumbled to put on his knickers, but his foot couldn't find the leg hole. He almost fell to the floor, and Louloudio helped him, holding the knickers by the waist. When the knickers were finally on, Minas cracked the door to take a look at Sideris's face. He wanted to check how drunk he was but didn't have a chance. The visitor shoved the door open with such force that it sent Minas sprawling to the other side of the kitchen. Sideris strode to the middle of the room; without a word he took his knife from his belt and jammed it deep into the top of the low table. He stuck it an inch into the wood, and the impact resounded from the kitchen walls.

"I want Kalliopo for my wife! What do you say to that, Mina Archountouli? Do you want me for your son-in-law?"

Minas and Louloudio were flabbergasted; they stood staring at Sideris with blocked throats, unable to sound a cry for help. All they could do was gape at the still vibrating knife nailed in the table, seeming to drip blood from the many times Sideris had sunk it in human flesh. At the end of every holiday, upon the intoxicated bragging of the strongest youths, Sideris would always find someone to cut. He was notorious for wielding his blade whenever he was drunk. The following day, sober, he would slap the wounded man on the back. "Water over the dam! Let bygones be bygones!" he would boom and buy raki all around.

Now his mustache trembled as he spoke."I want Kalliopo for my woman!"

He bent, seized the knife, and jerked it from the wood as Minas and Loloudio, still terrified, hurried to nod their heads in assent.

Sideris bared his teeth in something like a smile and thrust his knife back in his belt.

"The engagement ceremony will be tomorrow, Sunday," he said.

He yanked Minas's hand to seal the bargain. His father-in-law to be was nearly thrown off balance by the force of the handshake.

"And, look here—the wedding will be next Sunday!" he said.

"Whatever you say, Sideri," Minas whispered. "Whatever you say."

The son-in-law solemnly bent and kissed his hand.

The village buzzed with the news. Everyone praised Sideris, but Giannakos was furious with such behavior.

"What things folks find to say when they fear someone!" he groaned.

Minas Archontoulis and his spouse Louloudio were all bright smiles and elaborate arrangements. The scent of roasted lamb and pastry wafted through the village. Everyone was invited to eat, drink and give their blessings to the newlyweds. Sideris, grave and dignified, kept his eyes on the men who were giving Kalliopo a congratulatory kiss. After the feasting and dancing the couple hurried off. Maryo blushed as she entered the bride's bedroom, but she had to see this mismatched couple during their first moment alone.

Sideris, with his broad mustache and large hands, taller by a head than his older brother Giannakos and by two heads than his bride Kalliopo, stood with his eyes lowered and his limbs shaking. He was trembling not from his angry, if bloodless, encounter with the youth who asked to dance with the bride, but on account of the immediate circumstances.

Kalliopo was extraordinarily lovely. Her black hair hung to just below her waist, and her hands were white and graceful. Her eyes were pools of sheer sweetness and her lips tender cherry blossoms. Her form was lithe and pert as a flower's stem. The sight of Kalliopo, all softness and distilled sweetness, overcame Sideris. In the bedchamber he sat down awkward and unmanned on a cedar chest as his bride stepped behind the decorated screen. He hardly dared look on as she shed each article of attire, draped it over the top of the screen, and then emerged wearing a fine white nightgown which she tied with a white ribbon at the neck. She tied the bow with those delicate white fingers and Sideris hid his own clumsy, chilled hands. He longed to speak, but his coarse mustache seemed to be blocking his mouth. Oh how he yearned simply to utter her name. If he could only say, "Kalliopo—my Kalliopo," but his throat was sealed. She, however, with an easy motion lay down on the bed, pulled aside the pristine white coverlet, and whispered: "At last, Sideris! Come, my husband—come!"

Maryo tiptoed to the door and out of the room.

From that moment Sideris was a changed man.

"Well now, m'Kalliopo," he said each daybreak before leaving to labor in the fields.

"Well now, m'dearest, don't go to work on such a freezin' day."

"Well now, m'Kalliopo. Don't go tirin' yourself at the loom; I'll buy you a dress at Smyrni. Well now, m'Kalliopo," said Sideris.

Kalliopo walked with him to the end of the lane.

"Well now, m' Sideris. Today I'll cook boureki the way you like it... Don't be late hoeing too much ground. . ."

"Well now, Kalliopo. . .," Sideris said. He paused, as if there was something on the tip of his tongue."

"Well now, m' darling. . ." she said.

"Well now, there's a marriage for you!" Maryo exclaimed with a smile.

Despinyo was all alone. She was completely alone at the fields in Pyrgi, hurrying to finish her work. All day her boys had gathered the ripe tobacco leaves and carried them in heavy bundles to the shed. Seated on the ground with legs crossed, she was busy stringing them together with a large needle. All day she had hung the leaves in rows on the drying racks that Giannakos had built. As daylight began to fade, few leaves remained of the stacks that her sons had left on the dirt floor.

In the afternoon, thin, soft, white clouds were sailing in the sky. Now, thickening and darkening, they began to close and descend. Thin streaks of light and flashes of thunder came sporadically through the slats in the shed's side, and Despinyo pushed her needle more swiftly through the soft leaves. She kept biting on her mantilla as the lightning flashes grew more frequent and intense. The donkey, tied to the fig tree outside the open door, pulled restlessly at its tether and snorted anxiously.

"Don't worry, little fellow; we'll make it home before the storm," she spoke gently, hanging a batch of leaves by the door. "Don't fret," she said, glancing at the animal, "this is the last batch for the day."

The first shot of pain struck her in the back. She remained motionless with her arms outstretched. She stilled herself to heed her body. Was that a contraction pain? Her body as yet vibrated from the penetrating stab which shot up from her waist to her back and then rolled down between her thighs. She remained alert, and when she was certain that they were birth pangs, she froze. Immobilized by fear, she dropped the tobacco leaves and felt her belly. Tensed and arrogant, her belly announced that its hour had arrived.

"Aid me, Mother of God," she whispered. She carefully lifted the small rag rug from the floor, draped her shawl over her shoulders and left the shed, closing the door behind her. Her eyes flashed anxiously. The dusk, crammed with black clouds, was swiftly turning to night.

"Aghios Panteleimonas, be by my side!" she prayed to the saint she knew so well. She untied the donkey, mounted with difficulty from a rock, and adjusted her position. The beast set off at once. It trotted swiftly along the road to Alatsata, chased by thunder and lightning. Despinyo's second bout of pain came at the midpoint of their journey. The pangs were stronger, more painful, than the ones before. She held on more tightly to the donkey, uttering tiny cries of 'ach!ach!' and the animal slowed its pace to a careful walk, as if it wished to ease the woman's discomfort. Just as they reached the fig trees that line the vineyards nearby the village, the third phase of pain came on. It was deep, extended, and its end marked the coming of Despinyo's time. With a thrust of the uterus the waters broke, drenching the woman's thighs and the animal's sides.

"Gracious Mother of God, I bear this child in your name!"

Despinyo made the sign of the cross and tapped the animal's neck. The donkey halted; and with great effort amidst constant throbs of pain, the woman slid to the ground. She spread the rag rug under a fig tree and quickly made a nest of vine leaves. She raised her skirts and rolled them around her midriff. Upright, bending her legs and arching her back in effort, she entered the rhythm of birth. The throbs determined her response. She took sharp deep breaths with each shot of pain. The hurt struck at the midriff, rose to her back, turned downward and for a moment rippled away. The woman, artful in birth, waited for each separate stroke; when it arrived below she seized it with her muscles and fiercely pushed it outward from between her thighs.

There remained only a split second to catch her breath. The pains with pitiless rhythm smote her rabidly, but she pushed the pain and the child out of her body with equal determination. A bank of dark, dense clouds bent low along the entire horizon. They were a dark streaming womb like her own body. A light zephyr touched and cooled her bare parts. She moaned.

Lonely and dark was the hour of birth, broken only by moans and distant flashes of lightning. A faint roll of thunder accompanied her effort, and she bowed, panting in quick short breaths, knowing the time of release had arrived. Her frame doubled over, and with her hands gripping her thighs, she pushed and pushed, covering her hands with blood. She felt her child fiercely pushing. It pushed to come out, and the woman, assured now, waited. A sweet, fine pain arrived, and the child slid into her spread hands.

With the crying of the child, Maryo felt a rush of awe. She moved slowly toward the spot of the birth and probed the darkness to see the child. It was her mother, Panagiota. Maryo extended a hand trembling with emotion. She reached down to touch the babe, but in the pitch darkness she could not find where it was—she could not see, she could not touch. She could only hear. She clearly heard the babe crying in the darkness.

"The gates of life have opened for me, too!" Maryo shouted and sobbed in wonder toward the miracle before her. "I, too, am within that child. Somewhere, I, too, now exist." She wept uncontrollably and felt the terror—the movement of time.

Time galloped, it galloped forward, it licked her body, devoured it, obliterated it, but she, evaporated by its fiery breath, before she disap-

peared completely, became a miniscule being, placed and protected in velvet sheaths. Around her were streaming waters. Time continued galloping, and now she was becoming. Her body grew and suddenly was swept by tides. Powerful rivulets of warm water caught her, carried her, thrust her into narrow channels, and bumped her against soft hills. They parted, and from there she slid into a more frightening place, her frame was pounded, harried, tormented. Maryo ached in the exodus of birth and rabidly clenched her tiny fists, hopelessly opposing nature's movements. Abruptly her lighted place darkened. Woman's fragrances faded; red, savage, hard hands gripped and pulled, detached her from her mother's insides. "No! No!" she wanted to call. "I don't want to be born!" But only a slight cry came from her mouth, words did not form in her green throat.

Maryo lay down. She lay down in the place which had just been vacated. She was completely prepared to accept the pains that were hers. Her time had come. Her hour was here. She had embraced, she was embraced, and her body greedily sucked in the seed of life. Dark and deserted was the emptiness of space and time. She was frozen by fear. Endless pains drilled her; and the waters, her warm waters, slowly flowed from within her. She began to move rhythmically, to push the pain downward and out of her body. Seized by tremors, she broke open like the earth the moment of a quake. Maryo opens. Her whole body opens, and gaps and deep cracks break apart and pieces become detached. She clenches her muscles and begs them not to let her warm insides go out into the open air. Her insides ripple and explode; they become lava, burning lava that scars her guts. The child breaks the final resistance and its head emerges. She gently touches it and tries to catch its soaked little body, but it slips. It slips from her body, from her hands, escapes and falls onto the vineleaves, and she bleeds and bends to take it. As she extends her arms and stretches her entire being toward the child, it escapes, crawls and laughs, hiding behind vineleaves and grapevines. The human wound opens and hemorrhages, a river of blood, and she runs to catch the child, but it just watches her and laughs and hides again. It stands upright and grows, and her soul trembles to catch the child, but it bounds away, racing into the distance, while Maryo shouts hoarsely with broken breath. When she sees the child the last time, she is a tall woman with a round belly, ready to give birth. Inconsolable, Maryo keeps her eyes tightly shut, wailing in pain.

"I suffer.. .I suffer. . .I suffer. . .I suffer. . ."

The sound shoots to the four corners of the horizon and the echo comes back faint and transformed.

"I offer. . .I offer. . .I offer. . .I offer. . ."

To the east of the village, the darkness was shattered. Exhausted, Maryo dragged her feet behind Despinyo, who was mounted on the donkey. She was firmly holding her newborn baby, wrapped in her shawl. Thunder sounded in the distance like the echo of a painful cry, and bolts of lightning crossed the gray sky of sunrise.

The regular gait of the animal brought them steadily closer to the house. From the bend in the road, Despinyo saw the lighted lamp hanging from the eaves. She sighed with relief. They had lighted the yard for her return. Now the lamp's light was dissolving as the illumination of dawn poured around it. With great effort Despinyo climbed the steps and entered the kitchen which served as their bedroom. Giannakos awoke, lifted his head from the pillow, and gazed at her with half-closed eyes.

"What happened to you, kale?" He was upset. "Where have you been all night?"

"My time came," she said.

Now he saw the babe in her arms. From the neighboring room Maria came running into the kitchen. The other children stirred on their pallets.

"Is it a girl or a boy, kale mana?" she breathlessly asked.

"It was too dark to see," the mother answered, placing the child in Maria's arms.

Maria lovingly cuddled the babe and looked.

Maryo looked at Maria and the two of them smiled.

Maryo was awakened by the shuffling of bedroom slippers across the tiled area in the yard. She had become used to sleeping lightly, and the slightest noise awakened her. *Mother must be walking in the yard*, she thought and started to get up. Aching all over, her body refused to move. *What is going on?* she wondered. *What's wrong with me?* A flood of realization washed over her as her memory returned, pounding her like a cataract. *I have gone back in space and time! I have been sleeping on a pallet in the storeroom of my mother's childhood home. The person outside shuffling along is not my mother. It can't be my mother. She has only just been born.*

Maryo arose painfully, threw something over her shoulders, and went out into the garden. She found an old woman climbing the stairs, and again she was shocked. It was a small woman with a bent back dressed in black. It was her mother! That moment she heard a baby crying.

What is going on? Which one is my mother—the baby who is crying, or this old woman going up the steps?

She rushed to the steps and mounted them two by two. She reached the old woman on the top step and touched her shoulder. She turned and glanced a moment at Maryo. Bearing her toothless gums for a moment in a smile, she turned her eyes toward the kitchen and called out: "Despinyo! Mori Despinyo! Where are you, mori?"

Despinyo sleepily opened the kitchen door. "Welcome, kalomana!"

"You haven't come to visit me in a long time, mori!" the old woman said. Catching sight of Despinyo's flat belly, she added, "So, you had it, kori mou? You had the ill-fated one?"

"Yes, the child came, Kalomana!"

"Well, may it be blessed, mori Despinyo! But where have you been all this time? We can't manage anymore, me and your old father. That goat of ours will be our ruin. It broke into the garden and gobbled up everything we have! Come, my child. Come and help us."

"I will, kalomana! I will!" Despinyo pronounced heartily. "And if I can't come myself, I'll send one of the boys."

"Send that smart lass," the old woman said, glancing at Maryo as Despinyo stepped into the kitchen.

"Don't you worry your head about a thing," Despinyo reassured her while she thought, *My old folks aren't with it any more.* She returned with her apron full of raisins, figs, and almonds. "Some goodies in thanks for your blessing," she said, and the old woman overflowed with good wishes for the child.

"May the child live like the tall mountains! But don't forget that greedy goat—it will ruin us, devouring all our vegetables!"

She descended the steps with great care, and before closing the garden gate, she paused, turned, looked at Maryo and motioned her to approach. As she eagerly stepped to her side, the old woman whispered:"You come, dear girl; the boys are small and don't want to do a thing. Let's go together to see what can be done."

"Of course I'll come along, kalomana," Maryo agreed. "Where is your house?"

"Not far. It's there past yonder field," she said, pointing up the road.

"Let's go, then! Let's go!"

They took the road bordering the field and leading out of the village.

"And who might you be?" the old woman asked.

"I'm one of the clan, kalomana. I'm just one of the clan."

"But of what family?" the old woman probed.

"Of your family, in Despinyo's line."

"I don't remember you, my girl."

"But how could you, granny? You've never laid eyes on me before today."

Maryo laughed and the old woman was irritated.

"How could it be I don't I know you, since you are family and sleep in the storeroom? I saw that you sleep there; don't tell me differently. I saw that with my own eyes. You can't fool me."

The old woman was indignant and Maryo was confused. How should she approach such an old woman? How could she understand?

"Listen, grandma—I've come from your line but many, many years later. I've come to see you."

"Is that so!" she responded. "And now that you've seen us—what do you think?"

"When I say I've come to see you, I don't mean just visit."

"Is that so! Well, what is it you want, then?"

"I'll tell you, kalomana: I want to get hold of life from way, way back." She halted, hardly knowing how to proceed. Then after a moment she went on. "I want to understand. I want to trace the tread in the pattern to its source; I want to reach life's thread at its beginning and catch its meaning."

The old woman stopped, turned, and gazed at her. She searched Maryo's face to test her sincerity. She saw that she was perfectly serious. The old woman smiled and then began to laugh. At first the laughter was quiet, but the more she considered Maryo's words, the more intense her laughter became. She doubled over in mirth. It was a mean, sarcastic laugh, like Maryo's mother's laughter. It filled Maryo with bitterness. Thorns of memory pricked her body. Whenever her mother laughed at her doings, she felt torn to shreds. A thrashing would have been a thousand times preferable to that cruel laugh.

The old woman did not turn and see Maryo's face as it was darkened by bad memories. She walked on, continuing to laugh.

"So, you're looking for the thread, kori mou? You want to reach life's thread at its beginning and catch its meaning—that's your story, my little soul?"

Her thin body shook with laughter as her footsteps became more and more rapid. She was running now; she was running so fast, it was impossible for Maryo to keep up. Heavy beads of perspiration rolled down her brow, her damp clothes clung to her and impeded her movement. The little-traveled road petered out in a field, becoming a vague, pot-holed, rock-strewn path. Maryo kept stubbing her toes, stumbling, and twisting her ankles. She was about to turn back, and the old woman seemed to divine her thoughts. She stopped running and turned.

"Let's sit down under yonder fig tree," she told Maryo, pointing.

Right in the middle of this dry, barren place there was a solitary fig tree. Sickly, scaly, and yellow-leafed from lack of water, the tree was lean-ing, ready to fall. Maryo was amazed. How could she not have seen that tree? She must have been running with her head lowered. Quietly she came up to the old woman, who had already sat down right on the stones at the fig tree's roots.

Leaning against the trunk, the old woman was munching raisins. She filled her hand from her pocket, brought the raisins to her mouth, and shoved the handful in, but some repeatedly fell into her apron. She meticulously picked them up one by one, brought them back to her mouth. She was chewing the same way Maryo's mother did. The movement of her jaw seemed to set her face in motion, moving her nose and shutting her eyes. *She wouldn't be able to chew almonds*, thought Maryo with a feeling of vindictive pleasure that the chewing provoked. It was as if the old woman again guessed her thoughts. She took an almond from her apron, cracked the shell on the rocks, and between two flat stones ground the kernel to powder, putting that in her mouth and eyeing Maryo with an ironic glint in her beady, hawkish eyes.

"Where is your house, giagia?" Maryo asked indifferently.

"You can see it right up there." The old woman gestured.

Maryo was suddenly jolted. That remote little house, white-washed, with faded sky-blue shutters, and framed by two oak trees—its image was somewhere in her memory. It had always been a part of her, though she did not know where she had seen the house before or if she had ever seen it at all. Yet it had been with her for years. Its image brought her intense nostal-gia, and like a fever the nostalgia cut her feet out from under her.

"Let's go, kalomana! Let's go!" she urged.

She wanted to see the house from up close, to enter it, to touch the sideboard, to drink cool well water from the enamel cup, to see the small wooden bathing trough, and gaze at the damp wooden floor. She did not know where and how she had come to know these things, but they were part of her.

"Come!" she said, "Come!"

The old woman tried to stand but couldn't manage. "Help me a bit, my child," she said, extending her hand.

Maryo gently pulled her to her feet, and the old woman leaned unsteadily and wearily against her. She hung on, dragging her feet as Maryo pulled her forward. Anxious to proceed, Maryo lifted her from the waist and she hung on Maryo's shoulders. Dragging along the path, the tips of her toes made a line in the dirt, disturbed pebbles, and raised puffs of dust. As Maryo lifted her somewhat higher, she climbed onto her back, and Maryo bent her head as much as she could to avoid that sour smell on the old woman's breath which time brings up from aged guts. With great effort she strained forward, pushing her body, and begged her soul not to despise the old women. "Don't," she said. "Don't despise her. Don't feel disgust." The old woman brought her arms ever tighter around her, pulled herself higher on her back, and kept her face glued to Maryo's, as if she wanted breath from her breath, life from her strong body.

Near to the house Maryo lowered the old woman onto a rock by the old man who was awaiting them. He was dressed in black with Cretan knickers. His hair, mustache and beard were snow-white. His small eyes dripped anger.

"Just look at that goat, the devil take her!" he snapped, flinging stones at the animal munching in the garden.

The stones which hit the white back seemed to be no more bothersome than the touch of a fly. The animal continued to feed hungrily on succulent roots and tender leaves.

"Get her out of my garden, lass!" he begged.

Maryo jumped the fence, looped the goat's lead around her hand and pulled. The goat did not budge.

"Smack it with a stick," the old woman advised.

Maryo grabbed a dried branch and struck the animal harder than she intended. Shocked, the creature leaped to retreat, threw Maryo down, and dragged her along the garden path. Her legs were filled with bleeding scratches and her eyes with tears of rage.

"Hold on for all you're worth, and hitch 'er tight under that olive tree !" the old man bellowed.

He had sprung to his feet and was hopping about enthusiastically. Scrambling to her feet, Maryo hauled the goat out to the other end of the yard and tied her up under the olive tree.

"Who is that girl, anyhow?" asked the old man, again sitting down by kalomana's side.

"She's one of us. Kin." Again she broke into laughter but abruptly grew serious. "Says she's come to reach life's thread at its beginning and catch its meaning!"

Then the ironic laughter broke forth again as she nudged the old man with her knee.

"Whose thread you say?" the old man blurted, cupping his hand behind his ear.

"The thread of life!" said the old woman, nudging him once more.

"Whose life, mori?" he asked loudly.

"The life folks lead, you idiot, you!" she pushed him with both hands bursting with laughter.

"Ah. . ." said the old man knowingly. "Do you think the rope might break?" he asked.

"I doubt it," Maryo said, anxious to leave.

These two old people had wearied her, worn her to a frazzle.

"I really must be going," she said, and without waiting for an answer she started to run.

"Hey, Maryo—can't we offer something to that lively girl? She's kin, after all," the old man said when Maryo was already at a distance.

Imagine that! That old woman and I have the same name! Maryo thought and ran even faster.

When she reached the fig tree, she stopped. She wanted to think, to look back and view again the house of her forbears. Her jaw dropped in surprise and her heart sank. The house no longer showed clearly from that spot; she could barely make out the black shadows formed by the two old trees with their enormous tangled branches. It was like her childhood when she would look through binoculars. How she loved to bring the world nearer, to shorten distances, and observe things closely. Then she would playfully turn the binoculars around and everything would instantly retreat, grow distant, out of reach, non-existent. How sad that was; now the same sadness struck her. How she missed those two old people, that little house, that blooming garden, and that goat! How far off it all was, how remote! "And I didn't enter the little house to take a look," she sighed. "I didn't go in, I didn't see. I didn't take the food they wished to offer me. Those old folks are so infinitely far away."

She ran. She ran all the way. Winded, she reached the wide lane, and before turning the corner by the house she heard the crying of the child. Her heart skipped a beat in joy. The baby was awake! A wide smile lighted her face and her hand trembled with longing to touch the child. She opened the garden gate. On the low wall around the verandah stood a small girl. On the tiles was another, somewhat older. It looked like Garoufalo. Could it be she? She certainly looked like Garoufalo, the way she was crawling.

But who was the girl standing on the wall, who looked so much like her own daughter?

"Get down, Panagiota! Be careful! Don't fall!"

Maryo stood gaping; it was her mother, Panagiota.

"How amazing," whispered Maryo, approaching.

The child was playing on the wall, balancing. Her arms were leveled on either side, and she was walking back and forth on the narrow edge. *The naughty girl will fall,* Maryo thought with that anxiety which children bring into their mothers' lives. The little girl paid no heed to Maryo's thoughts or to her sister's words. She just continued her play, now with eyes shut. Maryo held her eyes wide open, concentrated, as if she could see for the child. She wanted to send her thoughts to safeguard her as she did with her own children when they were far away. With her thoughts she protected them.

Maryo proceeded toward the wall. That moment the child lost her balance and Maryo barely had time to bring her shoulders under her. She fell heavily onto Maryo's back and then slipped lightly to the ground.

"Ouf!" the three of them went, Maryo from the pain she received on her back, Panagiota from fright, and Garoufalo from fear.

Simultaneously two doors opened. From the bedroom Maria emerged, and from the kitchen Aggerou, her hands wet with dishwater. She frantically flew down the stairs, picked up the child, saw she was all right, and set to beating her on her fanny, her head, and her back, screaming, "Haven't I told you to be careful. . . How many times have I told you to watch out?"

Maria rushed between the two, taking the child in her arms. Kissing and petting her, she cooed, "Ach, Ach—poor thing. . .our poor little girl. . .but she'll be all right. . .".

Aggerou raced to the verandah, seized Garoufalo by the hair, slapped her on the head and back, jeering, "You ill-born thing, why didn't you call us? Do you want our sister to die? Is that what you want?" she shrieked, cuffing Garoufalo.

Maria rushed between the two of them, embracing the child and crooning, "Ach. . .Ach, my poor sweet thing. . . my poor sweet thing. . .".

Aggerou, her wild mania cut short but still boiling in her blood, began to scream. She fell to the ground in spasms, thrashed, tore her hair, screeched. Her face went blue and froth came from her mouth. Maria had embraced her, and with shocked pain in her voice she soothed, "Ach, Ach. . .our little girl. Ach, Ach. . . our Aggerou!"

The other children, Maryo behind them, looked on with gaping eyes. After some time, Aggerou's spasms subsided as Maria continued to rock her in cradling arms as if she were an infant, tears running down her cheeks and falling on the cheeks of her twin sister, who was now sunk in deep, serene sleep.

Maryo witnessed the incident with despair. She wished to intervene, but what could she do? Nature has its laws which she could not transgress. Only one thought preyed upon her. *Is all this real? Are all these things actually going on or merely imagined?*

She remained on the verandah steps watching the little children pulling the exhausted Aggerou into the kitchen. The door closed and Maryo heard the water gurgling from the pitcher and a sigh released from a child's bosom—which child she did not know. But the sigh was real. It definitely reached her ears.

She slowly descended the steps and went to sit under an aged olive tree. She arranged a spot by brushing aside the hens' droppings with the side of her shoe. *No!* she declared to herself. *All that isn't real; I've imagined it.* But the sentence did not end as a sharp pain shortened her breath. *Pain, however, is real*, she thought. She accepted the thought as it continued to the cause. *That pain comes from the force of the child falling on me. Its body struck mine, and I hurt. Therefore it is real.* With both hands she massaged the painful spot in the small of her back, and the pain began to lessen, withdraw, fade. *Now the pain is no longer real*, she thought. *And what about the children's crying?* She returned her attention to the house. The closed door muffled the sounds of crying. Nothing could be heard from the house. *But there are smells. The smell of chicken droppings.* She took a deep sniff, but her nose had already accustomed her to the smell. The droppings had no distinct odor. There was only a chicken, a small hen pecking the ground. She was foraging for seeds and worms. Her avid pecking threw dirt that sprinkled on Maryo's legs. The hen attacked a white pebble embedded in the ground. She took it for a seed, and her beak pecked with persistent power. Maryo saw and heard the fowl. *" Is this real, then? But if it is not real, what is? How is that determined? What senses determine reality?*

She settled more and more comfortably under the olive tree and surrendered to memory. Endless images of life flowed before her. At her children she stopped the flow. Her children overpowered her mind. Her heart trembled in recollection. *My children are my reality*, she affirmed. Two small blond naked babes sweetened her sight. In one corner of the room was her young husband seated in an armchair reading, and the children, one smaller than the other, were seated on her knees. Pieces of red cardboard taped to her index fingers were little birds nesting on the table.

"I've got two little birdies in two little baskets. . ."

One hand flitted above her head.

"One flew far oh far away."

The other hand raised.

"The other followed after ..."

Abandonment, sadness and yearning.

"But came the happy happy day: the one flew back.... and the other followed after."

The two hands flitted back and the fingers touched the table. Joyous was the triumphant return. The room was filled with giggling and the clapping of little hands.

Maryo's smile faded. Riding on waves of memory, she pulled up before a tall youth.

I've got two little children in two baskets. The words filled her memory.

"I hear tell of King Solomon's treasures." He spoke hastily, seated on the motorcycle. "I'm going to find them!"

He gave his foot starter a powerful kick.

"Who needs King Solomon's treasures?" Maryo asked.

She shook with despair. Her voice was drowned in the thunderous motor as it raced, roared, then back-fired. She raised her hand in farewell to the cyclist's back. *One flew far oh far away from me. . .*

A little note. A slip of white paper with a few scribbled words: "There is not enough life to be shared."

Two little children . . . The other followed after. . . The memory died away.

The little hen went on pecking at the pebbles in the garden.

Are my children real or are they an illusory memory? Did I really have children? Maryo felt dazed. She was seized by fear and longing. Suddenly she journeyed, leaping to distant places. She saw herself seated between the roots of an extremely tall willow. She was resting her back against its trunk, stroking her bulging belly. The child moved inside her. It responded to her caress, was becoming her child, preparing for life, there on the campus amidst gothic towers in the middle of Chicago. She was working in a university library with battlemented towers and leaded windows. Its thick walls zealously secreted on dusty shelves knowledge of the ideas and souls of a myriad of people over the ages. Maryo touched, she touched the fragile volumes whose yellowed leaves were pulverized by so much time. With love and awe she touched the books, and her hands trembled as she sensed the human wisdom so carefully preserved and guarded. There, nearby those walls and books, her first child had been born. Yes, that was real, not merely some trick of memory, for she lived it still. She was seated under that very same willow tree with the smell of the grass, students dotting the quadrangle. She was seated with her first child in her arms and her second within her womb. It was moving, developing, growing, becoming taller, that boy of hers, when Madame Fermi came by.

Laura Fermi greeted her and patted her daughter's little head. Very graciously, she asked if Maryo would, if it weren't too much trouble, be so good as to find her some books on Mussolini. Mussolini had changed their life, hers and Enrico's, she told Maryo. The third button of her blouse was undone, an edge of white lace showing, drawing Maryo's eye like a magnet. She wanted to bend, apologize, and button that button. Indeed the dictator had disrupted their life, she continued, but here in Chicago their life had been filled with purpose, for here Enrico's experiment had succeeded in smashing the atom and setting off the first chain reaction.

"Certainly your Democritus had not suspected such a thing was possible, while Enrico—I'm writing his biography—earned the title 'father of the Atomic Bomb' right here at the University of Chicago," she said.

She pointed with her white hand toward the tablet on the Stagg Field stands not far off. It was a small tablet commemorating the smashing of the atom, "December 14, 1942." That moment came Maryo's own beloved, the young father of her children; he bent and kissed Maryo on her half-parted lips, and she sipped the taste of the kiss. He tossed the child high over his head and Maryo gazed fondly at her little back, at the little damp curls of hair on the nape of the little neck dampened with perspiration, she smelled the fragrance of the child's body, feeling the other child kicking in her womb. It was all a jumble: the tablet inscribed December 14, 1942, the Hiroshima bomb, the mushroom of death, and the child's laughter as the father tossed her into the air and lovingly caught her, the laughter cut by breathless excitement, Laura Fermi's unbuttoned third button, and the books closed behind thick walls, yellowing, fragile books gazed upon with wonder, that flash at Hiroshima... Suddenly the images dissolved. Were all those things real? She was no longer sure. She sighed, feeling her mind emptying. She saw that the chicken had finally loosened the little white pebble and was chasing it around the garden with her beak.

Panagiota and Garoufalo appeared on the verandah with bright, freshly scrubbed faces and damp hair. One child sat on the tiles, the other on the verandah's low wall. Both girls had a thick slice of damp bread covered with sugar. Sitting quietly, they studiously licked off all the sugar and then chewed happily on the bread.

"How I love children enjoying bread and sugar!" Maryo exclaimed.

She left her seat on the olive tree's roots, shook the dust from her skirt, and went to sit beside Panagiota on the moudi. She was so delighted to be near her mother and her sweet aunt.

That evening, Maria told her mother about the incident involving Aggerou.

"Froth came from her mouth, mother. I tell you she was screaming and frothing at the mouth!"

"Never you mind," the mother said wearily. "Never you mind."

Heavy drops of water fell on Maryo's face. Water splashed on her cheeks and she suddenly awoke. She sat up on her makeshift bed. *Can it be raining?* she wondered and then remembered. *I am in the storeroom and the kitchen is over my head.*

It was very early Sunday morning and the children were bathing in preparation for the festivities. It was a glorious day. The village was excitedly celebrating an ethnic holiday. Flags were waving and enthusiasm was filling the streets.

Maryo bounded up the steps and glued her nose to the window. The air in the kitchen was steaming from hot bath water. Panagiota went to the garden to fetch firewood, and Maryo seized the opportunity to slip into the kitchen. Seated on grandpa's and grandma's bed, she looked fondly at the steamy forms of the little children. In the wood stove dried branches glowingly burned and sent up sparks, a large kettle sang a high note on the stovetop, and the children bubbled over with sing-song voices of fussing and fun. Their bath itself was a cordial festival.

Aggerou's quick hands scrubbed their small bodies and shampooed their little heads, while Maria brought the water for rinsing and the towels. She toweled the children, dressed them, combed their hair, and one by one their baths were completed. Now it was Maria's turn, then Aggerou's. Maria bathed quickly and it was time for Aggerou. She stepped into the bathing trough and water sloshed onto the floor. Her figure gleamed whitely; her small breasts were slight swells on her chest. Her womanhood was modestly hidden under a triangle of brunette down. The two girls were taken by these miraculous sights. Embarrassed by the persistent direction of their gaze, they turned their eyes elsewhere and resumed the bath. Maria poured water over Aggerou and threw hidden glances at the slight bosom and soft down. Aggerou soaped her hands and with soft movements cleansed her body. Her foamy hands passed over all her curves, over each magical little channel of flesh. Both girls felt their touch grow gentler as their bodies thrilled to a strange little pulsation. Those sharp but delightful feelings troubled the girls, and they constantly shifted the movements of their hands, which became swift and cool, and more water overflowed onto the kitchen floor.

The schoolroom was packed with villagers. Those who had arrived very early in the morning had secured seats on the chairs and benches arranged in rows facing the front of the room. The latecomers stood leaning against the walls, sat on window ledges, or crowded into doorways. Most of the celebrants were massed in the school courtyard.

Everyone was inspired. The teacher, wiping her overflowing eyes with a large handkerchief, delivered a speech depicting the terrible sufferings of Greece, and immediately thereafter "Hellas" appeared. Aggerou, tall and proud with a sparkling white sheet neatly draped over her like an ancient Greek toga, her hair tied behind with a blue ribbon, mounted the platform. With arms spread, she recited:

Small in size, rich in glory,
I am known throughout the world;
All the nations know the story
Of my bold intrepid soul!

That I rise once more to struggle
Not a single doubt can lurk;
I ask naught but to do battle
'Gainst the cruel tyrant Turk!

The glorious mountaineer fighter, "Long Rifle," sprang onto the platform. He knelt in fealty before Aggerou. It was Tsortsis in a white kilt, wearing a red fez. Aggerou grew faint, as he proclaimed:

Great of soul I am your fighter,
I am Hellas's vaunting gun;
I have come to serve your banner,
I am forever freedom's son!

To Hellas I vow my honor,
I endure the fearful strife;

'Gainst all foes and for all brothers,
For Hellas I pledge my life!

"Hellas" gave her hand to "Long-Rifle," who pressed it dramatically to his heart. There was Aggerou thrust into the midst of all these people with Tsortsis trapping her hand against his chest. The pounding of Tsortis's heart exceeded the thunderous waves of applause.

Aggerou was overcome with embarrassment. Mortified, she forgot her remaining verses, fled from the platform, and dashed into Maria's arms. There was not room enough for her in Maria's embrace; there was not room enough in the schoolroom, though she was showered with compliments by the villagers and her classmates, who eyed her jealously. "Bravo, Aggerou, our 'Hellas'!" they all shouted, as she rushed out of the school and down the lane to their home. She felt that somehow there was something at home which she had forgotten, but she found nothing there and raced back to the schoolhouse. Once more she felt Tsortsis's eyes upon her and sensed the beating of his heart. Again she fled. The noise deafened her, disturbed her; she felt a strange excitement.

Her mother's hand came down heavily on her head.

"Home you go, you stupid thing," she said, pulling her hair and untying the blue ribbon.

Aggerou was stunned. She was stunned by desire nestled yearningly deep within her, and the sharp edges of that newfound longing pierced and pricked her, increasing as night came on.

That night as she went to bed with the rest of the children, while removing her toga, she felt that somehow she was undressing herself as she never had before. She felt stripped and completely naked, with her insides warm and steaming. She heard her sisters drop off to sleep, one by one. Maria was the last to softly cross the border into sleep. Aggerou was left alone,. completely alone.

Frightened doves, her two hands flew restless and inexperienced in unknown places filled with mystery. Fearfully and awkwardly, her two hands searched amidst low bushes, thick growths, delicate blossoms, and damp petals. They probed for a place to build a nest. Two doves fluttered into the air and Aggerou flew with them so high it took her breath away. Now she was panting, panting on a magic path, heaving breathless as she reached the peak of the climb.

Aggerou watched the sun break intensely in the East before she sank into sleep. She got up late that morning and was shocked to find her panties soaked with blood.

In tears, Maryo stroked Aggerou's head and tried futilely to reach her little aunt.

"It's nothing," she told her again and again. "It's just that your period has come; you have entered the woman's world."

Kneeling in the stable, Aggerou stuffed a clean cloth into her panties and with terror felt the cloth become soaked with her blood. Four days she sneaked into the stable and fell on her knees.

"Forgive me, O Lord," she prayed. "I won't do it again ever!"

At the end of the fourth day, the Lord forgave her, and the blood ceased to flow from her guts. Despinyo sighed with relief. *Holy water of our Lady of Mercy is a strong antidote to the Evil Eye*, she thought, seeing Aggerou return to normal and go about the usual housework. Aggerou's eyes shone; her face was radiant. *This is an intermission—an intermission in her life.* Maryo mused. With this thought sadness come upon her. She attempted to hold it back. *After all*, she thought, *isn't our life in general an intermission?*

Aggerou carefully observed her body. She took great care to prevent its carrying her away. God was watching her sternly from on high. His forefinger raised, he told her sternly: "Take care, Aggerou. Beware of sin!" And Aggerou prayed. She prostrated herself and fasted. She went to church and lighted candles, and the new priest, a heavy six-footer, took her by the shoulders, blessed her, and pinched her cheek. She kissed his hand in reverence.

At night she traveled to strange places. Searching for something, seeking, she raced along broad streets, climbed hilltops, descended to the sea and rolled in the surf, cooled off, and calmed herself. In the morning with black circles under her eyes and faint limbs, she would go regularly about her chores. One afternoon, when she was seated on the verandah facing the road, Tsortsis passed by. Walking along their lane by chance, he caught sight of Aggerou on the verandah. The girl froze. Their eyes interlocked and that bursting gaze overflowed into their bodies. They said nothing; both were speechless. The youth took to his heels and disappeared around the corner, while the girl dragged herself in a daze to the bedroom. She felt so heavy, so weighed down, as if her heart and all her guts had sunk to her feet and held them in place.

That night she went to bed at the same time as all the children. God was the first to go to sleep. One by one the little children followed him, and finally, light as a feather, Maria drifted to rest. Like wild birds, Aggerou's hands fluttered over her body. Now they knew the place, they knew their nest, and they flew there instantly. In the morning she awoke with the hand of the Lord upon her, thrusting her into the furnace of hell. She could not lift her head from the weight which she felt upon her. God's face was livid with wrath—his eye pierced her with rage.

Her mother at once gave her Holy Water of our Lady of Mercy, but when Aggerou stayed in bed for three days they summoned Kanelios, their doctor.

"The girl has simply begun to menstruate; she's a woman now," the physician said. He took his fee and left.

"Out of bed, you lazy idiot!" the mother said sharply.

She rushed to the bed, pulling and slapping her prone daughter. With the third slap, the girl began to scream. She screeched, wriggled, thrashed on the mattress till her eyes rolled upward and her mouth foamed. The foam, mixed with her screams, flooded her pallet, overflowed to the bedroom floor, poured out through the door, onto the verandah, down the stairs, through the yard, into the lanes and throughout the village.

"Saints preserve us," blurted the mother. "Shame is on our heads!"

The family withered. Full of shame, they lost their rhythm. Then they became angry; their overwhelming rage broke out upon the guilty child.

Maryo awoke drowned in tones of twilight. She was deeply distressed in this hour of fierce emptiness. Her soul, a small, frightened animal, seemed to withdraw into emptiness, and the body without a soul at once emptied; her chest sank, her belly dried up, and her limbs hung like snapped branches.

"I'm afraid, "Maryo cried in the darkness of the storeroom. "I'm afraid for this body I've carried so many years."

The grayish illumination of twilight stole through cracks in the door and the small dirty window beside it. Maryo was choking—her breath was short. She had to escape this constricting space. She gathered her strength, aroused her courage, and commanded her body to rise at once. Heavily she dragged herself out into the yard, opened the outer gate and entered the lane. She turned eastward to meet the light of day that would dispel this dream light.

She found herself in deserted fields and on a road. It was a hard, straight, road that glittered from many footsteps.

What a host of people have walked this very road, Maryo thought and pounded her feet so her echo would be heard. Silence. The ground absorbed the sound and only the energy she exerted turned back, electrified her soles, and charged her spirit.

Maryo was completely alone. There was not even a shadow cast by her body. The place harrowed her. It was alien, totally alien. She thought of returning to the storeroom to await till daylight.. There she would hide herself under the thick hay.

Turning a corner, she found herself on a very narrow path. Low stone walls divided field from field, making a deserted meander. I'm seeing this soil for the first time, *she thought. Her pace increased and turned westward. In the distance a white chapel stood out, silently and mistily projected against the bare landscape. A small bell tower, and around it dry cypress trees, also without shadows, dominated the space.*

Suddenly Maryo caught sight of a huge shape in the distance. It was rushing toward her, and she stood motionless in the middle of the path, frightened, astonished. The shape approached with great speed and from up close resolved into the figure of a horse.

A huge, extremely white horse was galloping right at her. The road absorbed the sound of its hoofbeats but from its movement Maryo sensed its weight and power. Its sharp shoes sunk into the path, forming ridges wherever its wild hoofs struck.

Maryo was helpless. Stunned and frozen with fear, she fell to her knees in the middle of the path. She raised her head and gazed upward with awe. The approaching animal was massive. Lather in bright strings streaked the horse's flanks, its mane blew in the wind, and Maryo kneeling and motionless felt its heavy breath searing her face and its saliva gouging her cheeks and neck. Its muscles, steel cords, rippled across and down its hide to the very spot where Maryo riveted her gaze, the end of its shanks. As it reared, prepared to trample her, she just managed to turn. She turned her body slightly toward the right side of the path, and the horse passed by looming above her. It galloped on and she remained kneeling and dumb, its image oppressing her.

The fearsome image filled her mind with sadness. Time is always galloping! *she thought.* Behind us or ahead of us, time maintains the same unrelenting pace!

This knowledge weighed heavily upon Maryo's heart. With great effort she raised herself from the path and slumped on the low wall. After a few moments she noticed that her knees were badly scraped. Absent mindedly she touched her fingertips to her tongue and wiped off the blood.

A refreshing image from her childhood years blew over her: When they would fall and scrape their knees or elbows, they didn't stop—they would pause hardly a moment in their game there in the dirt streets of the neighborhood with its low houses and flowers, the flowers blooming in every yard. They would spit on their hands, hastily wipe their bleeding knees, dry hands on their shirts and continue with time agonizingly hovering over their heads. Soon it would get dark; it would get darker and darker and their mothers would come into the street and summon them home, though they hadn't finished the game.

The years were winds blowing in the memory. Endless were the images of moments, flashing, casting an illumination, erased by darkness; and Maryo shrank, she trembled, before the galloping of time, just as she had trembled before that bed. Memory immobilized; time froze. Thick white clouds, white surf, and his hair turning white. Pure white were the sheets covering the weakened body of her brother. His loved ones side by side formed a ring to ward off death.

Their taut nerves and strong bodies sought to form an impenetrable wall, but death pierced through. Scarecrows, the empty bodies of the guards collapsed in a heap. Their mouths opened and emitted sharp cries before the ravaged body.

The mind leaped up, the heart revived, grew determined. Maryo jumped down from the stone wall and raised both arms, palms upward, toward the sky. She tried to push away the weight of memory from her body, her mind, her spirit.

"That event," she cried, "appeared unreal! I couldn't believe it was taking place. Yet from that moment I have lived it countless times. Within the memory it is real. That image, that scene, that final instant, that slow, heavy, unbearable time, are present!" The cry could not escape from her mouth. The anguished feelings were trapped inside her. They seemed to be lodged within her like shards of glass.

"Giorgo-o-o!" She opened her mouth to call his name but found she had no voice. Yet she was not in the least surprised when in the distance his figure clearly appeared. She steadied herself and sprinted in that direction.

"Giorgo-o-o, wait, I have something of yours I want to give you!" It did not bother her that the sound of her voice was not audible. She was certain that he heard her and she was filled with joy. She raced towards him, taking a turn in the walled path to reach the path he was on. One more turn as yet separated them and she increased her pace, rounded the corner, but now there were branching paths and she turned breathlessly, turned again and again. The paths multiplied, she couldn't count them. She would never reach him! Winded, she stopped, keeping her eyes steadily upon her brother. She was glad she could see him from head to foot. She saw clearly *his curly hair, his bright eyes, and that smile of his. For the first time she perceived that his smile was made up of little bits of joy and a great weight of sadness. Her brother's moments were running out; his time was utterly spent.*

Maryo's soul withered as she watched him disappear into the gray light of the dream.

At the entrance to the village the sun had risen ten spans above the horizon. Day arrived pale and warm as Maryo hastened to return to her mother's house. At the crossing of the wide lane, an elderly blind woman approached her. She was carrying several loafs of blessed bread in the deep pocket of her apron. She reached in and broke off a piece of bread.

"Eat and be at peace, my little soul," she said. "Today is the day of all-souls."

Among the sisters, Aggerou's beauty drew all eyes. It was splendid: charged with magical chemistry, overflowing with femininity. Her eyes, large and playful, combed the village for the perfect male. Her mother was appalled. "Saints preserve us!" Despinyo exclaimed. She spat thrice to cast a spell against misfortune. She fell to her knees in prayer imploring the aid of God, the Virgin, and the saints to save the family from shame. In bed at night she whispered to Giannakos: "We've got to keep a sharp eye on Aggerou! We must arrange a marriage as soon as possible!"

They surveyed the eligible men of the village. Which of them would wed Aggerou and what would be her dowry?

"It will be the land at Pyrgi," urged Despinyo.

But Giannakos shouted his refusal: "No! That we will give to no one!"

His eyes fell on the smallpox marks on Despinyo's face. He recalled his words to his father on that subject at the time of the engagement, and that moment the scene with Chroustallo once more rose vividly within his thoughts.

He was drinking from early evening at Galanis's coffee house with Petros Lelemis. They had already put away a number of glasses when they were joined by Sideris's friend, Vagelios Christofakis. As Giannakos kept lifting his glass, something strange began to happen. Out of the corner of his eye he could swear he caught flitting glimpses of Chroustallo. It seemed to him that she was peeping at him around the edge of the coffee house door with her shawl held tightly around her shoulders. Then, sure enough, she was standing outside the window and beckoning to him. Giannakos was shaken. He jumped to his feet, lost his balance, and almost sprawled on the floor, but Vagelios caught him. Slurping his last glass of raki, he said goodnight to his pals and made for the door. Vagelios also stood up to go, but he pushed him back into his chair.

"Stay where you are, my friend," he said. "It's still early."

He left the coffee house, mounted the mule, and headed home. Giannakos was to swear that though he reined the mule toward the upper village, the mule had taken him to the lower village. It had gone to Chroustallo's street and stood outside her window. He hadn't pounded on the shutters; he didn't have time to touch them as they instantly opened and the girl lowered herself into the street.

"Be my man, Giannako! Marry me!" she pled. Standing on the road, she hung onto his jacket. Her very words seemed to be dripping with tears. "Take me away, Giannako, take me away! Tomorrow, Sunday, they're marrying me to the old barber with his wagon load of brats."

"I've come to take you, my heart!" Giannakos sang out.

He lifted her onto the saddle in front of him. He would take her to the church in Smyrni. He held her tightly in his arms so she wouldn't fall. He pressed against her. His heart clamored in his chest: by all the saints of the upper and lower village, may they forgive him, how exciting and fragrant this girl was! The daughter of that nobody, Anestis Dimoulas, smelled of roses and cinnamon. She was driving him crazy, making him tremble, sending his veins pounding. . .

"The land at Pyrgi is mine, I tell you!" he shouted at Despinyo.

Even now, so many years later, he still felt that pounding in his heart. He turned toward the wall, but before settling his head on the pillow, he again spoke severely to Despinyo. "Look here, woman! Don't ever mention that land again! It's mine! All mine!"

Despinyo was the first to awake. It was as if a whirlwind had broken out in their house. Yesterday afternoon a gentle breeze had come from the sea. It was refreshing, cool, and smelled of brine. Toward sundown the weather changed for the worse. Now the wind blew from the hills and a chill set in. The villagers hastened to hole up on their homes, to get under warm covers. Those who were still outside hunched their bodies and blew on their hands against the chill.

The malicious storm broke out past bedtime and found everyone asleep.

Mad winds buffeted the village and tossed things every which way. Tin roofs went flying, shutters and doors were ripped off, trees were uprooted. As night came on the wind finally subsided.

"Mercy upon us, Christ and Mary," Despinyo breathed, crossing herself.

She got up to check on the animals. They were making an awful racket. Tying a shawl around her shoulders, she opened the kitchen door. It was pitch black outside and unseasonably cold. She again crossed herself and let her feet find their way to the verandah steps. Feeling Despinyo leave the bed, Giannakos also got up, lighted a lantern and stood by the door. At the top of the stairs Despinyo's legs locked. Her feet would not move; it seemed they were not under her control. Frozen on the spot, she fearfully strained to see by the weak light of the lamp Giannakos held in the doorway. The lamp's flame trembled in the air, casting faint illumination downward into the yard, and there at the foot of the steps Despinyo saw the demon crouched and glaring at her with the infernal leer of its razor fangs, bloody gums, and savage crimson eyes. Its peaked ears stood upright and it waved its tail like a wand.

The terrified woman could not even manage to make the sign of the cross as the creature reared up, assuming gigantic size.

"Save me, Mother of God!" Despinyo screeched.

The bedroom door flung open, and her son Constantis, a powerful lad of fifteen, appeared, holding a heavy stool. Stepping to his mother's side, he hurled the stool toward the foot of the steps. The demon shrank backward and with a wolf-like growl retreated and vanished, leaving only a gust of air passing harmlessly over shutters and doors, which still trembled in fear.

Despinyo stayed awake all that night praying continually. When the sun rose, she went out into the garden to examine the great damage wrought by the demon. Amidst the debris in the yard all the hens lay with their necks broken. The roosters all remained unscathed.

"An evil omen!" Despinyo shivered.

She summoned the newly arrived priest. Coming at once with all the appropriate means for exorcising the demon, he showered the family with a surplus of Holy Water brought from Aghios Panteleimonas church, and they gratefully kissed his hand, bringing raisins and almonds, and pressing coins into his open palm.

Maryo witnessed all these goings-on with a certain uneasiness; she felt there was something amiss about that priest. She felt that something untoward was brewing inside him.

Panagiota was angry. Her mother, Maria, and Aggerou were going to the convent, while she had to stay at home to look after Phtychio and the other infant, Liapis. Garoufalo would help, but it was Panagiota who had to care for Phtyhio, who was ill-born. Phtychio was almost three years old but had not begun to walk. She could only crawl, and worst of all, she was always coughing. At times someone had to hold her up so she wouldn't choke.

Panagiota wanted to sob or to lash out at someone. She wanted to jump over the wall and be the first on the way to the convent, but Giannakos grabbed her and held her hard by the shoulders. "Watch your step," he warned. "Keep a sharp eye on Phtyhio."

She sullenly nodded her head and went to sit in the kitchen. That way at least she could avoid the sight of them leaving for their excursion.

"You arrange things with Sophia," Giannakos told his wife. He always referred to his wife's sister by her secular name. "Tell Sophia that if she likes we will pay the fee for her cell at the convent or have one built for her at once. We'll help do whatever she wants, provided she keeps Aggerou."

Giannakos passed through the gate first with his sons, heading for the fields. Before he hit his stride he paused. "And hey!" he shouted. "Don't come back without taking care of everything!"

"Don't you worry, kale," said Despinyo.

Despinyo was praying to herself. She felt a deep unrest. She feared that ill fortune was looming on the horizon.

Without mother and Maria the house was deserted, and Panagiota was on the brink of tears. She decided, after all, to watch their departure. From the garden gate she viewed them moving off into the distance, mother on the donkey's back. Returning to the kitchen, she kicked Phtyhio, who began to cry. On the moudi again, she shouted furiously toward the road, "The demon take you all! All of you, I say!"

Turning, she found Garoufalo seated on the tiles, Nikolos sitting on the verandah wall, and Phythio with the infant Liapis nearby Garoufalo. All of them were eyeing her anxiously. She puffed out her little chest, stared through the slits of half-closed eyelids, clenched her tiny fists, and drank in the scene before her. *They are all afraid of me*, she thought, feeling the tension released from her chest.

It was already past noon when they reached the convent. No voices were heard. There was total silence within those sacred walls, which hid the courtyard. Only the bell tower of the little church showed, snow-white and surrounded by the deep green tops of cypress trees. The girls waited restlessly outside the high wooden door with a cross in its center. By the door was a small bell. Despinyo pulled the string and soon an eye appeared through a peephole in the door. The eye seemed to smile when it encountered the woman and girls. As the heavy door began to swing open, the girls pushed it all the way with great enjoyment and repressed giggles. They found themselves in a courtyard filled with pots of basil and honeysuckle vines.

They hugged and kissed the little nun, and she approached Despinyo with head lowered.

"How is my mother, Aunt Despinyo?" she inquired anxiously.

"Very well; she sends her love."

"And the children?"

"All are well."

"And the mute—how is he? Is he still unruly?"

"No, my dear, not any longer," Despinyo told the lie, in spite of the holiness of the place.

The little nun joyously embraced her cousins and led them to her cell.

Despinyo went on to the Mother Superior's cell. She climbed the short flight of stairs, stood on the small landing, and deeply inhaled the aroma of blossoms. The landing was overhung with flowers. The convent's beauty pierced Despinyo's soul. *Why*, she thought, *didn't I listen to my mother? I could have been in Mother Agni's place, and she would be visiting me with her troubles!*

The narrow door of the cell opened, and Mother Agni held Despinyo's shoulders with her soft white hands. "The bitter cup is for all of us, Despinyo; it takes faith, great faith, to drink."

Despinyo fell into her sister's embrace and burst into tears.

The girls entered the convent courtyard. In the center was the church of Aghios Sostis, surrounded by two-story balconies with rows of cells. Outside the walls of the convent proper were stables and pens for the animals raised on the premises. There were also gardens and sheds, and everything was surrounded by the outer wall. Twenty nuns, all young girls from neighboring villages, attended to the work of the convent.

Maria wandered through the courtyard enchanted by the surroundings. A slight breeze moved the bell rope and a gentle note came down from the bell tower, going straight to Maria's heart. Nearby Aggerou paced restlessly, irritated by the silence of the courtyard and the monotonous vibration of the bell.

Aggerou entered the church and immediately backed out through the ornate open door. In the dim candle light, the figures of the icons seemed to loom before her. They seemed swollen by the dampness of the walls, and the odor choked her, taking away her breath. The church smelled of mold and incense. Aggerou strolled with relief in the open, sunny, air.

Maria entered. She felt an increased rhythm in her heart. Her heart always beat faster when she was inside Aghios Sostis church. Holy fragrances made her knees tremble, the dim light sweetened the faces of the Saints, and the Virgin Mary as always awaited her with a smile. Maria bowed before her as one of her own folk.

"Grant a blessing upon all our children," she whispered.

She looked at the Virgin Mary's child and wanted to tell her how much happiness their own son, Liapis, gave them. She wanted to ask the mother of God to make Phtyhio well, to bless Garoufalo, and heal Aggerou. Something bad was happening to her that she couldn't explain. If that foam coming from her mouth could stop, Maria would be grateful. A noise outside the church drew her attention, and the smile seemed to vanish from the Virgin's face as Maria looked anxiously out into the courtyard. She hurried out to find Aggerou in spasms on the ground, her body thrashing and her mouth opened to scream. Phlegm had blocked her throat, so neither sound nor foam came from her mouth, which was twisted and blue. Gradually her body's spasms decreased and she lay still.

When Aggerou came to, her head was enclosed in a wide white bandage and Maria was by her side.

"Aggerou, my Aggerou, you will never scream or have froth come from your mouth again. The Virgin Mary has healed you," Maria soothed.

As Maria embraced her sister, kissing her cheeks, lips, and hair, Aggerou knew deep within her that indeed she was completely well. She searched for that hum in her head that ran through her body and come out of her mouth as foam, but nothing of the sort had remained within her. Her body no longer trembled within; it was completely tranquil. She sighed in enjoyment of that stillness.

Despinyo followed the Mother Superior's directions to the letter. Each morning she gave Aggerou three tablespoons of holy water from the church of Aghios Sostis, not from the church of Our Lady of Mercy. Then she read the exorcism at four points of Aggerou's body, the head, feet, right and left arm, so as to trace a cross above her daughter. In the meantime she had sent funds to build a two-story cell at the convent; and, on her own initiative,

looked for a husband for Aggerou. Despinyo also did something not speci-
fied by Sister Agni. Each Wednesday and Friday she and Aggerou went to
the church of Aghios Panteleimonas and lighted votive candles.

Gray, heavy, the clouds closed in from mid-afternoon. Despinyo beckoned to Aggerou and they at once set off to church for their ritual. Maryo's
pace was heavy behind the quick light steps of the tall, lithe Aggerou, and
still farther behind was Despinyo, wrapped in her black shawl and mantilla.
From the dampness in the church their bodies quivered. The sanctuary was
dim; only a few candles were burning. The mother approached the cande-
labra with reverence and lighted each of her candles with care. The priest
nodded good-evening and took the daughter aside for confession.

This newly arrived priest, Father Vagelis, was young but stout, with
brown hair. His long beard was reddish in hue. He had come to the village
as a fugitive and had taken over from Father Nicolas, who was over eighty.
The old priest, who had served in Alatsata for over half a century, could no
longer manage his duties. To perform weddings became increasingly difficult, for people were getting taller and taller. He could not reach their heads
to place the ceremonial crowns. Baptisms were impossible. The infants
were so heavy he couldn't hold them up. Even performing confession was
hard; his hearing was failing, and he fell into the habit of rushing confes-
sions. Services seemed endless, and his knees ached from standing as he
read the gospel. In the end, Father Nicolas only presided at funerals. He
was very close to those who were departing, and in that weak, tremulous
voice of his, he bid them farewell on their way to the Lord, the Virgin, and
the hour of Salvation.

"Save a place for me," he whispered before saying good-bye.

Every Wednesday and Friday the new priest, Father Vagelis, awaited
the arrival of the two women. He blessed them with the flames that shot
from his eyes and the panting breath of his large torso.

That Friday darkness was closing in swiftly. Despinyo beckoned to
her daughter and the two crossed the yard, stepping into the lane. Maryo
breathed hard keeping up with her young aunt, admiring all the while
Aggerou's quick graceful step. First the daughter entered the dark church,
behind her the mother, short of breath and dampened by the light shower
that had just begun. Aggerou withdrew into the shadows to say her confession. Despinyo lighted a candle before the icon of the Virgin. Maryo cringed
in the darkness and tried to warm her hands under her sweater. Suddenly
she grew faint with awe and almost collapsed in the pew. Staring at the

icon of the Virgin Mary she whispered to herself,

"Lord, God, will I be struck dead before I am born?"

The eyes of Mother Mary were blinking as if they were adjusting to the feeble rays emitted by the candle Despinyo had just lighted. The Virgin bent down the better to see the supplicant before her. Recognizing her at once, she carefully lay her babe down on her throne and emerged from the surface of the icon. She stepped out of the frame and approached Despinyo.

Despinyo, who was kneeling with her eyes cast downward, did not see the Virgin standing before her. Maryo had come from the pew and had prostrated herself before Mother Maria, kissing her worn gingham dress.

"Help me, Mother of God. Help me with this difficult child," Despinyo prayed.

The Virgin nodded her head.

"You call this child difficult!" she told the kneeling mother.

Her memory raced into the past as she addressed Despinyo:

"What would you have done if my child were yours?" she asked.

She bowed her head in deep grief. She removed a handkerchief from her dress pocket.

"If a mother has ever suffered from her child, I was that mother."

She wiped her eyes, blew her nose and returned the ragged handkerchief to her pocket.

"Everything he did troubled me. That holy day, when was barely twelve years old, he disappeared from the house. We rushed madly here and there to find him. When we heard there was a young boy at the temple, I was first to get there, first to enter the temple; and when I saw him absorbed in discussion, I was hurt. 'Jesus, my child,' I asked, still trembling with worry. 'Have you given no thought to me? 'Don't you know how distressed I've been?' And can you imagine what he did, Despinyo! He just looked at me, merely threw me a glance, and mumbled something about his being in his Father's house. I will always remember the look he gave me! It was so remote! That moment I realized that this child was not mine any longer, he had begun to become God. Yet his mouth still smelled of my milk, and his body, his flesh, still gave off the warmth of the womb that had held him. At twelve years of age he immersed himself in knowledge and left me; he wearied me, he destroyed me. I was orphaned, kori mou, I was orphaned by the child I had just borne."

The Virgin nodded her head thoughtfully, overcome by memories. Despinyo, still unaware of the presence, spoke of her troubles, the daughters who would grow up and must find husbands, the boys who must leave the village to avoid service in the Turkish army. They killed the boys. Not a single lad ever returned from the Turkish service. In a broken voice the Virgin went on.

"Torments.... I have suffered torments. May no mother face such misfortunes as mine. When my boy grew up, when he became a man and left our home, then I was truly engulfed in terror. Do not think of me in the peace of this sanctuary. I had my fill of terror. There were always the neighbors, those heralds with messages of doom shouting to me from the corner. 'Run, Maria, run!' they cried with vicious glee. 'Run, Maria, to save him. The Romans will drive spikes into him.' I ran with burning heart, raced through the thoroughfares and byways. I dropped my broom, the cooking, all the housework, and rushed to find him. From a distance I would see my wearied boy. My son shone; he stood out amidst the crowd. I am still smitten to the core by the ache of the radiant sight of him. How my soul yearned. How my soul ached with sorrow and ecstasy. His countenance filled me with endless joy. And my eyes streamed from enormous grief. My arms grew long, they grew long to reach him, to touch him, to feel the joy of his warmth and to protect him. My arms grew long to shield my boy from the savage thoughts people had, the bitter words they said about him. I was terrified by the mob, so terrified, and I leaned toward him with outstretched arms. For hours, many hours, I stood in the sweltering heat, the rain, the rising wind, to protect him. My son, the first-born. The sweetest flower of my garden. . .".

She fell silent. From her pocket she again withdrew her handkerchief. She brought the damp handkerchief to her eyes, wiped her tears, and blew her nose.

"His words. It was his words that made me tremble. Words of wisdom are terrifying! 'Human beings have no use for wise words!' I shouted to him, trembling. My whole body shook with foreboding. His words wove a shroud, his own shroud. Is there any mother who could bear to see her son sew his own shroud with words before her very eyes? I saw it enwrap him, cover his splendid face and body. I couldn't bear the horror. I collapsed to my knees and called upon God. I implored Him. Save me, O my Father, save me. Blind me so I can see no more. Make me deaf, to hear no more. And He granted my prayer, Despinyo. He blinded me and made me deaf for the sake of great love. So deeply did I love my child that I separated him from myself. I began to look on him as another person, a person with a right to his own destiny. To the life he had chosen. I loved that young man simply for what he was. My boy was no longer mine, but humanity's son. His words were sweet as honey; they sweetened me to my very depths. The prince of the world shone. My son was all aglow. I don't want to speak of what took place later. I can't bear to think of that scene. I became a black bottomless well and I fell into an endless void. But think, mori Despinyo; that splendid young man in the final hour who was suffering for the whole world felt pain for me. He thought of me, my tender boy. 'Behold your son,' he said, to comfort me, and pointed to sweet John. But how would it be possible, how could I do it? How could I change and see another child as the one to whom I had given birth, to soothe my darkened, heavy heart? Even if I could have begun anew, only he would be forever the one I would bear."

She looked upon the babe seated on the throne.

"Thank you, my boy, for blessing me with your sweet birth."

She lowered her eyes toward Despinyo, who was striking her forehead upon the cold tiles of the sanctuary.

"Love your children, Despinyo. Love them not as a mother but as a human being. See them as your fellow human beings. Believe in the life they have chosen."

Maryo barely managed to kiss the hem of the tattered gingham dress which the Virgin abruptly pulled up as she withdrew. The Virgin disappeared into her icon, behind the luxurious silk robe they had put her in. Maryo humbly raised her head and beheld her gaze. It seemed to be withdrawn, lost in time and in suffering. Maryo dragged herself back to her pew. Her legs and her heart were trembling. She was deeply shaken by the encounter, deeply shaken by that truth . For the first time she understood that this son who had raised his mother to heaven, the son who had made her a saint, was the same son who had first taken her through the flames of hell. "Giving birth is a cursed blessing," she thought. Her soul was filled with sadness.

She wanted to cry. She wanted so much to weep, but could not; the sadness was too great for tears. She remained still in the pew, thinking of Mother Mary, of all she had suffered, and of grandmother, all she was to suffer. "When a woman becomes a mother," Maryo realized, "her life is transformed. Her fate is tied to her children's fate." She thought of her own children, the memory a sweet pain.

Despinyo arose from the floor and crossed herself many times before the icon of the Virgin Mary. She was relieved. Her troubled heart released a sigh and a smile. It seemed to her that the Virgin had given her a sign. She was convinced that all would be well. Taking Aggerou by the hand, she left the church. Outside in the wide cobblestone lane they were engulfed by a dense black rain.

Breathing hard, the new priest stopped outside the garden gate. A swift glance up and down the lane assured him that no one was watching. He pressed the latch, opened the gate, stepped into the yard, and noiselessly shut the gate behind him. Inside the yard, he looked up at the moudi; he found all the doors shut and no one in sight. He moved behind the stairs toward the storeroom and there, before the small door, he found Aggerou. She was holding her apron before her filled with chick peas for the evening meal.

The sight of the priest puzzled the girl. Such visits never occurred. A priest would come only for a funeral, a blessing, some special occasion. Special events calling for a priest were rare, particularly in the morning when everyone was off working in the fields. Aggerou's face held an expression of bewilderment.

A huge untamed beast loomed before her. His massive belly rose and fell impetuously; and above that his red beard seemed to be throbbing. He was panting as if he had run a great distance. His chest heaving, he stared at her. The girl was frightened by his eyes. Glowing like red-hot coals, they penetrated, wounded, her; and the pain was paralyzing, cutting her legs out from under her.

"Is your mother upstairs?" The words were rushed, hoarse.

"Tsk!" The girl clicked her tongue negatively.

"Where is your mother? Is no one else at home?"

"Tsk!" Aggerou repeated.

"Why, mori, haven't you been coming to confession?"

The priest's tone was extremely angry. He shoved Aggerou violently against the little door, and as the upper hinge was broken, the door swung wide open and hung askew. Trapping the chick peas more tightly in her apron, the girl stepped back, stumbled on the threshold, but Father Vagelis bent forward and grabbed her. His large hands scooped her up; he crossed the threshold and kicked door shut. Dragging her across the room, he headed toward the straw pallet.

Maryo leaped up and stood tall before the priest; he could not push the girl onto the pallet, the way she was kicking and struggling. He swung her violently upon a low bench in the dark corner, lifted her skirts over her head, tore her panties, and fell upon her. The chick peas went rolling across the floor.

Aggerou's whole frame was numb and rigid from terror. Incapable of the least movement, she felt as if she was nailed down. She felt as if her legs were tied to his and tightly bound with wire, fine wire It was like the scene she had witnessed a few days before.

Less than a week before, on Easter Sunday; she was in the storeroom at dawn when her father entered carrying their goat. He held the animal high, very high. The all-white goat was dangling in his grasp. He held it by its front legs, and as it was hanging it could not move. It could not move in her father's grip; its legs were bound with wire, very fine wire, and it could only revolve its head, which it snapped left and right, attempting to catch a clue, to fathom what was going on. It did not grasp why it had been taken from the meadow, why its little legs were bound, why it had been brought here and slammed to the bench in the dark corner of the store room; they lifted its muzzle, stretched it high, and stepped heavily on its bound legs, and Aggerou, hiding within her body, shrank back in fear as she watched her father's sharp knife. Keen steel, its blade sank into the immaculate white neck. Now the neck was covered with bright blood which sprayed on the wall and ceiling, and the goat could release no sound, made no movement of resistance, as the blade sank in furiously again and again, reaching ever deeper and deeper.

Her blood gushed, forming a rivulet on the floor. She throbbed and screamed in agony. Father Vaggelis pressed hurriedly against her body. He rushed to the finish, gathered his robes, and arose. Hurriedly he laid the back of his hand against her lips, and she kissed the hand, making the sign of the cross.

"Save me, Mother of God," she whispered, hearing the priest shout:

"Come, mori, come to confession regularly!"

As Aggerou closed her eyes she saw the goat. Breathing hard as his muscles tightened, her father hurriedly slaughtered the animal. His experienced hand killed it, skinned it, gutted it, ran the skewer through its body, and leaned the skewered carcass against the garden wall, prepared for the hot coals.

All day as Aggerou watched the spit revolve, she was in deep pain. She felt an incredible ache seeing their white goat browning, shrinking, becoming dark bronze, the color of death. Tipsy village men came by their yard and pealed off strips of the goat's flesh, leaned their heads back, opened large mouths and with many crude jests sucked in the strips of hot flesh. The goat disappeared piece by piece into the deep gullets of the men, and Aggerou opened her eyes again on the present scene. Abruptly everything went dark.

Maryo sprang upon the priest like a lioness.

"Curses on your soul!" she cried.

She pounded him on the face, head, chest, wherever her fists could reach. The man rushed from the store room, moving swiftly through the yard and cautiously through the gate into the lane. Still there was no one else in the vicinity. Gathering his robes, the priest rushed away up the deserted street. Maryo just managed furiously to sink her nails into the offender's neck and claw down to his shoulders beneath his robe. With a vengeful smile she saw the priest's blood form eight lines oozing with red drops.

Feeling a burning on his spine, the priest touched the hurt place with the palm of his left hand and viewed the blood aghast.

"Lord, have mercy," he whispered, "What devil has struck me?"

At his back, Maryo continued to curse.

"May you burn in hell, twice and thrice damned!"

Her screams so close to his ear threw him into confusion. A burning wind penetrated through his ear deep within him, plunging him into horrendous vertigo.

Terrified, racing up the hill toward the church, he chanted,

"Mercy, oh mercy, Lord!"

As the black-robed figure disappeared, Maryo returned to the storeroom to aid her young aunt. Maryo's mother, Panagiota, was staring through a crack in the shutters into the storeroom.

With little cries of pity, "oh! oh! oh!" Maryo approached Aggerou. A stream of blood was steadily emptying the warmth of life from the girl, who, with gaping eyes fixed on the ceiling, emitted a great silent cry. The cry came from her depths, filled her mouth, split her lips and poured out; her tongue extended, and the cry came continuously hot and steaming from her lips; without sound, without frothing, it shot into the air and streamed onto the floor. Her face the image of terror, the long silent cry dispersed slowly in that space. The girl's body emptied. The blood drained from her; her form remained absolutely immobile, rigidly tense. The pupils of her eyes were directed rigidly toward the ceiling and her wide open eyelids remained fixed.

Maryo sped to the well of the Virgin, drew cold water, added vinegar, and sponged away the dried blood and the priest's filth. She changed Aggerou's clothes and lay her ravaged body down gently on the soft hay of the pallet. She sat beside her, and with kisses and warm caresses slowly revived her. First the tense muscles recovered. With a light tremor they began to function normally again. The eyebrows vibrated, the heartbeat became strong, and the body moved with life. As Maryo made the girl comfortable in the hay, she saw her eyes close, sealing the image of violence within. Finally Aggerou fell asleep.

"Rest. Rest, now; this is only the beginning," Maryo said, wiping tears from her eyes.

Going into the yard, Maryo was disturbed by what was happening to her mother. Panagiota was seated at the top of the verandah steps, her eyes set forward in a blank stare. The scene she had just seen was etched on pupils of her eyes, erasing all other images. The child's little body was in convulsions. It was as if she was trying to vomit the scene she had just witnessed, to expel it from her mouth; but it remained in her eyes, and instead of coming out, dispersing along the ground and in the wind, it stayed trapped under the child's skin and seeped down into her body, and Maryo watched the image of the monster aggressor pass through the child's throat, which swelled as if it would burst and spew filth over the floor. Down it sank, tearing through the child's larynx, distending the chest, and sinking into the belly. There it became a small balloon changing form, and Maryo saw it turn still further downward to seek a place to lodge in the guts. It found unclean waters and there it curled like a snake, settled, and lay in wait. The savage monster-image lurked deep within her mother.

Wearily Maryo climbed the rocky side of a small hill outside the village. Wishing to calm her soul at a distance from that sordid scene, she set her sights on the top of the hill, but she had not mounted halfway when she came upon the old blind woman of the village, who was lying fallen from her donkey's back by an olive tree. The animal stood nearby munching leaves as the old woman lay unable to rise, her weak knees offering no support. Hearing someone approach, she called out in anguish:

"Are you coming at long last? I fell an hour ago and all this time I've been waiting for someone to appear."

Maryo rushed to the old woman's side.

"Are you hurt, giagia?"

She gently took the old woman under the armpits and lifted her to her feet. Through her tattered robe Maryo could feel her knobby bones.

"Are you all right, giagia?" she repeated.

"Yes, Angel of Our Lady, I'm all right. It's just that I couldn't get up. It wearied me to lie there, and I just kept shouting and shouting. At first I yelled for anyone at all to come, but when no one appeared, I asked Our Lady to send her Angel, and now you have come."

Maryo set her firmly on her feet and leaned her back against the trunk of the old olive tree. The old woman extended a bony hand.

"I want to feel your face; I want to know what family a lass like you comes from."

Maryo was disturbed. Shrinking before the old woman's touch, she moved backwards, and the old woman groped in the empty space.

"Merciful Mother of God, I thank you. You did send your angel. You always answer my prayers."

She bent over and felt for her cane and the donkey's harness, finding both.

"Let's go, you blessed beast," she commanded the animal.

She jerked the harness, and the creature started off slowly, close to the old woman's side. Side by side they took the path to the village. As she watched them go off together, the donkey and the woman close by its side, moving carefully along amidst the olive trees with their green and silver leaves, Maryo savored the painful sweetness evoked by beautiful images of life. The pair went slowly into the distance, disappearing behind trunks or branches, and again reappearing further on, their outline more hazy, their footsteps fainter, till they vanished around the turn of the path.

Maryo breathed a sigh filled with happiness and she too continued on her way. She scrambled to the hilltop to enjoy the panorama of the village. Now she felt relieved, buoyant, and her entire body drank in the fragrance of tilled soil, wildflowers and olives. Her eyes relished the colors that the sun tinted the scene as it turned toward descent. The landscape, the trees, the soil, the rocks, took on a scarlet hue. A light breeze arose, and Maryo felt the melody sent up by the earth. Like light tympani notes came vibrations from the depths of the earth, a melody of strings, the rustling of the leaves, and several wind instruments the delicate voices of birds. Maryo's heart, wild with joy, roamed the broad natural scene. Her heart went out, extending the limits of her body, stretching her skin, opening it wide, pouring out feelings, hearing, vision, touch; and reaching out beyond her, sensations drew her into a oneiric world. So Maryo wandered within the world of nature.

She must have been in this state of arousal for a long time, for suddenly her body felt extreme weariness. It grew heavy and again came down to earth. The sun was below the horizon and the colors were no longer reddish. Now they had become dark gray. Maryo was on the hilltop by the village mill, standing near its small window. Inside she saw Kyr Thymios, the miller, seated on a crate by his gigantic mill wheel. Kyr Thymios was a thick-set man around fifty with a bushy black mustache covering his mouth.

Sitting with spread legs, belly falling between, he was waiting for customers. His face bore signs of endless sadness. A sadness containing anger and total frustration.

"Kyr Themio! Hey, Kyr Thymio! Are you there?"

The heavy figure snapped upright.

"Good to see you, my dear Kyra Zaharo," he smiled.

"Good for you to see," she replied, dropping the sack to the floor.

Her figure was fleshy and she was breathing hard.

"You mill corn, I hear tell!" she smiled and nudged him in the belly.

"Yes—among other things. I mill whatever you please!" he said and answered her nudge with a two-handed push on Kyra Zaharo's shoulders.

"Quite a guy, aren't you," she said, doubling over with laughter. Again she pushed him playfully with both hands.

"Quite a guy to say the least!" Kyr Thymios nudged her a bit below the shoulders.

Maryo turned and scrutinized the scene below. The gray light of dusk had fallen like light down over the village. Misty figures, the village men mounted on donkeys, were returning home. Slowly, silently, joylessly, indifferently, doors opened and shut. No sounds were heard; there were only shadows, the shadows of human beings growing darker and fading as night descended. Soon everything would be gone in darkness. Maryo released a sad sigh and turned back to the mill. A small candle stuck in a mug, placed on a box, cast light on the parted bodies of Kyr Thymios and Kyra Zaharo. The chubby woman was studiously removing wheat seed husks that had stuck to the seat of her skirt. The miller was counting coins on his outstretched palm.

"We agreed to five and you gave me three," he complained sullenly.

"That's enough! It's enough!" she mumbled in hasty confusion.

The door flew open and a little boy rushed into the mill. His head was shaved and he was wearing a long threadbare coat.

"Hurry, father! Hurry home! Mana's worse!"

"All right, I'm coming," the man grumbled, blowing out the candle.

The whole scene instantly vanished.

Maryo caught up with them at the path on the western slope. The boy trotted ahead, and Kyr Thymios trudged along, head bent and hands clasped behind his back. Kyra Zaharo was nowhere to be seen. Maryo followed the miller, her course tracing his black shadow and heavy footsteps. Passing down through ancient olive trees they reached the first village lane and Maryo saw a two-story house which was overflowing with women of the neighborhood, a large lamp blazing on the verandah. All the downstairs rooms were fully lighted but the bedroom upstairs was plunged in darkness.

"My wife Koulio is gone," moaned Kyr Thymios. "That damned consumption destroys families," he cursed and spat on the ground. "Who will have me now, an old man with four children?"

He wiped his eyes and heavily climbed the steps.

On the west side of the village, far from familiar territory, Maryo was little concerned with who had died, who was left widower or orphan, and who would marry the miller. Her only concern was how—at such an hour, in such darkness—she could find the road back to her own neighborhood. One maze of lanes led to another or out into the fields. Virtually feeling her way along, she strove to reach some familiar sight to guide her.

After some time a landmark appeared in the distance, the black form of a cypress tree looming in the night sky. "In our yard," her father had said, "we had the tallest cypress tree in the village." Maryo guessed that it could be that very tree which now stood out darker than the outlines of the houses lining the lanes. Her eyes glued to the top of the tree, she picked up speed, jumping walls and cutting through side streets. When she arrived at the Well of the Virgin, she remembered: "Our house is just opposite the Well of the Virgin," her Grandmother Zgouraphenia said years later. And there it was! Maryo was at the doorway of her father's house.

Maryo's Aunt Malama was seated on the doorstep. A little child, she was blubbering and moaning in a sing-song voice:

"My brother fell from our ro-o-o-o-o-f; my brother was hu-u-u-u-u-u-rt!"

Maryo rushed past the child into a small room dimly lighted by a single candle. Her father, a small boy, was lying on a heavy woven blanket in the middle of the room. That moment he released a small sob and drifted into sleep. Mayro saw there was blood at the corners of his mouth and his eyes were swollen from crying. Swept by a surge of tenderness, she knelt by the boy, lovingly caressed his curly black hair, and kissed his forehead.

"My sweet little boy," Maryo whispered.

Then she heard a voice outside. Kyra Giasemi, from across the street, had opened her window and was shouting to Malama:

"What's the matter with you this evening, mori?"

Malama continued her sing-song moan:

"My brother fell from the ro-o-o-o-o-f!"

"And where on earth's your mother, child?"

"She's at chu-u-u-u-u-rch!" the child continued the same tune.

"My, my, my!" complained Kyra Giasemi, closing the window.

At once her steps were heard descending the steps.

"You hush, now. I'll fetch your mother."

Maryo got up and went outside. Since she could easily find her way home from the church, she followed the neighbor woman, who complained all the way of Grandmother Zgourafenia leaving the children alone all the time to go to church while that story-teller husband of hers hung out at the coffee house.

At the church Maryo had her first encounter with her paternal grandmother at that age; she was a beautiful girl, hardly twenty years old, caring for the scratches on the priest's neck.

"Look, Giasemi," she exclaimed, "see what happened to our pastor!"

Kyra Giasemi, rushing into the sanctuary to tell Zgourafenia what was what, was taken aback by eight rivulets of blood running down the back of the priest's neck.

"What is this!" she cried, "Is it the work of a demon?"

The two woman gazed anxiously at the injury as Father Vagelis murmured a prayer.

"Did you cleanse it with Holy Water from the Festival of Lights?" asked Kyra Giasemi.

The two women hastened to make compresses with special Holy Water from the icon of Aghios Panteleimonas as well as oil from the icon of the Virgin and various other saints. Father Vagelis blessed the water once more before the compresses were applied to his burning neck. Rather than improve, however, the lacerations seemed to become more inflamed.

"Scratched by Satan's nails," Kyra Giasemi affirmed.

She made the sign of the cross. Maryo examined her nails. They were rounded and neatly trimmed. Yet they appeared extremely sharp. They didn't look at all like her own.

"Mori Zgourafenia!" Kyra Giasemi suddenly recalled. "Your boy fell from the roof!"

"He couldn't have been hurt," said Zgourefenia, turning her eyes to the icon of Aghios Panteleimonas. "He is under the protection of the holy saint," she explained almost casually, as she applied oil to the priest's cuts.

Maryo sat in a pew and gazed at her grandmother. How beautiful she was! When she met her later, many years later, she always thought of her puffed face hidden behind a black scarf. Now she was a fresh-faced transparent-skinned girl of innocent loveliness. That loveliness, as Maryo knew it, would go on for two generations. This girl blushed for her white skin, red lips, sparkling eyes. She hid her curly luxuriant hair under an embroidered white scarf and always kept her eyes lowered. At church festivals which she always attended with her mother, young men recited verses to her, and she was so embarrassed she could hardly hold back her tears.

Giorgakis, the man who married her, did not recite verses to her, nor did he approach her directly. Instead, following one of the festivals he went directly to her home to speak with her mother, Kyra Malamato.

"Kyra Malamato!" he called in his cheerful voice from the lane outside. "How are things with you, Kyra Malamato?"

The woman had emerged on the second-story balcony.

"What do you say, Kyra Malamato, do you want me as a son-in-law?" he boomed from the yard below.

"Come, Giorgaki. Come on up. We'll drink to the engagement!" answered Kyra Malamato.

The mother-in-law to be, who was Giorgakis's age, was full of smiles. Giorgakis was a merchant in Smyrni and everyone knew he was a highly eligible bachelor.

"What do you say to this Sunday a week?" he asked climbing the stairs.

"Blessed be the day and the hour," she replied, reaching out her hand.

With a broad smile, the merchant bent over and kissed the extended hand.

Her mother did not tell Zgourafenia immediately. Fearing the arrangement would be jinxed, she kept her lips sealed and simply had her daughter tidy up the stable, clean up the yard, and set the house in order. Then, on Thursday, toward evening, Malamato said:

"Well, now, Zgourafenia, we have a wedding coming up on Sunday!"

"Who's to be married?" asked the girl.

"You, my daughter! And Giorgakis will be your husband!"

"Well, all right. . ." was the simple reply, but it seems she had a bad night, for she came down to breakfast very early with eyes red from sleeplessness.

"Mori mana, when I marry Giorgakis, where will I live?" the girl asked.

At this time Maryo's grandmother was fourteen years old.

"Why, here with me," her mother reassured her, and thus Zgourafenia was comforted.

She married Giorgakis, who was around forty years her elder. When a year had passed, her mother aided her in giving birth. She had Asimakis, Maryo's father, and three years later she had Malama. All would have been well had her mother not taken a mortal fall from the mule. Everyone in the village said that had Zgourafenia not taken Giorgakis as husband but some humble villager, her mother would have fallen from the donkey and would not have died. At the most she would have broken some bones, but the fall would not have been deadly as it was from her son-in-law's tall mule. At the funeral Zgourafenia appeared inconsolable.

"Mori mana!" she moaned, "how will I manage two children by my-self?"

On the fortieth day following her mother's funeral, Zgourafenia decided to appeal to Agios Panteleimonas.

"Holy Saint," she addressed the icon resolutely, "take care of my children, and I will care for your church."

The saint's countenance appeared blank, uncertain. It seemed to tell the girl he knew not a thing about children. The responsibility was great, he didn't want such job. But the girl was adamant; and from that very day she began to busy herself about the church. Each morning she lighted the icon candles, swept the sanctuary floor, and dusted the relics. Thus, the saint, in turn, was obliged to watch over her children.

"Shouldn't you go and see to your boy, Zgourafenia?" Kyra Giasemi insisted.

"Don't worry, I tell you. The boy's all right," Zgourafenia replied, sweetly smiling at the saint.

Kyra Giasemi was relieved, and turning to their task, they continued to care for the injured pastor.

From the church it was easy for Maryo to find the house. She had taken the route many times. She moved off toward the house, but at mid-point changed her mind, turning toward the main square. She wanted to see her grandfather, and he was at Galanis's coffee house.

Before him on the small table was a tumbler of raki. Giorgakis took a little sip now and then, and sometimes only wet his lips, which were dry from a plethora of words. Grandfather told stories and all the villagers seated around him listened with open mouths.

"Bless you, my story-teller grand-pa!" Maryo hailed.

She watched Giorgakis admiringly through the low window of the coffee house. He was a handsome man—tall, powerfully built, with a dense, deep-black mustache. His words took on the color of dreams from the blue cigarette smoke in which he enveloped them. Maryo was deeply overjoyed to have a grandfather who was a story-teller.

She took the lane, and when she reached the cross-street she turned left. The house at the end of the road was her mother's. It was the last home before the fields. She opened the gate and mounted the stairs. The house was completely dark; the hard-working farm owners were asleep. They always went to bed early, for there were many fields to cultivate and the workers need their rest. She took a deep breath and sat down on the top step. She wanted to think.

Thoughts and events crowded her mind, perplexed her judgment. She put them aside. What good were her thoughts, anyhow? What could she do about what was going on around her? She had no influence on the lives of her family; all she could do was feel for them. She opened herself to a flood of feelings and all of them were of love. "These are my people!" she felt with joy. "These are my roots, the farmer and the story-teller. I am these people with some slight variations due to time." She stood up and slowly descended to the storeroom to sleep. Before lying down on her pallet she quietly asked, "And, after all, aren't these really everyone's roots?"

It was Sunday, mid-morning, and before the liturgy ended, the town crier took his place in a lane nearby the church where he could be heard by all. His voice resounded like a bell: "Listen, one and all! A rare experience awaits you! Giorgakis Karabounas has captured the strangest of seals! Come and see the marvel with your own eyes. The amazing creature is kept in the Karabounas stable on the road to Agrilia. Villagers all! Bring your wives and children! Don't miss out! Come this very morning after church service to the Karabounas stable!"

The evening before Giorgakis's koumbaros, Grammatikos, had dropped by to see him. He was wearing a frown that sagged all the way to the floor.

"Hey, what's wrong, koumbare?" asked Giorgakis, all smiles. "Did someone sink all your ships?"

Grammatikos was poor—poor as poor could be. He barely survived by working around the village as a handiman. The jest was galling.

"What have I got, you joker?" he bitterly replied. "I have no ships to sink. All I had was a donkey, and it up and died!"

"Why, my friend? How on earth did that happen?"

"Don't ask me—I'm not a vet! All I know is, my donkey just stopped eating and kicked the bucket." He heaved a huge sigh.

"Isn't that the way things go! But don't take it so hard. If you lost your donkey, get yourself a mule!" Giorgakis counseled with a smile.

"You're out of your mind, you idiot!" Grammatikos spoke angrily. "I haven't got a single coin in my pocket."

"Don't worry, my friend," the other replied, "you are lucky it's already Saturday night. Early Monday morning we'll go to Smyrni for a mule."

"Listen, one and all!" the crier continued when the priest had concluded the service and all ears were tuned to his voice. "Giorgakis hired three caiques and sent them to sea to net that strange seal—three caiques manned by twenty bold youths. . .".

Soon the Karabounas barnyard was filled with men and children. Attired in his Sunday best Giorgakis welcomed the crowd outside the stable door.

"One by one," he cried, "the critter is skittish. Enter quiet as a mouse, one at a time."

He cleared his throat and went on.

"Pass by my dear koumbaros here, and throw your coin of eight into his hat. Children enter last and don't pay nothin'."

He slipped into stable leaving Grammatikos outside, his face glum and his hat in his hand. The first in line entered to find Giorgakis standing before a rag rug hung like theater curtain. Throwing his arm around the villager's shoulder, Giorgakis gave him a hug saying how pleased he was to see him, fine, upstanding citizen that he was. Then he moved him gently forward and raised the rug curtain. Open-mouthed the spectator found himself facing Grammatikos's dead donkey hung from its hooves on a beam and painted all the colors of the rainbow.

"What kind of shenanigans are these, Giorgaki?" the villager barked angrily, but the reply came swiftly,

"Pipe down, pal! You don't want to be the only fool that gave a coin of eight to see a dead donkey strung up by its heels! Besides, we're not concerned with Grammatikos's late donkey but his future mule which will earn bread for his children. Thanks for your help," Giorgakis concluded all smiles, pounding the man on the back. "Come to the coffee house this evening, the treat's on me."

All the village men paid full admission to see the curiosity, and that night at the coffee house Giorgakis began the tale of the wondrous seal. The episodes lasted all winter long. Giorgakis himself, went the tale, had launched three boats manned by twenty bold lads for that strange seal which they netted and brought ashore. In the Polis, the pasha heard the news and commanded that the rarity be brought to him as a gift. Giorgakis obeyed. In the pasha's palace he wandered into the harem and there he set his eyes on a ravishing concubine.

The coffee house audience was filled with yearning, passion, sighs and heartfelt tears when the concubine revealed to Giorgakis that she was not a Turkish girl but a Christian. Suspense mounted as the hero plotted to spirit her away from her keeper. The tears swelled to a river when the vizier ferreted out the plot and slew the girl in Georgakis's presence, the drama becoming more horrible than that of Oedipus who slew his father and married his mother or—could it be possible?—more touching than the love of Erotokritos and Aretousa.

Grammatikos alone did not follow the tale of the harem and the curious seal. After purchasing a mule, he snubbed the coffee house. He stayed at home plotting how to increase profits, purchase property, and gain prestige in the village.

A half-moon was declining over the horizon. Deep orange in hue, it sank into the sea and Maryo, seated on the rocks by the water, watched it sadly. "This summer is also disappearing like the moon," she sighed.

Yet another summer was debited on the balance sheet of life, a summer filled with hidden messages. Maryo's thoughts gathered in a mass, blended with feelings, and reached an impasse. With great clarity she saw how people's lives become tangled in a knot, restricting their paths of experience. She heard the sound of galloping time. Wild, aggressive, stormy time was racing forward, and fumbling inexperienced life trailed behind. Breathless life hastily strove to coordinate its movements with the maniacal galloping of time. "Life and its meaning. . ." mused Maryo.

Human experience seemed vacuous, flawed, amorphous, and Maryo strained futilely to arrive at some conclusion. Her mother again came to mind. She appeared suspended at the center of Maryo's thoughts with that slack, withered body of hers. "How can I free her if I cannot pinpoint the meaning she seeks?" Maryo wondered. She was choked with anxiety. She turned her head from the sea toward the hill behind her. A small white house on the hillside, and around it a vegetable garden. It was her family's summer house in the fields at Pounta. It was dinner time and the whole family was gathered at a table outside under their tall fig tree. Her mother, a small child, was standing on a stone bench pulling branches down to pick their clustered figs. The father had hung a kerosene lantern on a branch over the table.

The mother held the baby, and around the table the other children were preparing to eat dinner. Their voices, like water gurgling happily amidst rocks and trees, reached Maryo like a sweet memory. As the light darkened the children's forms gradually began to fade. The father raised his hand to the lantern, applied a match and turned up the wick. Again Maryo could see the children's gestures, faces, movements. She was so glad to see them there. So very near her. She turned her head back slowly toward the sea. She gazed at the moon. It had become a thin white curve etched on the horizon. The rock on which she was sitting suddenly became very uneven and uncomfortable. Shifting her position, she extended her legs and the sea rushed to lick them. The waves playfully splashed her with steady rhythm and force. With endless motion the sea struck the hollowed rocks on which she sat. They were crossed by a network of cracks, gullies, and holes. Continuing its game the sea sent streams surging into the bowels of the rocks, gouging their body. Maryo felt the water thrusting deeply into the rocks and hungrily devouring them as they powerfully spit the water out of their dark hidden parts back into the surf. A deep roar full of threats and implications burst from that implacable embrace.

Giannakos had been keeping a surprise for the family. The day before, as supper ended and bedtime approached, he told the children,

"First thing in the morning I want you to get ready. We're leaving for Pounta."

Bursting with joy the children's voices drowned out their father's final instructions. Her eyes fixed on the window, Panagiota waited for the sun. It was taking a long time to erase the darkness, and when she finally awoke she found it risen a span above her window ledge. The others were up and about, and everything was ready for their departure. In a single leap she flew across the moudi and down the stairs. Hardly aware of what was happening, she slipped and fell face-down. Her forehead was cut and her face was covered with blood.

"Vexer, you crazy thing," Aggerou seized her and took her to the kitchen. "How could you run like a chicken with its head cut off and fall on the stairs?" Aggerou yelled. She pushed her sister's head into a basin of water in the sink. "Everyone is ready to leave, and look what you go and do!" She roughly scrubbed the bloodied forehead as Panagiota struggled to free herself from her vise-like grip. Maria approached with a strip of white cloth which she wrapped around the child's head and gently tied. Above the injury a red circle of blood stained the bandage. Ready, now, and free, the child descended the stairs. Her father was waiting in the loaded cart prepared to leave. Seeing Panagiota with damp hair, wet bodice and bandaged forehead, he took her in his arms.

"Are you hurt, Giota?" he asked in a laughing tone."

"Tsk!" she clicked negatively.

Her father was pleased with her pluck.

"Askousoum! Good for you!" he said, lifting her onto the highest bundle in the middle of the cart.

"Askousoum!" the child repeated proudly to herself, her face beaming. Her mother came with the baby in her arms and the house key hung from her neck. "Get the child down from there; we don't want a calamity!" she snapped.

"Nothing bad will ever happen to this child," said the father, helping the woman and babe onto the cart.

Closing the garden gate, he climbed to the driver's seat and set the horse into motion. Panagiota did not turn to look at the other children but she heard the donkey behind the cart, its wooden carriers squeaking from the weight of little Nikolos, Garoufalo and Phtychio. Further back the older children walked pulling their animals, a sheep and two goats with their kids skipping along, and bringing up the rear was the dog Arapis, head lowered and tail between his legs.

Now at summer's end, sitting on the rocks, Maryo thought of Arapis. He was black, deep black, skinny, sad. His eyes showed a sad nostalgia toward the memory of lost wild, primordial life, but for Arapis it was more than the sadness of loss. The present also carried burdens of its own. At Pounta he was kept tied up by the chicken coop where he was on guard. After the first two weeks this summer, Despinyo had discovered that the dried scraps of bread she fed him each evening were not enough to fill his belly. He was eating the fresh eggs which she had believed the hens had ceased to lay on account of the change in the weather. Pushing the eggs out of the coop with his muzzle, he cracked them skillfully and lapped up their nourishment.

"Bad, bad dog!" Despinyo shouted.

Constantis grabbed the animal, circled his waist with a rope and strung him up on a high bough of the fig tree. There he hung all day. The children's hearts ached from his whimpering, and when Constantis at last went off for the evening, Maria dared to untie the rope. The dog landed heavily, and with the rope still tied to his middle went racing toward the distant hills. He was gone for three days. On the third day, toward evening, he was seen on the path to the Chapel of St. John the Baptist. The rope was gone, and his filthy body was covered with cuts and bruises.

Starved, miserable, red-eyed, he moved slowly with his tail between his legs. Panagiota saw him coming down the hill and heading toward the sea. She saw him jump into the water as if he wanted to wash his cuts. He sprang the water, and so did Panagiota, and when she saw him swim farther and farther away from the shore, she shouted urgently,

"Arapi! Arapi! Come here! Where are you going?"

Joining her on the beach, the other children plunged into the water, all of them crying,

"Arapi-i-i-i-i-i-i-! Arapi i-i-i-i-i-i-i-! Come here! Where are you going, Arapi-i-i-i-i-i ?"

Their voices were very sweet and hid the anguish of shame.

"Arapi-i-i-i!" they cried.

But the dog looked not once behind him. It was as if he no longer knew the voices. The following morning the sea, calm and indifferent, brought the swollen corpse of the dog to shore and deposited it on the beach. Panagiota's eyes opened very wide. Her heart trembled and cracked like the dried earth.

Maryo shifted her position on the rock, and the moon, suspended on the horizon, as yet did not sink. The summer's images continued to bombard her mind.

The young fisherman stopped beneath the fig tree. His glances were darts flung at Aggerou's beauties and she felt them strike her stooped form. She ceased scrubbing the flagstones and stood up, motionless and alert.

"Good morning, m'lady," said the muscular lad, taking a step forward. "I have brought you a gift."

He presented her a basket heaped with fish.

Aggerou's gaze settled on the youth. He had very dark eyes, black as ebony, glittering like jewels. White teeth gleamed beneath his black mustache. His bare breast steamed like that of a perspired steed stopping after a gallop in deep shade by a river. Aggerou's knees grew watery, her heart throbbed and the feeling spread throughout her body.

Immobile, Aggerou stared at the youth.

"What is your name, lithe willow?" his voice dripped honey.

A dark shadow fell across her sight. Aggerou's little sister stepped between her and the fisherman.

"Out of our yard!" she ordered.

"I brought you a gift, Aggerou," breathed the youth.

"Both your gift and you, out you go!" Panagiota cried, shoving the intruder from the yard.

It was a bad morning. Garoufalo awoke needing the comfort of her mother's arms. She crawled to her mother who, half-asleep, embraced the child. Her sighs of pleasure awoke Panagiota. Anger was in her eyes. Rising from bed she stood by her mother's side.

"Kale. . . Kale, mana. . ." she said with quiet urgency. "Mana, are you awake?"

Her mother opened her eyes and her father turned from the other side of the bed.

"When you were working in the vineyard yesterday, kale, the fisherman came bringing fish as a gift."

"Which fisherman?" asked the mother.

"The one father calls a scamp."

The father jumped out of bed. "Who was here?"

"The fisherman came to see Aggerou," the child cooed.

The man sprang to the mattress where Aggerou was sleeping and grabbed her by the hair.

"What is going on!" the mother screamed, leaving Garoufalo and hauling her husband away from Aggerou.

Antonis stood up and intervened. "No, father—no, don't hurt her!" he begged.

Constantis cursed and stamped out of the house; sobbing, Maria curled up in a corner of her bed. Panagiota set upon Garoufalo, pinched her and ran out the door. The sobs of the younger sister were covered by the screams of the older. Panagiota scrambled onto the bench, took the basket from the bough of the fig tree, and ran down to the beach, to look for crabs. Standing stiff and angry on the rocks, she waited for crabs to emerge shyly, hesitantly from the cracks, whereupon she grabbed them and tossed them in the basket. Maryo watched the crabs fall on top of one another, skitter across the bottom of the basket, and with panicked motions try to climb out. Their claws tangled and they thrashed in a trapped mass.

Anguished voices from the house filled the air. Maryo went up to the house and sat on the stone bench by the large table, which was crowded with plates holding scraps of food. Flies buzzed around bits of bread sopped in gravy and strips of cantaloupe rind. Panagiota was coming up the hill carrying the basket on her shoulder and shouting,

"Look at all the crabs I caught! Look at all the crabs!"

As the child rushed excitedly forward several crabs scrambled to the rim of the basket, held themselves suspended and, dropping onto their backs in the path, waved their claws in the air.

Setting the basket on the table, Panagiota cried, "Kale mana, come see the crabs I got! Look at all these crabs!"

Her father came out and sat on the bench. He was pale and tired, his face sharp with anger. His wife followed carrying the sobbing babe whom she comforted with a warm embrace and gentle caresses. One by one the children emerged from the house, their bodies shy, their faces pale. Aggerou's hair was uncombed, her eyes very red. Crabs jumped madly from the box, struck the table top and strove to escape. Aggerou approached, she grabbed a food stained bowl with both hands; she raised it high and rabidly began to pound and smash the crabs on the tabletop.

Repulsed by the broken crustaceans and their sticky innards, Maryo dashed down the hill to the beach. She wanted to ponder what was going on around her and put it into some sort of order. Why all this violence? she wondered. What was its source?

"It comes from fear," she concluded, "fear of the violation of honor. And that fear is greater than the power of love." She stepped into the water and the sudden cold sent a chill through her body. As she jumped back her thought continued with great bitterness: "Love lacks power." Shaken by these words she turned toward the hill to observe her family. They were all outside eating breakfast.

Aggerou was frying eggs and Maria was spreading slices of bread with butter and honey. Milk was heating in a pan over the fire and its smell filled the area around the house. How loving they all seemed. The argument was like a sudden storm that had hit them and now had apparently completely gone, vanished.

Maryo looked more closely at the faces. Nothing was erased, nothing was gone. It was all etched on the children's skin, their countenances, their souls. And Maryo imagined the soft tissues of their brains scarred and channeled, and the channels becoming wilderness ravines inscribed by bitter memories. Only the sound of the argument had gone, the wound remained.

"Yet they do feel love for one another. Why does it not control the other feelings?" The thought chilled her soul. "Love brings up the rear in human relationships. First all the other feelings march by. They parade in fancy uniforms, under flashy banners, which skillfully obscure the steel armor, bows, barbarous spears and sharpened fingernails of primitive men. These all march in the relationships of people and when they are exhausted, then, as if in a truce, as if by agreement, humble tattered love comes in at the end of the line."

"Is love really so slighted in people's lives?" Maryo stepped on a sharp stone which cut her foot. She washed off the blood and continued to walk back and forth along the beach. "I am wrong," she cried. "I am terribly wrong. Love cannot be so slighted as that. Haven't I loved? Hasn't the whole of my life been loving? I have felt so much love, an overwhelming love, especially for my children." Their beaming countenances appeared before her and she leaned over and kissed them. "Yes, I loved my children so much, and my only concern as they were growing up and preparing to go out into the world was that they would be happy." She shouted the last words: "I want them to be happy!"

Her beautiful daughter appeared. She was seated on the top stair at the front of the house. Her eyes were red and tears were running down her cheeks and neck.

"Why are you crying, kori mou? Why are you crying?" Maryo's heart brokenly cried. "Why are you crying?"

There was no reply.

"I want. . ." Maryo continued making a speech by herself there by the sea. "I want. . ." she suddenly stopped. A great light dawned within her.

"I want nothing; I want nothing from anyone. I will accept with gratitude whatever direction their nature takes them."

She swiftly threw off her clothes and dived into the sea.

It was Maryo who first heard the rapid hoof beats of the mule. Coming swiftly down the road from Litzia, the town with healing springs, was her grandfather Giorgakis with her father, Asimakis, riding behind him.

Maryo was glad. The children's faces glowed but their parents scowled.

"The storyteller will keep us up all night!" Despinyo complained.

"Don't worry—I won't let him get started," Giannakos reassured her.

"Welcome, Giorgaki!" they spoke in the same breath.

"Health and happiness to you all!" Giorgakis boomed.

He dismounted, plucked Asamakis from behind the saddle and placed him the bench amidst the children. Panagiota saw that Asamakis's hair was stiff from saltwater and uncombed. His knees were dirty and scratched.

"I caught some crabs," she said, giving him a shove.

"So what?" said the boy, shrugging his shoulders.

"And I saw a couple of snakes, too!" Panagiota persisted.

"I know a charm you tell a snake that makes it tie itself in knots and shrivel up!"

"What's new, Giannako?" Giorgakis asked, observing the look set in his eyes. "The seal is still on his mind," he thought. "He's still thinking of that filthy coin missing from his pocket."

Maryo strove to guess whether Giorgakis indeed wanted Asimakis to marry Panagiota. He didn't live to see the marriage. In Athens, far from the village after the expulsion, Giannakos wanted Asimakis for his daughter.

"Marry him, my girl; he's from the old country, after all!"

He reminded her, too, of the saying:

"Wear a shoe from your homeland, however patched it may be."

"I'll have the dirty patched shoe," Panagiota replied and everyone roared in laughter.

"So, how is your dead donkey doing, anyhow?" Giorgakis ribbed Giannakos to his chagrin.

"What are you talking about?" he replied somewhat sharply.

"Just shooting the breeze, koumbare," he said, thinking, "He's one of the few villagers who never became, and never will become, my koumbaros."

The children were restlessly awaiting a story but Giannakos held Giorgakis back. He turned at once to the matter uppermost in his mind.

"I've got over 2000 kilos of Sultanina raisins. "

"A fine crop!" said Giorgakis. "The wholesaler from Smyrni will give you a good deal, but you've got to give the raisins to him on consignment. After he sells them in Athens he'll pay you what he owes. I trust him."

"Well I don't!" said Giannakos sharply

"The mainland Greek middle-man will eat up all your profit, and all your work will go for nothing."

"A bird in the hand.. ." Despinyo put in.

"And what do you care about profit, Giorgaki?" Giannakos asked ironically "What do you know about money?"

"Nothing, I admit, but in the end money is worthless. Time is what has value. Time. . ." he said with gravity, shaking his head sadly.

"So, he has a premonition that little time is left for him. . .". Maryo pitied Giorgakis for the first time in her life.

"We'll see how you can live without money," said Giannakos, looking at the children for whom his words were intended.

"When death knocks at the door, money can't stop him," Giorgakis said. Smiling upon the children, he asked,

"Tell me, little ones, have you heard of the story of Erotokritos and Aretousa?"

He didn't wait for an answer but at once launched into the narrative.

"Now we're in for it," Despinyo sighed, biting her kerchief.

Indeed, Giorgaki was at full pace and didn't stop till the villains were dead and the lovers were wed. Then he stood up and took his leave.

The children sat very still in their places, their hearts filled with awe. Giorgakis lifted Asimakis high into the saddle; then he lighted the lantern and handed it to the boy. Asimakis raised it high in his right hand and lighted the path all the way to the turn. Giorgakis patted the mule's muzzle and took the reins.

"Till we meet again, neighbors," he said, setting off.

"You didn't even offer the man some raki," Giannakos told Despinyo, who was already putting the baby to sleep.

"A lot you care!" she told him angrily.

In their beds the children heard wisps of talk and laughter carried on the wind from their Uncle Nikolo's yard. Giorgakis had stopped there. He had to find raisins for the Smyrni merchant. Aggerou could not sleep that night thinking of Aretousa, and Antonis, too, tossed and turned on his mattress admiring the courage of Erotokritos. Panagiota recited over and over again the charm she had learned from Asimakis:

Be-dee, be-dee,
be-dum, be-dum,
two-headed, three-headed,
Johnny Saint John,
tie the snake fast
with the slim asp,
with crawly stone
the scorpion smash,
the bogie man,
the rabid hound,
be-dum, be-dum,
be-dee, be-dee,
fagots five times five,
briars twenty-three,
till sunrise be.

A full moon was declining over the horizon. At the end of the summer, seated on an uneven rock, Maryo pondered all the summer had held. The fruit, the fish dinners, visitors, swimming, work in the vineyard. She thought of the laughter and the tears. "Summer is behind," she mused. "Tomorrow we return to the village and a hard winter. Spring will be even worse for all my people." A great pain knifed all of her cells. Knowledge of the future was hard to bear, and even harder the inability to intervene, to change the course of the future. There were forces like gravity and weight which determined the course life would take through the generations.

The baby's crying was heard and Maryo turned toward the house. Everyone was outside sitting under the fig tree. They were dressed for the fall, eating a supper of chick pea soup, onions, olives, and olive oil in which they dipped freshly baked bread. The wooden spoons hitting the wooden bowls made Maryo's mouth water with thoughts of spicy chick peas, whole wheat bread and olive oil.

"Happy will be the man who marries you, Aggerou," Giannakos said. "You bake the best bread in the world!"

Her mother stroked Aggerou's hair and Maria hugged her warmly. The lantern, hung from a low branch, lighted their faces. The little children's faces and her mother's childhood face glowed. They all glowed. Maryo was overwhelmed, completely overwhelmed by the great love she felt for them all. The sight of them was too much for her to bear. She turned toward the sea. She was delighted to see her brother seated on a rock nearby her. Nostalgia waxed within her. She wanted to touch his curly hair, which was soft as sea foam, a tuft of spring clouds. She reached out her hand but with a smile he pulled his head away.

"Enjoying bread again!" she told him and both of them laughed.

"How you love bread hot from the oven. You are always munching on warm loaves."

His mouth was full of crunchy crust and his jaws kept chewing as a wide smile spread across his face.

"I have something of yours," Maryo sadly recalled.

"You don't have anything of mine," he told her with his eyes.

"Oh yes I do!" she insisted, extending her left hand, fingers closed, toward him.

"This is yours. How much I long to give it back to you!"

"Nothing is mine any longer," he declared to her with his sad eyes.

"But this is yours, your last breath that Friday a few minutes, only a few minutes before that Saturday arrived. It was pitch black outside, and all of us who were guarding you were unable to protect you. Remember? Just as I touched your chest you released your breath to me. You left me your last breath."

"Let it go, let it out into the universe where it belongs."

The ground shook from his powerful voice. Tearfully Maryo looked at her clenched hand. She tried to spread her fingers and release the breath she had held so many years. The fingers refused to obey the mind's command. They remained rigidly closed. "I can't open my hand," she turned to tell him with deep anxiety.

But he was no longer there. In the place he had been sitting was a small crust of bread. That was what was left of him. Maryo leaned over. She bent down, took it gently between her right thumb and forefinger, and brought it to her mouth. Her left hand relaxed, the fingers moved slowly, stretched, opened. Like a caress the warm breath slid across her fingers and suddenly her palm chilled. That breath, his last, dispersed into the universe and at once Maryo became less. Her body became incredibly less, her soul weakened, and she felt a little breeze caress her face, go down her back and tangle her hair. A little breeze swirled around her a moment and left her, flowed toward the sea, struck the waves and lifted the sand, growing stronger and stronger till it was a powerful wind. A storm was rising. Suddenly she was filled with anxiety. She looked toward the house to see what her people were doing. They had all risen from the table. The father held the lantern high, its trembling flame lighting the road. The mother was holding the baby tightly in her arms, and bent over she was entering the cottage. Holding to one another's shoulders, the children followed, straining against the wind. The lantern disappeared through the doorway and Maryo heard the door shut with a bang. Now she was in total darkness.

The air continued to blow. It struck the ocean, which swelled angrily sending waves pounding onto the rocks, the beach. Maryo clung tightly to the rock. The water smote her to the bone. Her soaked clothing and hair stuck to her body and face, blocking her sight.

She held herself tightly on the rock, she held on and waited. The water struck her, covered her, reached beyond the rock to the bottom of the hill. Everything was covered by churning water, and Maryo held on persistently. Hours passed till the wind weakened, died down, became calm. The sea withdrew into its place and lay serene. Maryo timidly opened her eyes. All was peaceful around her, but her spirit was exhausted from the effort to hold against the storm. With great pain she pulled her body erect and walked heavily toward the hill. She needed the haven of her mother's little house where she could rest for a while. Her feet were sucked into the wet sand and as she dragged them out the sand and water rushed in; those two elements competed to see which would fill the cavities left by her feet, which would manage more quickly to erase her tracks.

Maryo wearily climbed the little hill and searched for the small cottage by the dim starlight just before dawn. As she climbed and searched she became more and more anxious, running now to the right and now to the left, but the house did not appear. The spot where her people's house had stood was just sandy ground with a few bushes and a huge stump where the fig tree had been. The vineyard and the fine pasture were arid ground covered with sand and dry branches. There were no signs of people there, just weathered branches, thin dry porous branches which looked like skeletons of trees. Everything was at the mercy of the wind. All was at the mercy of the storm. Maryo was terrified. Her soul was terrified by this ravaged place. Her eyes filled with tears of nostalgia for the children's sweet little faces. Seized with panic she rushed to the other side of the hill.

The sun rose over the sea. The light of fresh new day broke in the heavens. She felt relieved. She caught sight of the path leading to the village, and that calmed her. With each stride down the path her fears lessened, her spirit revived, her body felt relief.

The path, all white before her, worn smooth by the steps of her people, led to the village. She felt grateful for the sunlight, the path, the sweet, peaceful day that had dawned.

"Thank you," she whispered, "thank you."

Feeling a lightening of her body, she began to run along the path. She raised her head toward the sky and shouted with her whole body.

"Thank you. . . Thank you. . . Thank you-u-u-u-u-!"

Despinyo awoke disturbed.

The dim pre-dawn starlight shone through the small transom above the kitchen door. She lay still in her bed, her gaze fixed on the little window. Her chest felt heavy, as if she were being cut in half. Each shallow breath was cut short and heaved in and out of her mouth. Her body, immobile, debilitated, sought the relief of death.

"What can be wrong with me?" she felt with amazement and fright. "What can be making me feel so heavy?" She strove to remember, to think of what was happening in the household, what dream she may have had. A hint of a dream passed hazily, vaguely through her mind, made no image, disappeared and left mounting anxiety. Biting her lip, she forced her thoughts in the direction of the dream and somewhere deep inside her dark forms began to move. They dissolved at once, however, and were completely lost.

She wanted to get up, to go and sit on the low wall and look up high into the sky and see the stars—how they were fading with the coming sunlight. "In the sunlight I will remember the dream," she thought. But she was afraid to move. She feared that Giannakos, sensing she was awake might want to make love.

"Oh that I could stop giving birth and be reborn!" she sighed the thought which was brewing within her. With great emotion she quietly arose and went outside.

The night before she had picked up the child, her boy, the little bird of her heart, as she called the blond, blue-eyed boy, to whom she would croon: "Oh, last little bird of my heart, lucky child of mine."

Late in the night she took her small son in her arms and noiselessly tip-toed to the middle of the room. Through the shutters slid the slight illumination of the pale moon. All of the children were asleep, and she stood thinking where she would lay the sleeping infant. Usually it slept by Maria, but Panagiota had again slid in beside her sister and there was no room for the small boy. Despinyo turned to Garoufalo, but Phtyhio was by her side. Finally bending over Aggerou's side she lay Liapis down there. Aggerou was uncovered. Leaving the child, Despinyo emerged troubled from the room. Sitting now all alone on the verandah under the sweet night sky, Despinyo was wide awake. Suddenly she jumped up. She shot erect as if bitten by a rabid mongrel, a deadly asp, or the words of an evil man. It was the last impression which hit her now as she recalled the scene, standing by Maria, then by Garoufalo and finally laying the child down beside uncovered Aggerou. Now she saw with utter clarity the naked body of her daughter. She saw her belly. A round swollen belly and enlarged breasts. "Why, it was like she was carrying a child!" Despinyo clapped both hands over her mouth to block the voice which burst within her breast and heaved within. She sprang from the verandah ledge into the room. It was pitch black inside. Nothing could be seen. Her steps took her to Aggerou's mattress, she bent over and touched the sleeping form; she couldn't be absolutely sure. She left the room and slumped to her seat on the low wall. She was trembling all over. Her teeth were chattering as if from a fever, or as if deep winter had suddenly come. She crossed her arms and pressed her hands under her armpits. She was waiting for the moon to cross the sky, to give way to the sun, so she could enter the room, approach her older daughter, examine her belly and confirm that it had been nothing but her imagination, nothing but dark shadows in the night playing tricks. Of course her daughter Aggerou was not pregnant, couldn't be with child; it was merely a suspicion, and then the dream flashed, forming in her mind. She had dreamt that she was marrying again. It was a man who was not at all like Giannakos, she didn't know who, but this other groom brought her the wedding band and it was a black wedding band, jet black, which he slipped onto the middle finger of her right hand.

Panagiota bit her lip in fury as she watched her younger sisters and brothers. Garoufalo was seated on the floor sewing dresses for her dolly, and Phtyhio was by her side. She had a cold and every so often sneezed, wiping her drippy nose with the back of her hand. Liapis, in a harness held carefully by Garoufalo, was taking his first steps.

"That's right, precious," Garoufalo coaxed, urging her brother with a gentle tug.

"Precious" was a word which Maria had brought home from school. It was a term of affection which the schoolmistress, Kyra Pelagia, reserved for little Elenitsa, daughter of the village doctor. "You recite the poem, Elenitsa precious," Kyra Pelagia would say.

Maria took a liking to the word and brought it home. Garoufalo made it her own, applying it to Liapis, especially to him. "Come here, precious," she would tell him, and he would beam when she would add, "Come to your Garoufalo!"

Nikolos viewed the whole ceremony with an attitude of amused boredom.

Panagiota was furious. With eyes blurred by confusion and anger she gazed at her sisters and brothers. A lot had happened that morning, and she was trying to make some sense out of words and events. Only dim suspicions, dark and elusive, whirled incoherently within her.

Today mother was not mother.

It must have been very early, just at the break of dawn. Panagiota awoke and from her pallet heard father and the two older boys in the yard. They were preparing to leave for the fields. Father was harnessing the horse, while Constantis and Antonis were putting the tools in the wagon. Mother was up preparing breakfast, and Panagiota heard the horse snorting before setting off, then its hoofs beating as it turned off their lane onto the main road. That instant mother burst into the bedroom.

Today mother was not mother. A wicked witch flew into the room, leapt to Aggerou's pallet, grabbed the sleeping girl by the hair, hauled her nightgown above her waist with one hand, passed the other palm around the curve of her belly, scolded in a shrewish voice, and began to beat her.

Mana was someone else today, for she had never meted out a beating so hard, angry, vicious. With both fists, with her feet, and even with her head, she pounded Aggerou.

"Who was it, you stupid thing? Who shoved a baby inside you? Who? Who—"

It was á hard, harsh voice.

"Curse you, girl! Better the single sorrow of your death than the hos

100

of sorrows you have brought down upon our heads!"

She began to beat the other children, too, screaming

"I didn't bear children, I bore coiled snakes!"

She hissed like a snake, heedless of sobbing cries for pity. She heard not a single plea. From a corner of the room, Panagiota observed her face and found it unrecognizable. The pockmark scars on her face had become channels. Her hair tangled across her face, mother was a vicious, savage witch.

"What has come over mana?" Panagiota wondered.

When the fit of flailing and cursing had subsided, the mother ordered the older children to saddle the mule. Gathering some changes of clothing, she threw a few things in a bag, immediately exited to the yard and swung into the saddle.

Aggerou walked ahead holding the reins and she was, ugly, awfully ugly from her tears and runny nose; her face was puffed by crying and her breasts seemed to be swollen by sobs. Aggerou led the mule through the gate, and Maria, her features tense with fright, slapped the rump of the mule to increase its pace. As they entered the lane, the mother appeared to remind herself of something; she turned and shouted to Garoufalo,

"Look here now, girl. When your father comes, tell him my sister Agni is ill, and I've gone to see her."

The mule hurried to pass through the gate and climb the cobblestone grade that lead out of the village. Panagiota sighed. The sigh emerged from deep within her. Her stomach was churning, she felt nauseated. As she descended the stairs to the yard, the large rooster caught sight of her from a distance and came racing at her. He was an unruly bird and Panagiota had always feared him. Now she stood firm and stared at him. She was glad he was coming toward her. She tensed her muscles and glared at him out of the corner of her eye. The fowl pulled up, moved his head nervously and puffed his comb. Opening his wings, he flapped them in the dust and took short hops in her direction. Pangiota held her ground with muscles alert. She awaited the bird, welcoming its attack. It was the first time she was not afraid. The bird and the girl exchanged angry glances, and then the bird composed himself. He turned his head away, and seeing a young hen he raised his wings and sprang on her. Nailed on the spot, the hen puffed her feathers in panic and averted her head from the attacker. The rooster mounted her spine and his weight ground her head in the dirt. The girl's face darkened; she set upon the fowl and aimed an angry kick at the its posterior. The fowl dropped startled to the ground, and the hen skittered to the chicken coop as Pangiota jumped and landed with both feet on the cock's back. With a powerful vault she came down on the bird's spine and heard his small bones crack and a squawk come from his throat and snapping bones, and the beast in her guts, caged, lunged fiercely back and forth, just as Father Vagellis moved on Aggerou, with those filthy robes and that fat belly of his, and that flabby, sweaty neck, in which Maryo had sunk her nails, and now Panagiota jumped on the fowl harder and harder, ever more rapidly, and felt his body and feathers spread on the ground as she went up and down hoarsely shouting:

"I know how babies are shoved into a belly, I know how babies are shoved into a belly. . .".

Garoufalo, Phtyhio, Nikolis and Liapis sat thunderstruck on the stone bench and stared open-mouthed at Panagiota. Not a word, not a peep came from their mouths, and Pangiota kept jumping and shouting,

"I know how they shove babies into a belly. I know how. . ." she screamed, till the fowl was still.

It was totally inert, not a sound came from its body; and Panagiota ceased. She ceased jumping, she ceased shouting. She went to the corner of the garden between the chicken coop and the dung heap, bent very near to the ground and vomited. She vomited a long time. Her stomach emptied and the beast inside her was pacified. It curled up in serene repose and remained so, till the next time.

Her eyes fell upon the mill. Framed sharply on the hill to the north of the village, it peered out over the red tile roofs between which wove the snaky white road that lead to the main square. Maryo breathed a sigh of relief. From the rise on which she stood she could now locate the lane to her mother's house. She stood for a while savoring the sight of her mother's village, which was becoming a deep part of her, becoming her village. Beyond she could hear the sea rhythmically sending its eternal waves onto the sand and dissolving into foam. "Praisé for the sea, who shall say?" She recalled the poet and suddenly she was seized with joy; joy hit her like a cataract with the thought that she would again be seeing her family. With long strides she jumped rocks and bushes descending the hill to the village. Before reaching the wide lane she saw the mule with her grandmother in the saddle, her aunts Maria and Aggerou trotting along behind. Excitedly Maryo began to shout,

"Wa-a-a-a-a-a-it! Wa-a-a-a-a-a-it for me!"

She caught up near the fig orchard dividing the village from the open fields, the place where her mother was born. Breathlessly she reached out to embrace the girls. Stunned, her smile froze and remained pasted on her face. As she softly touched their shoulders, she felt their bodies faltering; they were stumbling along awkwardly, about to collapse. The children's bodies were about to break, to shatter, to disintegrate. They were not the vital bodies Maryo knew but sacks stuffed to look like human beings. Maryo looked closely at the faces to verify it was her aunts. Each face was empty, vacant, lost. It was the mere shape of a face, without features. It was like a painting in which the artist had limned a silhouette in a single dark brush stroke. Maryo crossed her arms and followed. Like sadness she dogged their steps.

Maryo was literally frozen. Outside, snow was falling, and upon touching the ground, the flakes dissolved and turned to mud. Even here inside the convent, there was not a single warm corner to be found. Only in the chapel was the cold somewhat abated, especially on Sundays when candles were lighted. She was huddled under a thin blanket in the stable and was thinking of her Aunt Maria. She was thinking of her under her name in the order, Sister Theochtisti. How many winters had she spent in convents!

"How much she suffered from the cold in her life! And I never gave it a thought. How meager and limited people's feelings are! We never think of the suffering of others till we experience the like, and then we suffer for ourselves alone." Her face darkened and her body shivered with the thought. She pulled the old blanket up to her chin, and that uncovered her feet. Bending her knees, she curled up, continuing her dark thoughts. "One life isn't enough. One life is insufficient for people to comprehend what is going on around them." She smiled. "We need another lifetime, like the one I have now." Aggerou's moans froze her smile.

Aggerou's time had come. It was Christmas eve and the girl was giving birth. Her mother had just arrived at the convent. Her cheeks red from the cold, her body weary from traveling, her frozen hands pressed under her arms, she kept counseling her daughter. Her voice was curt and chilled.

"Be patient, Aggerou. Calm yourself; the time has not come. Do you feel cold?"

She turned.

"Quick, Maria, make more coals. Fill the magali."

Maria at once left the stable to gather wood and Maryo followed her. "She must be tired, very tired, indeed," she worried for the girl. Maria had just returned from the village, having rushed the whole way to fetch her mother.

Maria ran leaving dark footprints in the thin layer of snow. She was oblivious to the chill as she moved through the deserted countryside, but she felt a pleasant shock as the warmth of their kitchen fireplace softly surrounded her, enclosed her body, enwrapped her like a feather comforter. Her family were all gathered around the low table. Their bodies warmed the space even more, and the pot hissed boiling over the fire as the father played the old game with his boys. He was seated on the small stool and little Nikolos tried to push him off, while Liapis pulled at his legs from behind. The younger daughters commented all the while, and Maria rushed in, hastened to whisper to her mother, who jumped to her feet not needing a cue, dropped the stocking she was mending and seized her shawl. Dumbfounded by Despinyo and Maria, the father stared, and grabbing their chance the boys pushed him to the floor and swarmed onto his back, the other children laughing with glee till the man thrust the boys aside, barely with time to exclaim,

"What's going on here!"

Despinyo slammed the door behind her.

"My sister needs me," she was heard to say as she and her daughter Maria flew down the front stairs.

Scrambling to his feet and disentangling himself from the boys, the father swung open the door and leapt onto the moudi.

"Hey! What on earth can she want on Christmas eve?" he asked testily.

Maria was pulling the mule by its bridle.

"As soon as I find out, I'll tell you," Despinyo curtly replied.

"Curse her and her whole sisterhood!" he yelled after her in rage as the garden gate banged shut.

The road that cut across the countryside was covered by a thin crust of snow. The mule's hoof prints formed little pools of muddy water which Despinyo, trudging to the animal's rear, was careful to avoid. Maria, taking her turn in the saddle, inhaled deeply. She greedily sucked in and swallowed the damp air, which refreshed her weary breast. The snow-covered landscape was a soothing sight. And that sound also. The sound made by her mother's feet crunching on the snow crust comforted her heart.

Maryo shivered. She shivered from the tips of her toes to her chin. Her fingertips were puffed and blue, near to frost-bite. She was sniffling and her eyes were running as she thought of her Aunt Maria, the sweet nun Theochtisti, who had suffered so much from the cold throughout her life.

Now after all those years were gone, she pitied her. Her heart bled to see her now as a child search the frozen fields for branches, carry one armful after another to the outside stove, light kindling wood with chilled fingers, and fetch hot coals for the magali to warm Aggerou. Her heart bled too for the fifteen year old aunt who was in labor biting on a rag to muffle her cries of pain. "The way we live life..." Maryo smiled bitterly; ". . . the way we live controlled by others, with no will of our own, one life is enough. More than enough!"

Lying on a thick pallet, naked from the waist down and covered by a rough afghan, Aggerou was giving birth. Her body shook spasmodically with each surge of pain; her face swelled and distorted as she twisted hay or the edge of the afghan in her mouth to quell the pained cries which rose from her warm depths. Aggerou had fixed her eyes on the half-open stable door. She ignored the chilly air which passed through the opening, for her mind was set on her mother. She was waiting breathlessly for her mother to come and take the baby out of her insides so she could be rid of it, so the pain would cease.... Someone had swung a huge scimitar, cut her body in two, right in the middle, and she was begging for her belly to open up, to expel the child, but her belly, heavy and barred, refused to open, would not rid her of the child. Only her legs, each time the scimitar descended, sprang far away, violently detached, and came back again.

The door opened wide and a blast of icy air whipped Aggerou's body. A black shadow, her mother, stood on the threshold. Behind her, Maria gave her a gentle nudge and closed the door. The mother approached, lifted the cover and felt the girl's belly. The girl shuddered from that frozen touch; her stretched belly trembled and she shivered from head to toe. The mother drew back her hands, rubbed them together and warmed them under her armpits. Her eyes focused keenly on her daughter but she did not touch her face, which watched the mother, eager for a comforting word. Despinyo kept her lips tightly sealed. She breathlessly inhaled, drew in the cold air through her nostrils and almost at once expelled it burning hot. Aggerou formed words from that burning air, bitter words which cracked her eardrums. "Better the single sorrow of your death. . .

"Help me, mana! " she groaned as the pain mercilessly struck her body. "Take it out of me—I can't stand it any longer!"

Despinyo raised her eyes and gazed at Aggerou.

The mother's thoughts dwelt heavily upon her birthing daughter. In her she saw the hours, unending savage hours that were her own. Her child-births, her limits. Each birth further narrowed the limits of life, and now it was happening to her first daughter! She felt a sob that choked her deep inside, deep down, where all the bitternesses had settled. She wanted to speak to her child, to say, "Come, my daughter, let us sing together a lament of the narrowing of your life."

"Come, kori mou," she said sweetly, "Easy, now. . .".

She placed her warm hands on Aggerou's belly and measured the hours.

"It isn't time yet. Sshh. . .sshh. . ." she whispered repeatedly. "Your time has not come. There's nothing to worry about. Giving birth isn't anything for a woman! Look at how many times I've done it!"

"All right, mother! All right!" Aggerou said with her mouth, her eyes, her stomach, her entire body. "Take it out of me, mana! Take it out!"

"Patience, Aggerou. Don't fret. It's not time yet. Are you cold?"

She turned.

"Quick, Maria, make more coals to fill the magali."

Maria instantly rushed out of the stable and Maryo followed her. Despinyo turned to her sister, Mother Superior Agni, who was seated by the head of the girl in labor.

"There will be some time as yet before it begins," Despinyo told her with her eyes, and the nun responded with her gaze holding that serenity which comes in the presence of another's despair. Since deep midnight she had been there by her niece's side. With Maria she had prepared the girl, and now Despinyo had arrived to take charge. The nun rose.

"I'll go now," she said with some relief; "I'll go to the chapel, light a candle, and pray. . .".

Despinyo nailed her with a look.

"Yes! Go to the chapel! Light a candle! And. . .!"

Her voice rattled, frightening even Despinyo herself.

"Mother of God, forgive me," she whispered. "Yes, go and pray for help for us all," she said softly with a gentle voice.

Maryo followed Maria.

"She must be so tired. She must be so cold," Maryo thought as she pressed her back against the warm outer wall of the oven. Some distance from the nuns' cells, the oven was built flush against the convent's outer wall near the stables. Its hemispherical baking chamber was always freshly whitewashed, and kindling wood was always lighted in it early in the morning. When they began to prepare the young mother-to-be, Maria began to feed the oven with branches, thin sapling trunks and pine cones. Soon the fire was blazing, leaving large burning coals. In the morning prior to leaving for the village, the magali was well supplied with hot coals.

From a distance a dog caught sight of Maria and began wagging its tail. It watched her mournfully, moving hesitantly in her direction. Maria continued to feed the stove with branches, occasionally stealing glances at the dog which, ever bolder, came closer and closer. It was old and gaunt. Its exposed ribs showed starvation and its eyes told the sadness amassed in its lifetime.

Maria turned from the stove and concentrated on the animal. "How hungry he must be!" she said to herself. "The poor thing must be starving!"

"And you must also be hungry," Maryo whispered.

Maria had been fasting for three days. Christmas was approaching and she was preparing to take communion, but events changed her plans. The evening before she had been with Aunt Agni, who had given her sesame soup, but she had not touched it. She wasn't hungry; she didn't feel like eating at all. She took Aggerou's soup to the stable and forced her to eat it all. Then they went to sleep, and she must have been sleeping very deeply, as her sister spoke.

"Wake up, Maria, wake up I tell you!" she urged, shaking her shoulder.

It was a moaning voice. The tone was hectic and harsh, and Maria awoke in deep darkness.

"What. . .what is it?" she cried, fumbling for a candle.

The candle lit, she raised it high and cast its flickering light on Aggerou's face. How altered, how deeply altered it was; it was like a face she had never seen before! And the voice, it too had changed ! Maria could not grasp what that voice was saying. Did Aggerou say "hurting" or "birthing"? What was it Aggerou had moaned? Vertigo seized Maria; quickly, quickly she must light the wick in the little oil lamp. It had gone out. Why had it gone out? A draft had extinguished it and now it just wouldn't light. Maria's hand was trembling as she held the candle over the wick—she was trembling, and the Virgin blessed the lamp into light, which softened the atmosphere in the stable. What, she now asked herself, should she do? Should she go the village to bring her mother? It was a long way and at the witching hour the wilderness was full of scary shadows. Should she fetch Aunt Agni? What would she tell her—"Come, Auntie, Aggerou may be hurting or birthing"? Hadn't the nun said she didn't want to know a thing? They could stay in the stable at a distance from the convent—that was all. "How could you, my own sister, bring such shame on the convent? You may stay in the stable," she had said, "but I don't want to know a thing. Absolutely nothing."

That day she and Aggerou had arrived with their mother frantic, exhausted and sunk in bitterness. It was that morning when mother had cursed and beat them and wasn't like mother at all. They had reached Aunt Agni's cell, and mother had planted herself solidly at the doorway, speaking in that hard, harsh voice:

"Aggerou is going to have the baby here."

Aunt Agni, the Mother Superior, retorted in the same tone of voice:

"No! Here, never! The world is all too eager to blame us, and my nuns are innocent young girls. No! No! No!"

"I refuse to take her to Smyrni. They'll make her a whore there. Aggerou will have the child here."

"It can't be done here, I say! Here never! It's out of the question!"

"But no one will know but us two, you and me. . .".

The two girls, seated on the edge of their aunt's narrow pallet drew in their bodies to take up a minimum of space. They listened to the sharp exchange between their mother and aunt, and they watched their altered faces. Now there was no more talk of birth, only of sovereigns, the sovereigns the girls' grandfather had given Agni to build the convent, though she never even paid the old man a visit, managing only to come to his funeral. Who was it, however, who had rushed into marriage with Giannakos and rushed to give him their best land, while he did nothing every night but go to the coffee house and get drunk. On the other hand, who was it who never visited the grandmother, who was bed-ridden and took so long to die, while Despinyo was always by her side? Finally, Aunt Agni said yes:

"You can stay in the stable at the other side of the grounds. But I want to know nothing. Absolutely nothing. For your ordinary needs only Maria can come to my cell after vespers. But stay out of sight; we don't want the sisters to suspect a thing. . .".

At dusk Maria would head quickly for the cell. Not that there was any fear of demons here. On the grounds of a convent no such thing could exist. She hurried along, anyhow, and before she had repeated thrice, "Jesus Christ prevails; he casts out all iniquity," she would reach the wide stairway and take the steps two at a time to the door of Aunt Agni's cell. Her fingers would barely have touched the latch when the door would open and Aunt Agni's hand would draw her gently within, closing the door behind them.

How warm the cell was! The walls were lined with icons. The constantly lighted oil lamp illuminated Jesus's face in the embroidery which Aunt Agni had stretched on the wall above her bed and before him a small deer in a very green forest was looking at Christ. Maria would feel deep contentment at such moments in her aunt's cell. The nun would have her sit down in the big Mother Superior's chair and with a thousand kind words would always offer her something special to eat. Maria would eat hurriedly and again rush back to the stable where Aggerou was.

There, the night before, her aunt had sesame soup for her. But Maria was not hungry; she had no appetite at all; she just took the sesame soup to Aggerou, and she had to force her to swallow what was in the bowl. Aggerou kept wining and groaning in discomfort, her lips trembling from her sobbing and the stable's chill.

"Look how I've become!" she said. "Feel my belly as tight as a drum and heavy as lead!"

So she sobbed and pulled Maria's hand toward her belly, but Maria drew back; she didn't want to touch that belly. Fearing that contact, she just kept repeating,

"You're very near your time. The baby will come soon."

They fell asleep with the lamp lighted and thus Maria was shaken awake in dense darkness by Aggerou, her fearful voice strangely harsh, coming from deep inside her: "Hurting. . ." or "Birthing. . ." she had said.

Maria had searched for the candle, attempted to light the lamp and wondered what she should do. The Virgin blessed the lamp into light, which lent warmth to the stable. Rushing into the darkness, Maria had barely mumbled "Christ prevails" twice when she reached the top of the stairs and the little door of the cell. Aunt Agni sat up on her pallet and greeted Maria with sleepy eyes as she with heaving breath blurted out:

"She's hurting! She's birthing!"

The aunt rose slowly, came to the girl and spoke gently.

"It's raining, my child, and you are soaked."

She took her habit from the clothes tree, threw it over Maria's shoulders and embraced her tenderly.

"God is with you, kori mou," she whispered.

Maria rested her head on Aunt Agni's shoulder; her robe smelled comfortingly of incense.

In the stable they prepared the young mother-to-be. They put more straw in her pallet under its rough coverlet, loaded plenty of hot coals in the magali, and heated water. Maria gave her sister a sponge-bath, delicately touching her belly and whispering,

"There's a girl—there's our dear girl."

Aunt Agni murmured prayers on her rosary. Maria prepared to go to the village to fetch her mother. A light rain was falling, a very light rain which would soon turn to snow. The day was dawning gray and cold.

Maria steadily fed branches into the mouth of the stove. With one eye on the dog which was approaching with ever greater boldness, she heard the crackling of the damp branches in the fire combined with the sound of Aggerou's moans. The movements of her hands quickened as her eyes now fastened on the stray animal.

Maryo was grateful for the wall of the stove warming her back and hands as she leaned against its heat. Maria was crying and her tears struck old memories of things which were yet to come. In Maria's place Maryo saw a woman of another era. She tried to rid her mind of the image. With all her will-power she attempted to expel it, but it remained fixed in her mind's eye.

Once, far ahead in time, she met a woman. That woman taught her a lesson in weeping. She showed her how bitter tears are when the soul is crazed by great pain. The woman's eyes, very small and petrified by too many dreary years, were like a spring coming from a rocky mountain that suddenly exploded and burst open. It was as if she was bearing a cataract, such were the woman's tears. With awe Maryo watched her standing motionless, absolutely straight, the tears steadily flowing. Acid the tears, they etched, scored, punctured her flesh, forming deep channels everywhere on her face. Lava, they rolled slowly, dissolved the flesh till the meat was gone from the face. The sharp bones jutted brutally through patches of remaining flesh, the lava streamed onto the neck, the breast, the entire body. With horror Maryo watched the skin disintegrate, dissolve, the tears continuing to stream from the two eye holes over the fragile white bones, themselves now cracking, fragmenting. They too dissolving, vanishing. In the place where she once stood, a small pool formed. A little lake of black murky water. Nothing ever grew in that water. No life appeared. So salty, so bitter it was.

Maryo expelled the image, she pushed it away. She had to erase it, to inscribe another in its place. Another more human that she could bear.

Maria was crying; her tears were silver streams.

"That is the image I want to keep," Maryo exclaimed with ardor, and everything instantly froze. The place, time, the figure of Maria all froze.

Before the white-washed stove streaked with soot above its mouth, stood the girl. Her red cheeks glowed with light from the core of burning coals. Her black hair, gathered behind, blew in wisps over her face, and her bare forearms, her sleeves gathered above the elbows to facilitate work, had a roseate hue. With one arm lifted to throw a handful of branches into the stove's mouth and the other bent holding tongs, she was frozen so Maryo remember her. Behind her was the white snow broken by patches of bushes. Above were clouds, lead-colored—not ebony. The sun was partly seen sending its rays diagonally through cloud openings, hinting of its coming warmth. Maryo came up close to Maria's face. She came very close to her face and with great surprise confirmed the presence of a little smile. A faint smile promised to appear. It would be coming as soon as the present tears of bitterness would dry. "Maria is being born this very moment," the thought flashed. "In sadness," she mused, "knowledge is conceived. From knowledge the soul is born and then the person exists." Maryo was deeply touched. Then she heard the other girl's moaning. The sound spread through the air, reverberating around the stable. Within the stable Aggerou was giving birth. Her whole self appeared to turn only toward her body's pain. Maryo looked at her from close up. She observed how her face was distorted and tears were flooding down her cheeks, being absorbed by the pallet. "Bodily pain is quickly forgotten," thought Maryo. "It must touch the soul to become essential knowledge."

Maryo came out of the stable the moment that a gentle breeze was passing, rippling Maria's skirt rippling and lifting her hair, as her arms moved, feeding the stove and stirring the fire with the tongs. Then Maria turned toward the stray dog. He pulled back his head and released a dull howl full of woe. Maria could no longer endure the hound's sorrow; she threw down the tongs and broke into a run. She raced to her Aunt Agni's cell. With no thought of murmuring "Christ prevails," she bounded up the stairs, slammed open the latch, flung wide the door, and burst into the cell.

"What is it! What has happened, my child?" Aunt Agni blurted anxiously.

Maria was oblivious. She went directly to the cabinet where her aunt kept bread, broke off a large chunk and gripping it tightly leapt down the stairs. Following her on the run, the nun was confused by questions and fears. By the stove, Maria's eyes searched for the hound. He had vanished. He was nowhere to be found; there was just her mother standing in the low doorway of the stable calling insistently,

"Maria, bring hot coals! Hot coals, Maria! The girl is freezing!"

Maria's eyes darted frantically in search of the dog. Maryo came; quietly and gently she took the bread from Maria's hand. She, hands freed, took a shovel full of red-hot coals, carried them carefully into the stable and emptied them into the magali. She again rushed out, filled the shovel with coals, returned to the stable. She came and went again and again till the stable was filled with hot light. Her hands were seared, her face was reddened, her palms were burning. Kneeling beside her birthing sister, she rested her open palms on her round belly. Gently, like waves, she moved her hands. She pulsated them rhythmically and their warmth penetrated the skin, reaching the baby. Maria was leaning her head back with her eyes closed, concentrating her whole soul on the movements of this moment. She pushed downward, not abruptly, not forcefully, like a caress of life; she pushed and felt the belly give and soften as the wave of water broke over Aggerou's thighs.

The mother, Despinyo, with teeth clenched in a harsh voice urged, "Push. . . push . . . push!"

The daughter in pain and animosity pushed downward. With little shrieks she pushed downward. It was Maryo, standing behind Despinyo, who first saw the dark little head project from the narrow channel of the girl. The channel opened, tore, broke and filled the little head with blood and liquids amidst which Maryo now saw the little blue face of the child, the tiny eyes closed and sealed, the tiny nose flattened as if it had fallen face downward and had broken its little brand-new nose. The little neck was wrinkled, wrinkled like the neck of an old man of one hundred, and tightly wound around it was the umbilical cord. "The baby was hanged. It hanged itself," Maryo whispered to herself, as Despinyo commanded frantically,

"Push, Aggerou, push to save the child."

In agony Despinyo pulled on the fragile body, which slipped out, slipped like an eel in her hands; and she raised it high with the noose around its neck, its body bruised, dripping wet, and angled toward where it was held by the cord. Her hands moved the child in a circle. Thrice she brought the babe through a circle in the air, saying,

"Be baptized the servant of God, in the name of the Father, the Son. . ."

". . . and the Holy Spirit," Aunt Agni added, crossing herself as she entered the stable.

"What on earth could your Aunt Agni want with your mother on Christmas eve!"

Giannakos was furious and Panagiota was filled with despair. Maria had lunged into the kitchen looking at no one but mother. As she had opened her mouth in silent exclamation, mother had swept up her shawl and the two of them dashed from the room, taken the mule, and departed. Nothing had been said. Panagiota sighed as she looked at the three younger children. Here she was alone again, and again saddled with the three of them. "Cook us some nice hot noodle soup for this evening," her father had told her, leaving for the coffee house with the two older sons behind him.

Panagiota put the noodles on to boil, and standing on the stool to stir the pot she felt the anger inside her gather into a tight heavy knot. At the first sign of darkness, she arranged the pallets in the bedroom. Lining them up and spreading the afghans, she got her pillow and was the first to lie down to go to sleep. She wanted to be alone to shed the silent tears of her great bitterness. She also wanted to get hold of the quilt before the other children lay down. Phtychio would curl up beside her, pull the quilt to her side and again leave her uncovered. Panagiota clamped the cover between her knees and pulled it over her head. Alone in the darkness under the cool bedclothes she followed the sounds of the other children in the kitchen— Phtychio's bawling, Liapis's giggling, and Nikolos' vast silence. She heard her father coming round the corner of the lane. Drunk on raki, he was in a foul temper. She heard him curse the two boys, who were attempting to coax him along as gently as they could. They mounted the stairs, pushing him into the kitchen and slamming the door behind them. Antonios served the soup, and Panagiota heard her father slurping and continuing to curse. He cursed her pock-marked mother and her black-robed aunt and her silly sister Aggerou, who had up and taken off for the convent. And then there was tight-lipped Maria, who was always whispering woman-talk with her mother! Never a word to him! Yet he was the master of the house! Panagiota drew the cover even tighter around her head, blocking her ears. She couldn't stand the sound of her father's voice, she hated him so much.

A heavy murky sleep dragged her to the church. The sanctuary was asphyxiatingly full. Many votive candles had been lit. At the front of the congregation Panagiota awaited the priest and he came out wearing his stole and nothing else. His silvery stole hung on his nude torso, and in his left hand hung the censor. It frightened Panagiota to see his big bare legs covered with thick black hairs, his toe-nails long and in-grown, with dirt between the toes. As soon as he caught sight of her, he began to shake the censor very close to her face and the smoke of the incense with its choking aroma suffocated her. She began to cough, and she retreated, but the priest rushed after her, the censor striking her with upward sweeps as she dashed through the congregation round and round the church. The man kept right behind her but she got smaller and smaller, became so very small she could step under the seat of her mother's pew, so he lost sight of her but kept searching here and there, shouting, "You want to go to Hell, do you! So you want to go to Hell!" Panagiota stayed quiet as quiet could be in her hiding place. Then little Phtychio appeared. Her little sister was on her feet; she could walk, not merely crawl as before. She was dressed in white, a sparkling white dress tied with a blue bow behind. With a big white ribbon in her hair, she was dashing up and down the aisles of the sanctuary, the congregation parting before her, and every so often she jumped very high. Little Phtychio made bounding leaps higher and higher as if she was about to fly, and in unison the assembly cheered her on—"Oo-oo-oo— OOP, she goes! Oo-oo- oo-OOP, she goes!" and then they leaned their heads way back, opened their mouths doubly wide, and roared with laughter. Their mouths were black. They were deep wells. Without teeth or tongue their mouths were just a circus sound, "Oo- oo-oo-ooOOOP! as the child sprang higher and higher. Panagiota was frightened, terribly frightened that little Phtychio would go so high she couldn't come down. Leaving her hiding place she caught the child by her dress and brought her down hard on the stone church floor. With a hollow "F-f-f-f-OP!" she came down on her head and it split in two. "F- f-f-f-f-OP!" went the head, squashed and opened the way onions do when her father pounded them on the cutting board; Phtychio's head opened exuding membrane and fluid, and the congregation froze, mouths rounded ready to sound "Oo-oo-oo—OOP!" as Father Vagelis finally grabbed Panagiota by the shoulder, shook her and bellowed, "Look alive, my girl! It's already noon, and you have chores to do at home!"

Panagiota opened her eyes and found her father bending over her. He touched her kindly, squeezing her shoulders, and she wanted to cuddle in his arms, stay there and cry till she felt relief.

"Time to get up," he told her. "I killed the rooster. I want you and Garoufalo to pluck the bird and cook it for dinner."

It was Christmas day, but they had stayed at home. Panagiota was glad she had not gone to church and had thus avoided the shoving of the children for a place in the communion line. At the noon meal father declared he had never had such egg-lemon soup, and never tasted such savory fried chicken. He declared that his little Panagiota was the ablest of all the children, the best of the lot. She sidled shyly up to her father, and he, seated on the low stool, pulled her playfully onto his lap. Phtychio came over and her father lifted her up and set her down on top of Panagiota. Nikolos pushed at the stool, playing at toppling his dad, who lifted him up beside Phtychio and then hauled Liapis onto the pile, tickling them all as they kicked and laughed with glee till the tears ran down their cheeks.

With his second jigger of raki Giannakos's mood changed.

"Where is your mother on Christmas day!" he raged.

The house had become very small in Despinyo's absence. Casting a sullen look around the kitchen, Giannakos took his cap from its peg and stepped outside, slamming the door behind him. Constantis at once followed, and Antonios reluctantly brought up the rear.

The door remained open and Phychio crawled out onto the verandah. Panagiota shoved the door shut and jumped into her mother and father's bed.

"Open the door, vexer!" shouted Garoufalo, "The baby will freeze!"

"Open it yourself" Panagiota snapped, snuggling under the covers.

"Nikolo-o-o-o-o!" Garoufalo yelled, but received no reply.

She crawled slowly to the door, raised her body, stretched out her arm and pulled on the latch. The door creaked open slightly but stopped against the body of the child. Panagiota came out from under the covers, her eyes glued on Garoufalo, who slowly, with great care, planted the sole of her right foot evenly on the floor, straightened her leg, and firmly grasping the latch, pulled her body upright. With only a slight tremble her legs were supporting her. Panagiota got out of bed and rushed to her sister's side.

"You can do it! You can do it!" she clamored. "The doctor said you could. Come on, you can make it!"

Liapis dropped his playthings, staring at Garoufalo. Nikolos came running from the other room, took Garoufalo's hand, and she took one step. On the second she collapsed to the floor. With the children's eyes intent on her progress, she clung to the edge of a low table and again pushed herself upright. Heading for the sink, she held on to its edge, steadied herself for a moment as if she were gauging her course, again set off and collapsed once more. Panagiota's mind returned to Phtychaki outside on the veranda, took the child by the shoulders, pulled her inside and pushed her to her bed. Phtychaki watched Garoufalo spellbound as Liapis scrambled to her side. Panagiota extended her hand, and Garoufalo was supported by her brother and sister. Together, with great caution, they slowly circled the kitchen.

The children's eyes shone. And Garoufalo's face also shone as she walked entirely on her own.

Darkness was cast over her days when Despinyo lost Phtychaki. Gone! The poor child was gone! She had lost that tiny tormented child of hers, though Aunt Polyxeni Rougana kept declaring again and again that the child was not lost but had been called back.

"Woman, how can you carry on that way?" she angrily rebuked Despinyo. "Why are you crying and tearing your hair? Was Phtychaki yours alone? She was the child of One greater than you. He lent you the child for a time; she was with you awhile, gave you joy awhile, and then came the time He called her back."

Aunt Polyxeni Rougana was right; she certainly knew all about children that were only lent for a time. Of the sixteen infants she had brought into the world, only five survived.

"The children are not yours alone. Get that into your head," Aunt Polyxeni intoned.

Lying in bed in the kitchen, Despinyo watched the children endlessly coming in and going out. This morning she watched the children with sadness, thinking bitterly: "Is it possible that these children are mine?" None of the children looked like they were hers, except perhaps little Liapis. He looked like her child, though he was blond and blue-eyed. "He has Grandfather Alexis's complexion," thought Despinyo. "He looks like a child of mine. The others don't seem to come from my stock, in spite of the old saying, 'The family line is never lost; in fact, it multiplies.' Take Antonios, for instance. He's like a shy girl. There's never been such a man in our family, or for that matter, one like Constantis. He's a savage. Look what he did to Arnaoutis's billy goat because it bit him. He beat it to a pulp with his bare hands. The beating even made its meat inedible. You're hard and mean, my boy, but I feel deeper anguish for you than for my gentler one. And Aggerou, how wild she has become! How I fear for her! What men won't do to my girl when they get wind of her. My poor child, you don't know what it's all about. And my Maria?" The thought of Maria brought deep pain. She felt such dismay. "What can be wrong with my dear girl, my blessed child? This child did not come from my guts but from my heart. But what is happening to her now? From the time she helped at the convent she hasn't smiled. All my darling's smiles are gone. Yet somehow she doesn't seem sad." Despinyo pondered Maria's every movement, all her words and all her acts. She released a heart-felt sigh: "My child is not hurt; she is withdrawn." Despinyo was frightened. "It is as if she is no longer here. The girl has left us. She does not see us, she does not speak to us. She left without saying goodbye." Suddenly tears were gushing. Taking a piece of cloth from under her pillow, she wiped her cheeks and nose.

"Are you in pain, kale mana?" asked Garoufalo.

Her sweet girl was seated on the floor, writing with chalk on her slate, which was resting on a stool. She wrote, erased, and wrote again. That was what she had been doing from the first day she went to school.

"And this child is someone else's," thought Despinyo. "She couldn't

116

possibly be mine. From the day —Praise the Lord!—she stood on her feet, from the time He performed His miracle and the child stood on her own feet, she has been at it continuously. Frisking like a new-born kid. But the walking is nothing beside the talking. From the day she walked and went to school she has been speaking in rhymes. Like a book of nursery tales. What mysteries there are deep within a child! And—hah!—there is my capable Panagiota. But how domineering she has become. She's mean to them all. She has Nikolos under her thumb. She's always beating on him, and he keeps his anger pent up inside. And oh my Phtychaki, dear little thing!" She sighed so deeply that again she felt immense pain. "These are my children who came from inside me without being mine." Her eyes rested on the children gathered there in the kitchen. "Were they ever really inside my body? I don't know who they are. They were strange children attached to my flesh. Bound to my guts. One by one each child took a piece out of me. Phtychaki took her piece to her black, deep black, grave, and that's what hurts me so. And poor Aggerou's baby, even that one too took a piece of me, though it was our shame. What hurt I felt for the poor little thing! How did it all come about? How could my body accept all those children? How did they come to enslave my soul? Now I have no life. My life dispersed with their birth."

Again Despinyo was not feeling well and was resting in bed. Everything had happened so suddenly, so swiftly; and she simply couldn't cope with it all. It seemed that things would never be right again. First she discovered that Aggerou was pregnant. With endless precautions so the men of the house and the neighbors would not learn what had happened, she had taken the two daughters to the convent. Aggerou's child was born dead, they had buried the poor thing, she had cared for Aggerou; and just as she had begun to regain her composure, Panagiota came running:

"Hurry home, mana—our Phtychio is sick."

Again the sin and the shame weighed like mountains on her spirit. Reaching the house short of breath, she rushed to her little one to find the child close to death. The child's skin was scarlet, a hideous scarlet. She was red as a beet and barely breathing with great effort. It looked like the end was near.

"Hurry, Giannako!" she blurted. "Bring the wise Dr. Kanelios!"

So Giannakos rushed to the lower village and fetched the doctor. He looked sadly at the child and examined it; and Despinyo screamed when he told them in a low voice,

"May the Lord help this child..

"Run, Giannako," she moaned, "bring Vaggelio the medicine woman."

Giannakos galloped on the mule to the outskirts of the village and brought back the daughter of Tsipitis, Vaggelio, a tall unmarried woman who was known as a caster of spells. She entered the room with her slow walk, wearing a long skirt, gloves, a hat and many bracelets, all fancy things from Smyrni. With her she carried a big sack of herbs. Removing her gloves and her large black hat, she placed the herbs in a mortar with an onion, added ten drops of mouse-oil, made a paste with the pestle, coated a strip of cloth and wrapped it around the little neck of the child, whose breathing was ever more rapid and whose lips were black and blue. So was Despinyo's lip as she bit it to keep herself from moaning. Who was it that changed the bandage? And who was it that covered the child's face with the other cloth? Despinyo could not remember who, nor could she remember who screamed,

"We've lost Phtychaki!"

Was it Giannakos who screamed or was it her heart? She did remember, however, that the house filled with people; all the neighbors crowded into the main room. Everyone came and everyone was talking at once, including Giasemo, who had ten children. She took Despinyo's hand in hers and, moving it up and down for emphasis, said in her whining voice,

"God took pity on you, Despinyo. He pitied you and remembered you."

Then there was another woman, Kousoula's elder daughter, Annyo, who told her,

"May you live in good health to remember her always."

There were so many other women touched by Charon who seized the chance to whisper through the child messages to the other world that it infuriated Despinyo.

"How many things will you tell her? How can you expect such a tiny thing to remember it all?"

How Despinyo's heart felt for the child as she imagined her crawling here and there in the other world to find each and every child so as to deliver the greetings. She moaned and sobbed as she recalled she had not found time to sing the child lullabies. She had never lullabied Phtychaki; she wanted to do so now, and over the small body she began to sing a gentle cradlesong:

"Come, sweet sleep; sweet sleep, come to our little baby girl...".

Aunt Polyxeni Rougana took her by the shoulders, shook her roughly.

"How can you go on so?" she said. "Why are you crying and tearing your hair? Was Phtychaki yours alone?"

In a flash Phtychaki was gone and the funeral was over.

Garoufalo stood up. Holding her slate in both hands, she came to her mother.

"Look, mana! See what I wrote!"

With great effort Despinyo focussed on each of the large round letters and read syllable by syllable: "be-lov-ed-par-ent."

Her eyes shifting back and forth between the letters and her daughter's face, her mind somehow could not decipher the meaning of "be-lov-ed-par-ent." Then she again felt a stoke of pain deep within. The pain pierced her memory. She relived a dream she had the night before. She dreamed she was once again with child. Her belly was a large, transparent, luminous sphere, within which she saw a miniature child doing somersaults in the waters of her womb. Its legs were very small, but its arms were regular in proportion to its body. She saw clearly that the baby was like a kite held to her by the umbilical cord. It somersaulted like a kite in the wind. It turned head over heels within her belly, and the umbilical cord tugged at her painfully. But the child was indifferent to her pain; it was swimming in waters which must have been urine they smelt so terrible, so terrible that their stink awakened her. Despinyo felt the same pain now that she felt in her dream as her child pulled on the umbilical cord. She pushed Garoufalo and her slate aside, arose with difficulty from the bed, and went out onto the moudi.

The world outside was beautiful. What a blessing from God was this day. Despinyo raised her face toward the sun and took hold of a tuft of her hair. "As many as the hairs on my head be the years that pass before that nightmare becomes a reality!" Thrice Despinyo whispered the charm.

Maryo, seated on the low verandah wall, observed her grandmother's thinning hair. She smiled sadly. "My poor grandmother, your childbearing was your noose. To love with such abandon is both a blessing and a curse." Maryo's eyes seemed to turn inward, as she thought of her love for her own children. "And what was my life like?" she asked. " *Was.* Why did I say *was,* since my life is yet to come?"

Maryo's mother, a little child, was seated on the tiles of the moudi playing. There she was with Maryo's aunts and uncles, all of them now children; and all at once their lives passed, they passed before Maryo's eyes. Before very long their paths would part; some would hasten to leave this life, some would join holy orders, some would be married. Maryo saw too their children, how they grew up together and they also had children who were together with her own children. Her heart was flooded with nostalgia, nostalgia for the life she would lead. Like a blotter her heart absorbed life. It drew the world deep within her and inscribed in large calligraphic letters everything she loved. It was as if she found herself in a grand museum.

A vast dazzling white marble hall, the museum of life. The rooms were spacious and they were all filled with paintings. She was amazed at how many and how valuable they were. Beaming with delight, she sped through the high-ceilinged hallways with their open double-doors. She found a hall she wanted to see, and she paused to look with care and love at those works of human art. She absorbed into herself the simple faces of human beings, the simple faces that had become works of art. She received their images, the messages they were sending, but she could not pause to contemplate, she had to press on, for time was passing and the museum would be closing. She had so much to see, so much to learn. Breathing hard with her heart in her mouth, she ran excitedly, her feet blistering in her tight shoes, as the museum guards, black men and women from the South, politely told her to hurry, and she threw off her shoes. Barefoot now and free, she traveled the smooth marble tiles, popped in and out of rooms, some full of light and warmth and others cold and semi-dark. Savoring the variety every moment in all the details of human art, she felt herself overflowing with joy. She hid her sadness in the dark recesses of knowledge, she pressed it back down deep inside and she wanted to shout, "Stop time!" but it steadily, insidiously streamed on around her and penetrated her.

She reached a hall that was narrow and very bright. In the center was a sculpture of St. Teresa. It was very white under the abundance of intense light. In awe and rapture Maryo paused to look. St. Teresa, her soul drowsy, was falling into the final sleep. The angel who killed her, holding his bloodstained arrow, smiled on her and gazed lovingly deep into her eyes. Maryo remained there. She stayed in that hall admiring God's caress upon the human face. St. Teresa was smiling as death came upon her declining body.

A chilly draft passed through the room. A door must have been left open somewhere, letting in the cold. "It must be freezing outside," Maryo thought and felt a shiver run up and down her spine.

She was walking, walking lightly on the edge of the horizon as she had longed to do for many years. Her eyes played between the two worlds divided by its line. The one was recognizable; the other was blank and formless— so totally white, it was the same as darkness.

For many years her body prepared, it prepared her soul precisely for this game. For many years she saw the horizon beckon to her and invite her to its edge, and she honed the skills of the acrobat. Now her body, weightless, agile, walked the razor's edge which grew steep and narrowed her course. With every step she took, her soul's yearning grew, and Maryo surrendered to that yearning.

She leaned over a little to see her unknown world, and the emptiness greedily seized her, pulled her in. Maryo fell. She fell into the void; the white darkness blanketed her and she groped for somewhere to catch hold, her mouth gaping to release a powerful utterance. Harsh voices from her depths wounded her larynx, and barbs returned to pierce her breast and her entire frame. The void continually pulled her downward.

She awoke terrified. She awoke in terror and found herself in darkness. The chaos and the silence of her dream continued in the storeroom where she slept, below the verandah of her mother's house. Her terror increased in this unfamiliar place, and she started to scream.

Her breast swelled and she powerfully expelled her breath to release the sound, to hear her own voice and gain relief. The sound lacerated her throat and poured into her mouth but did not come out into the air. She waved her hands before her eyes; she could not see their form or their shadow; in anguish she brought them to feel her body, seeking its sound. She put her right hand under the bodice of her nightgown and touched her breast over her heart as if she could somehow get hold of the sound, but still the vibration stayed within her body. She touched her face as if she could convey her voice through her palms, but again there was no sound, and no sensation.

In panic she pressed her palms on her face. It was dry and stiff: She touched her lips; they were parched, cracked. She felt inside her mouth; the gums were shrunken, the tongue numb, rigid. She moved her hands slowly down her torso. The skin was hard, desiccated, covered with scales. Her belly was hollow, inert, and where the liver should have been, that dense cataract of life, she felt something small like a dried fig. Her blood was not flowing and the nest of delight was dry and empty.

Maryo's body was a vast black chasm of silence. Desperate, the soul begged the memory to fill her dwelling place with motion, with sound. The sea! It sought the sea, that vast fluid in movement, filled with wild sounds. Her memory reaching, its vital cells called forth the panorama of the sea. But there was only sand, fine, bitter, hot, stretching out before her, and that instant a wind arose, lifting the sand and piling it higher and higher about her. Its gritty particles stung her face, entered her eyes, clogged her nose and invaded deep within her mouth. She spit, she spit repeatedly, without salivating.

"Thirsty. . . Thirsty," the word formed on her lips as she dragged herself through the storeroom door. With difficulty she rose from her straw pallet; she rose to go from the storeroom to grandmother's kitchen. She yearned to sink her head in the bucket which was always full of water on the sink.

"Thirsty. . . Thirsty," her lips repeated as she dragged herself outside.

Outside, the distant light of the stars dimly spotted the darkness. Maryo took cautious, sluggish footsteps into the yard. She found herself in a strange place, a thick jungle of wild plants. Rising high above her head, the thick growth blocked her way. She forcefully parted the tangled greenery whose spines pricked her face and hands. With care she took a path which she recalled, trying to find the steps to the moudi. As she hauled herself in that direction, statues appeared through openings in the undergrowth. They were of white marble and she stopped to run her fingers with reverence over their cool surface. She cooled her lips, forehead, cheeks, on the marble, wondering how the statues came to be in this garden. What titans with crane-like arms brought them here? And why had she not heard the loud hoarse voices giving orders when they were delivered and set in place? Had she been sleeping so profoundly?

With hands held out before her face, she proceeded slowly, parting branches and vines, parting that heavy, dark silence. Her foot touched the bottom stair. She looked upward and her soul trembled. The weak, trembling light of the lamp shone from the middle room through the fanlight above the door. One of the children must have been thirsty. Grandmother had gotten up, lighted the lamp, filled the enamel cup with water, brought it into the room where the children were sleeping. She came to quench her child's thirst.

Maryo labored up the stairs and before she reached the verandah she saw the lamplight going away, slowly moving across the fanlight and disappearing behind the wall. She froze on the top step, her eyes now fixed on kitchen transom. Grandmother would come there. The fanlight gleamed softly, and Maryo hurried to pound on the kitchen door. With her fists she hammered with all her might but the door, barred and latched, absorbed all sound, and one panicked thought seized Maryo: grandmother would put out the lamp. "No! No!" she begged voicelessly and bent to look through the keyhole. That moment, her hand cupped around the lamp-flue, grandmother was bending to blow out the flame. She plunged the kitchen into darkness.

In a frenzy Maryo concentrated on the inner door where her mother was. She began to strike with her fists and felt their flesh cracking. The skin split exuding no fluids, no blood; it broke exactly as her heart was breaking "Mana!" she cried rabidly, "Mana-a-a-a! Open up—I'm thirsty-y-y-y-y-y-y!" Her voice broke, turning into sobs.

What fragments of remembered scenes, what nostalgia, seized her spirit! The dryness of her body was deeply painful. She wanted to curl up in her mother's arms.

She yearned for the security of a child's life.

"Open up, mana-a-a-a-a! I'm thirsty-y-y-y-y-y!"

Her mother must have heard her, not from the sound of her natural voice but purely from the call issuing from her soul. Something was heard from within the inner room, a hint that someone was getting up. Maryo ceased her pounding and shouting, took several steps backward and waited. She tuned her hearing to the sounds from within. Her mother woke up, arose from the pallet, felt for the candle, lighted it from the icon flame burning in the corner of the room, came to the door, pressed the latch, opened, and stood on the threshold. The child peered outside to discover where the voice that had awakened her had come from. She saw no one on the moudi. She raised the candle above her head. The area was more fully illuminated, and the child's eyes probed with curiosity to find who had called to her. Maryo collapsed on the verandah tiles. Her mother was so small Maryo would not fit in her embrace; her mother was a child and she was so old.

She dragged herself across the verandah, down the steps, and through the yard. She opened the gate and entered the lane, taking the road to the well of the Virgin. She would draw water alone, she would quench her thirst alone.

From a distance she saw the man. He was sitting on the ledge by the well with a full pail of water beside him. Tipping the pail, he sent streams of water across the tiles surrounding the well.

Maryo was stirred, she was moved to see the man whom she had loved countless years deep within her soul. She felt how deeply she had erred; it was he to whom she should have come to ask for water. She buried her face in her hands and approached him with lowered head. She was ashamed to face him, ashamed of her dry face, her dry body. The man stood up, dipped his cupped hands into the pail, and raised them slowly over her head. He released the water in streams which fell on the crown of her head and passed in rivulets down her chest and back. Her pores opened like a sigh, the man refilled his hands, and the water coursed over her greedy skin. She raised her head with eyes closed, let her hands fall, and received the water on her forehead. It flowed over her cheeks, her nose, the edges of her lips. The water flowed and its drops slipped into her slightly parted mouth. Like a snake awakening from hibernation, her tongue stirred and slid outward, seized on the drops remaining on her cracked lips, drew the drops in, and spread them throughout her mouth. The man drew more water and now poured it from the pail onto her body.

Like a bird hidden in thick dark bushes, her body yearned for released powers. It throbbed and drank in the cool drops. Her hands tore her nightgown, threw it off, and she lay back on the wet tiles. Her entire body yearned to quench her thirst.

The man knelt with his knees on either side of her body, he bent over her, bent down very close to her face, and her memory galloped as the ocean danced before her eyes. It was silent, as yet without sound. The line of the surf stretched endlessly. Its caress was hard against the beach. Its waves were huge like a wall that fell and withdrew into the depths. Maryo was afraid. She feared the water's mania to suck in whatever it found in its path. The waves pulled her like a magnet and she felt them carry her, dissolve her, break and pulverize her bones.

Terrified, she was struck by panic, but passion greater than fear carried her away, absorbed her, and left her free.

Lithe and poised was the figure of the young surfer coming straight at her on the surfboard. "The rider of the water! The rider of the water!" she cried from her trembling heart, watching the extremely tall youth bend his powerful form to hold stubbornly to the slim board as the water insistently swelled, lifting him high, tossing him from side to side, while he smiled, crouching and straightening his torso, savoring nature's sport, sliding below or again mounting the waves. The enraged sea now violently seized him, flung him to the bottom, and tossed him out onto the sandy beach, covering him with sand and foam. The sound of the sea which Maryo had yearned for was heard, and her voice which had been sealed in her body, in her soul, sprang out into the air, merged and spread in the sound of the ocean.

"Barba Giannako-o-o-o! Barba Giannako-o-o-o!" From far away, very far away, was heard the voice of her young son in the midst of her memories. The boy's voice was warm, soft, uniquely his own. Maryo awoke. How she longed to see her son. To see his slim body, his blond hair, and the crazy tricks his eyes played when he laughed.

"Is that you, yeh mou?" she shouted and her face awakened with love

She opened the low door and stepped out into the yard. The boy was on the verandah, a thin, tall boy with curly black hair. He was standing on the stairs and calling softly but insistently:

"Aunt Despinyo-o-o! Barba Giannako-o-o!"

She recognized Asimakis, her father.

"What is it, boy?" Giannakos's voice sounded hoarse from sleep. He stood in the kitchen doorway wearing a wool undershirt and long undershorts.

"What is it you want at this dark hour?"

The sun must have risen only a few spans below the village's horizon and light had begun to play dimly on the horizon's edge. When Giannakos saw the face of the boy he came fully awake. Realizing it was something serious, he approached the boy and touched his shoulder.

"Tell me, Asimaki—what brings you here so early?"

"Mother sent me..."

"Sent you for what?"

"Mother said..." The boy took a deep breath. "My mother said you are to send Constantis and Antonis to the Chapel of Aghios Giorgis outside the village to fetch the icon before liturgy begins and bring it to our house so the saint will lend a hand and my father won't die."

With the boy's last words his breath was spent; he fell silent, waiting. His sigh remained within him.

"What on earth. . .!" Giannakos gasped.

"The doctor. . . " the boy whispered, ". . . Doctor Kanelios said that only the saint's miracle can save daddy now."

Despinyo came out onto the verandah and gazed bitterly at the child. The door to the inner room opened, and one by one the children formed a circle around Asimakis. He had lowered his head and was staring at his bare feet. He moved his big toes up and down. Panagiota came up to him; she gave him a swift kick in the toes and he stopped his movement.

"When our Phtychaki fell, the saint brought no aid!" she snapped.

Asimakis lowered his head in confusion.

"I'm telling you;" Panagiota continued, "Phtychaki fell on the church floor and hurt her head. Her head split open and the saint didn't do a thing. Nothing! Nothing at all!"

"Liar—you dirty liar!" Garoufalo accused her sister. "Phtychaki died of pneumonia."

Glaring, Despinyo took the children roughly by the shoulders and pushed them into the bedroom.

"Get moving all of you—there's a day's work to be done!"

Head lowered, Giannakos descended the stairs, went to the corner of the yard, and brought kindling wood to light the kitchen fire.

Asimakis remained on the verandah. He stood with head still lowered, and soon his big toes began again to move.

Despinyo bustled out of the kitchen and stared at the child.

"What's going on here? Go away, you!" she said rather harshly.

The words were daggers in Maryo's memory.

"What's going on here?" is what she too had said, addressing the old man Asimakis. Then he was weighed down by time, by disease, and was departing slowly, reluctantly from life. He was afraid of death. He was afraid to cross the thin line between the known and the unknown. He shut all the doors and windows of the house and covered his head with their threadbare old coverlet so that the only thing that could be seen were his eyes. Eyes enlarged by the shocks of time, the terror of death.

"Maryo-o-o-o-o-o, Maryo-o-o-o-o!" he called to her, and she came running. She came down the stairs to the old man's room on the ground floor.

"What's going on here?" she asked him with feigned impatience.

She wished to reassure him, to say that nothing dramatic was going on. That's simply the way things are. One by one, we take our turn.

"You go home now," Despinyo told Asimaki impatiently." The boys will get up, have some milk, and immediately go to the chapel to fetch the Saint."

The boy did not budge from his place. He remained with head bent above his bare feet.

"Aren't you listening, my child?" Despinyo asked sharply.

"My mother told me," the boy said slowly and softly, "not to leave till I saw them get on the mule."

Constantis dashed from the room, grabbed the boy by the shoulders and pushed him toward the stairs, which the boy stumbled down, holding his arms up on either side for balance.

"Get out of here," he barked. "Don't you hear what my mother said. We'll get dressed and go right away."

The boy stood, silent, with his back against the garden wall.

Maryo approached and stood by his side. She put her right arm across the boy's delicate shoulders, and as she held him she felt the light trembling of his body against hers. Her mind was numb with so many sensations. She wanted to hug Asimaki close, very close. She longed to be able to offer him something, to tell him something significant.

"What a pity, father! What a pity life is so hard, so joyless!"

She could think of nothing else and could do nothing. The boy remained immobile against the wall looking up at the verandah. Antonios suddenly appeared, dressed and all set for departure. He hurriedly crossed the yard, entered the stable and readied the mule.

"Constanti!" he urged. "Get going, Constanti-i-i-i! The man's life is in our hands!"

Anxiety was etched on his face. He was thinking of Erotokritos. It was he that was chiefly on Antonis's mind—Erotokritos and his beloved Aretousa, the trials of that enamoured pair. If Giorgakis left the village, they would be lost.

"We'll make it. Just you wait and see! We'll make it!" he told the boy and again called out forcefully,

"Come on, Constanti! Shake a leg. Get moving, I say!"

Maryo sped up the stairs.

"Giagia," she said, "give the boy some milk."

Grandmother poured milk in a pan to warm as Maryo looked on.

"Can't you see the child's mouth is dry from anxiety. Give him some milk! Give him some warm milk, too!" she shouted in her ear, praying there would be a miracle and grandmother would hear.

Despinyo routinely went about her work, waiting for the milk to simmer. It came to a boil and overflowed onto the hearth.

"Stupid, watch what you're doing," the woman reprimanded herself.

She poured the milk into a dish in the middle of the small table. She sliced bread, sweetened the milk with sugar and called the children. When she saw them hungrily attack their breakfast, she remembered the other child.

"He'll be hungry, too," she murmured to herself and went out onto the verandah.

"Asimo-o-o!" she called. "Asimo-o-o-o!"

Descending the stairs, she crossed the yard and looked into the lane.

"Asimo-o-o! Asimaki-i-i-i!" she called again anxiously.

She received no reply, but now she saw the boy in the distance running toward his home; and she heard him shout,

"Father-r-r-r! You're going to get well, you hear me! They're bringing the saint!"

Grandmother Despinyo went slowly up the stairs and Maryo came very close to her side.

"You were too late," she told her harshly. "You were slow to think, and when a thought comes late it is as if it never came at all."

Maryo could stay no longer at that house. The day continued with its usual routine, but for Maryo the day was scarred. Her grandfather Giorgakis was dying.

Frantically she ran down the stairs and took the road for the square. The men for whom grandfather had been koumbaros were gathered at the coffee house, talking of Giorgakis's love of life. He had sworn, he had taken a sacred oath, never to let one single pleasure slip through his fingers.

"You've got to catch life before it sweeps you away!" was Giorgakis's motto, so he was always setting up dinners, theatrical events, festivals. He never tired of involvement, especially by relating to folks as the best man or godfather. Most Sundays of the year he was to be found at baptismal or wedding ceremonies. Now all the men with whom Giorgakis had shared in ceremonies were gathered sadly at the coffee house.

"Grit your teeth, Giorgaki," one of the men said. "Hold on hard! Don't let life slip away!"

"Life is not a banquet," another commented bitterly; "it's only a few measly appetizers."

"Let them at least be good appetizers," a third man added.

Maryo quickly left the square. The gathering there made her melancholy; its sadness pained her. She paused at the crossroads on the outskirts of the village. The one road, the narrow one, went toward memory. She feared pain and took the other road, which led to broad meadows. It was a scarlet sea painted brightly by waves of poppies. It was spring, St. George's day. With a light step and joyful heart she cut across the meadows. She listened to the poppies. Like cheerful children's voices their petals were opening.

The sun shone; it shone on the poppies' petals, which spread with the touch of its rays. Maryo leaned over and plucked a poppy as a lucky charm. She brought its red velvet to her lips and holding tight to its delicate stem she turned to go back to her grandfather's house. Outside the yard she looked down at the poppy in her hand. All of its petals had fallen off. But the black tips of the stamen, round and alive, held tightly to the stem.

The women in the yard had all been death-scarred. From the crack of dawn and even before they crowded into the small yard. They greedily stuffed their words into the wound which had scarred their life; they scratched the wound and made it bleed, and they bent to lick with rough tongues the hurts of memory.

Hanging against the wall along the lane, Asimakis waited for the saint. He heard neither the women's crying nor his mother's prayers. Zgouraphenia raised mountains and seas of supplication to all the saints.

Maryo entered and went to her grandfather's room. *White thick clouds, white the sea foam, white, pure white, the sheets that covered grandfather's body and his hair that was beginning to grow white.*

Sharp needles of memory punctured her body. Her body grew heavy. It became incredibly heavy. "How circular life is!" she thought. "I used to believe it went in a straight line!" She sat on the edge of the bed. She too was waiting as grandfather slowly, cautiously descended the stair.

At first Father Charalambis was unwilling.

"Come now, how could I let you take the Saint on his festival day!" he kept repeating.

But the boys refused to budge from the sanctuary.

"If the saint doesn't come," Antonios implored, "the man is lost."

Constantis grew furious. He grabbed the priest by his robe and shook him.

"Listen to me, Father Charalambis, we've come all this way to take the saint and take him we will!"

Fearful that his best festival robe would be torn, the priest answered soothingly,

"Very well, my child, you will take him, but after the service."

When the service was over, the boys discovered that the Saint did not want to leave his festival. The icon was immovable; the combined strength of the two lads could not even budge it.

"Do you see, you stubborn oaf, you—do you see now?" the priest shouted at Constantis.

He sprinkled holy water on the icon, mumbled prayers, and summoned his son. Finally, the four of them managed to lift the Saint. The mule's back bent under the strain, but when they reached home the boys easily carried the icon into the room where Giorgakis lay. His friends crowded in behind the brothers. Grandmother crossed herself repeatedly and shouted,

"Open your eyes, Giorgaki! Open your eyes! Look what the boys have brought!"

Beside the sick man, Antonios, trembling, held the icon.

"Open your eyes, Giorgaki. We brought you the saint," he whispered.

Sweet and warm, the voice slid like balm into the body of the sick man. Gradually, with great effort, Giorgakis parted his eyelids. His gaze fell on the saint, on the brothers, on the scene as a whole. His lips trembled in something like a smile. Maryo was taken aback.

"He is not distressed," she thought. "He seems to accept death."

"Take the saint to where he belongs," Giorgakis said softly. "Take him there, for it is his festival day."

Antonios was trembling.

"No!" he cried. "No! The Saint must be near you till he performs his miracle and makes you well."

Asimakis stood with his head rigidly bowed. Giorgakis ached for his son's sadness. He ached for the pain which would be Asamakis's, but what could he do? He was approaching another realm; it drew him like a magnet.

"Oh, Antonio," he whispered; "look what the saint has brought me. The room is full of angels."

Giorgakis's gaze surveyed the room. His eyes rested on the angels and then became fixed on the ceiling. In anguish and despair, Maryo observed his eyes rolling further and further upward, turning inward, becoming lost within his skull. There within his body he was seeing the angels. Maryo was covered by the shadow of the pain of death. The heavy shadow brought dolor, anger, and finally rage. She threw herself upon Giorgakis, seizing him by the shoulders. She pushed him, she shook him, frantically calling,

"Grandfather Giorgaki, papou, come back, come back!"

His body began to tremble, to throb, seized by spasms. She gripped him tightly and waited. Grandfather's body returned and became calm. He slowly opened his eyes, saw Maryo above him, and smiled.

Time froze. The women in the room, the brothers, Asimakis, all froze; they became a sculpted frieze on the walls of grandfather's room. Maryo fixed her gaze upon Giorgakis.

"Papou. . ." her voice trembled. "Tell me, what is death like?"

Giorgakis looked at her and smiled. It was a broad, ironic smile. Maryo trembled with impatience.

"Tell me," she insisted. "Answer me. This is terribly important to me. Perhaps it was this very question that led me to make the voyage. This question alone!"

"Who are you, and what voyage are you talking about?" asked Giorgakis with the same smile, the same ironic expression. "Who are you?" he insisted.

Maryo caught his ambiguous meaning, but she chose to respond simply.

"I am Asimakis's daughter."

She turned her eyes to the small, thin boy, and grandfather looked at his son as he was seeing him for the first time.

"You're telling me you are the daughter of my small son!"

Maryo realized that he was avoiding her question.

"Papou, I saw you descending the stairway of life. I saw you touch death, and I brought you back for you to speak to me. Tell me about death."

"If you are Asimakis's child," he continued, "then you have not been born."

"I was born. I was born much later, far ahead in time, and I have come to visit you."

"Ahead? How far ahead?" he went on.

Maryo tried to recall. She tried to count the years. She remembered nothing. Anyhow, what did numbers mean?

"Many years ahead. So many. . . . Do you see all these people. None of them will exist then. Neither your young wife nor little Asimakis. Do you understand: none of them will be there; they will have been obliterated by the passage of the great storm of time."

"None of them?" he said with amazement.

His voice held no sadness at all. That is the way he had said *none*—simply with amazement.

"None of them will exist then."

He gazed at all the frozen figures and then fixed his eyes on Maryo.

"Do you exist?" he whispered to her.

Maryo was shocked; she didn't know how to answer. She fell into deep thought.

"I do. . ." she said hesitantly.

"Where and when?" he insisted.

Maryo was upset because she could find no reply.

"You must answer me!" she blurted roughly. "You must tell me about death."

"Tell me about life!" he sighed. "What is life? What is life like? Did I have life? Did I? Was I really alive? I don't understand a thing. Nothing stands out in my mind. . .".

He began to sob. Maryo was frightened. She relaxed her hold on her grandfather's shoulders and withdrew her hands. She sensed that he was departing. Giorgakis was leaving, rapidly descending the stairway of life, and a little breeze began to blow as the women's mouths opened to emit a cry of mourning.

Maryo paid no heed to the weeping, the lamentations. That was the way it had been from very ancient times. There was weeping over loss until death took on another dimension, and the departed life became a sweet memory. Maryo was no longer concerned with these events; she was oppressed by other questions. Questions without words kept burning in her mind. She wanted to ask about a matter that was beyond those two things, beyond life and beyond death. Far beyond those things. She wanted to ask but did not know how. What words could she find to put the question and whom could she ask? Her heart was in turmoil, her mind shattered.

Giannikos woke early, very early. Before the crack of dawn. He kept tossing on his bed, but sleep would not return. He went out onto the moudi, looked high into the arch of the sky and burst into shouting:

"Come on Lord! Come on! Get that sun of yours in motion! We've got work to do!"

Awakened by her husband's shouting, Despinyo was irritated.

"What sort of work do you have to do on Sunday?" she demanded. "All you want to do is wake the whole family up."

"Woman, you can bet I've work to do," he replied good humoredly and went to the yard to fetch kindling wood.

He began to sing, and the keening sound of his melancholy Turkish *amanes* moved Maryo. A wave of nostalgia burst within her as she remembered her childhood Sundays when she was awakened by Asimakis's singing of such melodies. Those sweet tones with sad, plaintive turns were like a prolonged sigh, a hymn to human heartache. A heartfelt sob of love for life.

How much Asimakis loved life, and she kept telling him pleasantly, somewhat sharply, "Come now, what's going on here?"

Nothing was going on. You were born to die. And now Asimakis was fading. For some time he had plunged into the sphere of death. A magnet, it pulled at his being, cutting him farther and farther off from life, weakening his legs, his sight, his hearing; and seeking refuge under the covers, he would call to Maryo.

"Save me, Maryo!"

She, caught by the magnet of life, did not understand the grip of the other magnet. She did not understand that its jaws were powerful, powerful as the grip of life.

Climbing the stairs to see Giannakos, Maryo thought of Asimakis. She thought of him without sadness, simply as an event which had occurred in life.

"What's going on here? What's the matter?" she would ask him.

There, half way up the stairs, she received the answer: "Nothing's the matter, exactly, that final hour," she spoke out loud to herself. "There is just that space between the magnets. That alone is what matters. What can you do between the magnets? What can you do in that space?" She began to articulate persuasively, as if she were making a speech: "Fill up the space that belongs to you properly. Be very careful about what you fill it with, and don't take too long," she cried. No one heard. She bent down to the small window and looked inside. Grandfather was sitting by the fireplace.

His cup of coffee was steaming, and, chin leaning on his right hand and eyes closed, he was crooning an *amanes.*

Then he burst into a smile.

"Now I see. It's Manolios! Our farmhand Manolios!" he thought with amazement. "He's worked so many years on my land, but the thought never struck me. Manolios will marry Aggerou. I never gave her leave to go to the convent and put on a black sack! You barely missed becoming a nun, Aggerou. Manolios is a strong lad. A good boy. He's not so smart, but so what? Do we expect him to become a teacher or a priest? He'll marry Aggerou and work in the fields. He'll work just as he does now, but eventually the land will belong to him. How dumb can a man be? What a lunkhead I've been! But today it will be settled; after the church service the agreement will be made!"

"What do you say, Pantelio," he asked Manolios's father; "Why don't you and I become in-laws?"

They had barely sat down. They were in Pantelios's kitchen, not in the sitting room, because Pantelios thought that Giannakos had come to discuss farmland. The woman of the house had served them raki and had just left them alone to talk. Giannakos eagerly raised his glass high and with flashing eyes cheerfully announced:

"What do you say, Pantelio; let's unite our families!"

Pantelios's face was radiant.

"My Manolios is a fine boy, a hard worker, a home body."

He was very proud.

"You took the words right out of my mouth!" said Giannakos, raising his glass to toast the blessed hour.

"Your Maria is an angel," said Pantelios, raising his glass to touch Giannakos's.

Taken aback, the other man did not clink his glass to seal the toast.

"She will not be marrying as yet."

"Then who is it you are proposing?" Pantelios's voice was hard as steel.

"My Aggerou..."

"The one who had the bastard child at the convent last year..."

He broke off, looking with astonishment at Giannakos, who was thunderstruck. His face had turned yellow, then green and finally black.

His body swayed to one side and the other, his raki glass flew from his hand and broke at his feet. Catching the edge of the table, he just managed to avoid falling down at the feet of Pantelios, who was, after all, nothing but his handy man.

"What did you say, you foul-mouth!"

It was a strange harsh voice, the voice of Giannakos out of control. Standing up unsteadily, he prepared to set his feet in motion. Pantelios had reached out to help, but dared not touch the visitor.

"I had no idea you didn't know," he mumbled repeatedly and then added, as if to excuse himself, "Everyone in town is talking..."

The old women, seated on stools and leaning against walls, watched Giannakos, dressed in his Sunday best, white shirt, black breeches, wide belt, shiny, pointed shoes, weaving along the narrow lane. To Giannakos's eyes they were black, utterly black, ghosts that gestured to him threateningly. He saw their mouths opening and spitting black words which struck him square in the face: "Don't you know... Don't you know... Everyone is talking..." Striving to escape those barren lanes, Giannakos's feet brought him reeling against the wall on the right and then against the wall opposite.

Reaching the outlying fields, he took deep breaths till his heart was somewhat relieved, but his mind was racing: "That damn pock-marked wife has disgraced me, and that bitch Aggerou foaming at the mouth, and silent humble Maria. I'll wring the necks of the three of them to rid me of shame! I'll wring their necks!" His thoughts grew somewhat calmer as he ran all the way to his property at Pyrgi. The surrounding hills were smoothly carpeted with greenery, his large field was fertile red soil, and the lean-to under the fig tree was open to welcome him.

Sitting down on the earth in the middle of the lean-to, he fumbled to control the angry beating of his heart. Suddenly he shuddered with fear; his entire body thrilled with terror. Out of the corner of his eye he caught sight of a huge black-yellow scorpion. It seemed to be calmly looking him straight in the eye, and he calculated that he would stand up at once, slowly and carefully approach that waxy insect, lift his right foot, and bring the toe of his shoe forcefully down on the scorpion's back. He would bring the sole of his shoe down square on the back, press downward with all his rabid fury, hear the body break, see its juices spurt from under the sides of his shoe, keep pressing down till the body sank deep in the soil, till its juices and its blackish-yellow shadow sank deep in the ground and were lost. He went to stand up. Feeling pain in all his bones, he kept his eyes fixed on the ugly sight of the scorpion, which began to move. With slow, sideways movements it reached the edge of the lean-to, burrowed beneath a pile of wood, and vanished.

Giannakos sat back on the ground and burst into tears.

Panagiota sealed her ears.

Every evening she would put a pillow over her head and cover her ears. The voices pierced through the feathers and cloth; they pierced through her small palms, penetrated her head, reaching to her very bowels, obliterating her.

"Tell me, you slut..."

Her father's drunken despair exploded every evening after the closing of the coffee house.

"Admit the truth!"

He stank of ouzo mixed with rage and heartbreak, which he endlessly released upon his wife. He pounded the serving dish on the table, threw a pan against the sink, and kicked over the stool.

"What happened, woman! Tell me everything you've kept from me! Where is her bastard?"

"They've been telling you lies! It's all lies. People are vicious," Despinyo insisted.

"Who's the head of the house around here, anyhow?" Giannakos yelled.

"You're the head; but sometimes it's an empty head..." Despinyo breathed.

Giannakos was shocked to see his right hand lifting powerfully and descending on his wife's face. With gaping eyes he saw her bend and spit into her hand a dainty white tooth smeared with blood.

A wave of pity broke within him, his eyes filled with tears, and he did not see his little daughter, Panagiota, who was standing near the open door, hurl the small stool which he sat on as he played with his children. Its edge caught him on the forehead just below the left eyebrow, leaving an open deep gash. The blood coursed down his cheek and over his neck.

"Ah-hooo, you poor thing!" Despinyo exclaimed fearfully, taking a towel and cleaning the wound.

Dark were the hours, the days, the weeks. Dark were the months. Haunted was the house of shame. All its doors were shut. Its windows and shutters were sealed. The latch on the garden gate locked itself. A heavy silence weighed upon the house. The people, shadows, came and went without breathing, without speaking. Tearfully Maryo chased the spiders which were weaving heavy webs in all the corners.

That morning very early, in that silence, the door flew open. It slammed against the wall, and Nikolos burst onto the moudi. His face disturbed like a hurt animal's, he rushed down the stairs and climbed into the olive tree in the yard. His slim young body pressed against her trunk; and his head leaning far back, he gazed high into the sky.

For a long time he stayed in that position.

"A-ou-ou-ou-ou-ou!" the first scream came from his mouth. "A-ou-ou-ou-ou-ouou!" a profound, burning pain poured out into the air.

Maryo shuddered. It is this date, she realized, fifty, sixty, or more years later, the first day of the month, that Nikolos lost his first child. On this day Despinaki departed. She was his only daughter.

No one in the house heard the pain which wracked the boy, no one saw the effort, the enormous effort, his body made to become one with the body of the tree. No one perceived Nikolos's yearning to immerse, to be oned with nature, at a time of vast emptiness. Maryo alone understood. How packed the human soul is. How many aeons of knowledge and how much weight of lamentation it bears.

The doors opened wide, the shutters snapped open and scraped the walls. The windows opened and elbows leaned joyfully on the sills. The faces glowed with broad smiles. Kyra Violetta, Pitsoulas' widow, came up their stairs. She was coming as a match-maker. The match-making was completed, the sweets were served, the dishes washed, everything was back in place, and only pleasant small talk frolicked in the air.

"Giannako, my Giannako! At last it is accomplished! A match has finally been made!"

Despinyo's words were washed by grateful tears.

That evening after vespers, following supper, Giannakos, Despinyo and Aggerou were sitting at the small table in the kitchen. Nearby, on the edge of a bed, Maryo cocked her ears to catch what was being said. She couldn't hear a word. It was as if the phrases were coming from their lips without sound. She came to the table and brought her ears close to their lips. The sparks thrown by their words, sharp and searing, penetrated her ears without significance, utterly without meaning. She again sat down on the bed and persistently watched the faces, the mouths, so as to read the words. She saw their eyes protrude, grow narrow, and crawl across their faces like snakes and their heads nod spastically like wild animals seized in a trap. Especially Aggerou insistently rocked her head from one side to the other. She forcefully threw her head back. She threw it so far back it touched her spine. Maryo was terrified, for she feared the girl's neck would break where it bent, and her larynx would split open. Like thin paper her pure white neck would tear and blood would shoot up like a fountain and flood the kitchen.

The house blossomed before Sunday arrived. The garden walls, the ledge around the chicken-coop, the window sills, and all the flower pots were white-washed. The rooms shone, the floors, windows, and doors were immaculate. The house took on a festive mood and gay little words rattled in the air. Early Sunday afternoon, Kyr Thymios the miller, wearing a mourning ribbon around his left sleeve, mounted the flower-lined stairs. On his arm was the matchmaker Kyra Violetta, Pitsoulas's widow, wearing her best dress and holding a colorful handkerchief.

It began to blow at daybreak.

The wind swept down from the mountain top, raked the meadows, and tore into the village, rabidly swirling around the yards and the dark houses. The windows rattled and the gardens were devastated. The trees shuddered before the blast; their tops bent and humbly touched the earth. In their beds the villagers pulled their covers more tightly around their ears, and Maryo cuddled more deeply in her soft hay. Finally, wearied of weaving through the village and smiting the houses, the wind stretched across the meadows and took the road that led to the sea.

All at once the thick black clouds which spread tightly before the wind relaxed and released torrents that pounded on the roofs of houses and sheds. Streams channeled the dirt roads, the lanes were flooded, and the yards became muddy pools. The sun made a tardy appearance. Hidden in the mist, it quietly, unhurriedly proceeded to dry the roofs, yards, and fields with its warm breath. The land exhaled dampness and the villagers, like snails, emerged from their houses. Maryo came out ahead of the rest. Her pores opened, she stretched, and she greedily inhaled the aroma of the moistened earth.

At a great distance she saw the horse that was galloping toward the house. It swept past her through the yard and disappeared into the stable. Maryo noticed that the two of them, horse and rider, were soaked, completely drenched. She did not know whether it was by sweat or by rain. Maryo was frightened. Her soul was stricken because as the horseman had passed her he had had thrown a heavy shadow over her. It was the first time she understood how black and ponderous the shadow of a human being could fall.

It was the last Sunday in October.

Today, early in the afternoon, Aggerou, the first of the twin daughters of Giannakos Zanafetis, would be married. She would take as husband Kyr Thymios the miller, who was a widower with four young children.

Dressed in her bridal gown, Aggerou was trembling before the large mirror in the far bedroom which served as a sitting room. The mirror was massive. With its gilt frame topped by a crown, it almost touched the ceiling. It had been purchased in Smyni by her grandfather and was the first item in her mother's dowry. It was the first time that Aggerou viewed her body in a mirror. Trembling, she gazed at her large multi-colored eyes. Her straight nose, her red full lips. Her neck white, pure white. Her breasts two soft rises beneath the wedding gown. Her gaze gorged itself upon her face and fell lower, across her flat belly and down, down upon her slim legs. Slowly, shyly, she lifted her dress to drink in the curve of her limbs. She lifted her dress; she raised it higher and higher, savoring the smooth contour of her loins. She yearned for more. Letting her dress drop, with slow movements she unbuttoned the long row of small buttons down the front of her bridal gown. She unbuttoned them all, pulled the dress over her head, and let it fall behind her. She removed her slip, unhooked and cast aside her bra, took off her shoes and stockings, and finally jettisoned the last vestige of clothing remaining on her body.

A strong wind rose and made her shake. With uncontrollable joy she surveyed her completely naked form. Her hands reached out to the cold surface of the mirror. Her fingers trembled, thrilled, as they slid over each hidden part. Fingertips chilled by the cold surface, the hands turned themselves back, seeking the body itself, and Aggerou felt them, she felt them to be her own hands. The body to be her own body. They traveled methodically, touching the head, plunging into the hair, moving down the forehead, caressing her eyebrows, contacting the eyes and nose, playing with the mouth, the lips and tongue, descending the neck, reaching the rounded hills. The nipples of her breast and her finger's tips trembled. And her heart trembled too as she imagined that little baby sucking on the nipples with tiny lips that draw forth a spring of milk filling its mouth, overflowing, running down her breast and reaching her belly. She almost swooned. She softly stroked her belly and was swept away by the strength of her muscles and pull of her dove's nest. For the first time she claimed her body as her own. The girl shivered, and Maryo also shivered, hidden behind the mirror.

"What immense love you have for your body!" she whispered to Aggerou.

Tears wet Aggerou's cheeks and a great desire staggered her mind. "What am I like inside?" she wondered with longing. She pressed her nose against the mirror and shoved. She shoved with frenzy to get inside her body and see. She penetrated the pupils of her eyes, and they opened like doors. Aggerou passed through; she sank softly within her body, she slid through her soft insides. A red canyon the neck, a bleeding lake the heart. Ebony the spleen, the bladder, and the liver a boiling furnace. Coiled snakes the intestines. Aggerou passed by all those things paying slight heed. At one place only did she stop. There, in the middle of her body, she was smitten before a misty reservoir. Thick-streaming liquids in swelling blue pouches, steam and warm waters flooded and overflowed the womb. She bowed and first reverently touched the waters with trembling fingers, and then as if she were kneeling in honor and awe, with closed eyes she dipped her roseate tongue in the tidal waters.

"How could mere logic impede such a nature as this!" Maryo was taken aback as she watched the intoxicated, impassioned Aggerou. "All other human concerns will evade you. You will find nothing else; you will savor nothing else, only the body!" Maryo bitterly declared.

"Aggerou, Aggerou!" Soft notes of fright hung in the air.

Maria, her back pressed against the door, gaped at Aggerou, whose face was still glued to the mirror. The sound flowed in the bride's direction, and with great effort she came out of her body's depths and turned toward the voice which was calling her. Her eyes were unfocussed.

"Aggerou, Aggerou!"

Maria again spoke sternly but as quietly as she could. Aggerou's eyelids parted, her pupils focussed, and she caught the image of Maria in the mirror. Turning her head, she vaguely consented, and the other girl hurriedly picked up each piece of clothing, forcefully and hastily dressing her sister.

"What's wrong, sweet girl? What's the matter with you, my little heart?" her voice caressed.

"Nothing . . . nothing's the matter with me," came Aggerou's words with a false note. With the adjustment of her vail, the bride was again fully prepared before the large mirror. She stood with lowered eyes.

"Are you all right?"

"I'm fine."

The voice sounded strange. This was no longer Aggerou; it was another, older, woman. Maria scrutinized her sister's face with eyes sharp from anxiety.

"Don't worry . . . I'm really all right," Aggerou insisted, but Maria was still upset.

"I have bad news," she said hesitantly. "Some Turk struck Father Vangelis outside Aghios Minas chapel."

Aggerou shrugged her shoulders indifferently. "That's no concern of mine.

"But," Maria replied, "I'm afraid that Father Nikolas will perform your marriage ceremony. It might bring you bad luck."

"No one and nothing will bring me bad luck. Never fear for me again!" asserted that strange woman.

Maria and Maryo began to tremble.

"Despinyo-o-o-o-o-o!" screeched Kyra Harikleia, the ill-tider.

Her voice carried clearly from the far corner of the lane.

"Mori Des-pin-yo-o-o-o-o-o!" she boomed in her crystalline malevolent voice. "Some infidel flattened Father Vangelis with a staff, and when he was down he beat him black and blue!"

Despinyo was distressed. "What a terrible thing!" she said to herself. "And at a time like this!" As her feelings whirled she began to tremble with an awful premonition. Good lord! Where had Constantis been? Where was he off to so early this morning in that great downpour? Racing to the stable, she surveyed the stalls in a glance. In one corner, half-covered in a manure pile, was a stained pick handle. Despinyo crossed herself.

"Kyr Thymios is passing by-y-y-y-y-y. To the church he go-o-o-o-o-oes!" chanted the children along the lanes of the neighborhood.

Despinyo hastened back to the kitchen. She wanted something sweet to put in her mouth, which was so bitter that her saliva tasted like poison. The sitting room door opened and the bride emerged. She glowed in her white attire. To Despinyo she seemed to have grown so tall and slim, so splendidly beautiful. The mother looked very closely at her daughter; she wanted to hold this image in her mind. She wanted to remember always the bride descending the stairs, but there were shadows which blocked her view of Aggerou. Despinyo rubbed her eyes with her palms, attempting to see more clearly. It was like a dream, as if it was not the wedding day, as if everything was happening in some other time dimension, as if her daughter was not her daughter and she was not herself.

Aggerou moved very slowly downward step by step; one by one she left each step behind her. Never again would she ascend these stairs; the bride was departing from the parental home. Outside in the lane, Antonis was holding the mule by the harness. Giannakos took Aggerou's arm, they passed through the gate, and she mounted. With head held high, she looked neither at her family nor at the four Mylonas children lined up in the lane dressed in their Sunday best.

Each morning Maria awoke with a shock.

Her body trembled with her dreaming soul's return. Through her body like an electric charge ran the fluttering of her spirit as it penetrated deep within her in an attempt to sustain her joy. Her entire being pulsed. Like the end of a caress, her dream departed; it evaporated like summer mist, numbing her arms and legs, sinking her into a dull pain.

Daily she opened her eyes on the same room amidst her brothers and sisters. Panagiota's length pressed against her and she drew back. She didn't want the touch of the human body; she couldn't bear the weight and smell of flesh. She shrank back against the wall and sought to retrieve her thoughts, wishing to revive the dream which she had experienced. Where had she journeyed in the night? What glowing places did she visit at night, and in the morning why did it seem she was returning to darkness? What did her soul desire?

Her mind sped in frenzy searching for fugitive shadows. It raced in search of illusive visions but returned unsatisfied. Her spirit was inert, frustrated, and Maria clenched her fists to hold back the scream which arose from her depths. "After every unrealized dream," whispered Maryo, "comes rage. . . The soul quests, but the mind does not fathom the mystery of our nature. Only the yearning soul knows."

Daily Despinyo anxiously approached the children's room, cautiously peeping through the doorway to discover Maria's waking mood. She bit on her kerchief. "What is it you want? Who is it you are seeking?" Despinyo wondered in anguish, and she and Giannakos searched for their daughter's happiness among the young men of the village. Whom could they choose for her? Who was worthy of her? "What fate, what ill fate," Despinyo tearfully asked herself, "anointed you with the myrrh of such a special nature?"

Maria awoke instantly to her mother's words.

"Get up, my sweet girl. Today is laundry day."

Opening her eyes, Maria felt rested and cheerful. It was as yet dark outside and her spirit was still in the land of dreams. Could it be that she could catch her soul somewhere out in the open where it would reveal its secrets? She sprang out of bed, eager to join her mother on their washing expedition. Dawn broke on the horizon; and by the time they would reach the river, light a fire, and put the clothes in the pot to soak, the sun would have completely risen. Its warmth this day was given for the cleaning of their wash. The donkey, loaded with containers carrying dirty laundry, trotted along rapidly, its head bent low over the narrow path. Maria walked behind the donkey, and behind her came her mother, her mother's sister Marigi and her two daughters.

Her attention alert to her exposed soul, Maria did not hear the tittering of the girls or her mother's sighs; she heard only the rhythmic hoofbeats of the animal and the wild fluttering of her heart. These she heeded closely, anxiously. They had now reached the top of a low hill and were descending to the valley peacefully traversed by the river.

From the hilltop Maria viewed the land spread below them, and she caught the scent of bushes, oak trees and water. Nature's music washed over her: the gentle whir of the grasses and flutter of the leaves as they rose on their branches, better to see the sun. Everything entered her like a caress, and she anxiously ran ahead of the donkey to reach the river bank first. There she stood. She was overflowing with ecstasy. A miracle was unfolding. Divine was the gift she was gazing upon. In the middle of the meadow there were two rivers. The one was of water. Its surface was still and gleaming. The first rays of sunlight glittered upon it, and above that there was another river, the spirit of the water ascending. White, a pure-white stream, the fog climbed. The mist rolled to the call of the day. Dampness and silence. A soft melodic silence breathed seclusion. The girl was utterly separated from the world. In complete solitude. She fell to her knees and beheld the slowly flowing water.

The women arrived out of breath. They were about to approach but then held back. Motionless, embracing one another, they gazed at Maria. She was like light. Her soul, a white cape, enwrapped her. The women trembled.

Ceremoniously the sunrays lifted the mist from the river, spread it within their bright paths, and proudly displayed nature's glory. The birds, surprised by beauty, burst in unison into song, filling the holy silence at the coming of day. Maria rose, approached the water, bent her knees, and immersed herself. Three times she immersed herself in the water.

From a distance the women made the sign of the cross.

Maria fasted for three days. For three days she did not touch even a drop of water. On the fourth day, clad entirely in white, she went to her mother and father.

"My name is Theochtisti," she said. "My life is in the convent."

Giannkos was smitten. Losing control, he slumped onto his chair. Despinyo stuffed her mantilla in her mouth, knowing that if she released the cry that was within her it would startle the entire village. So she bit down on the cloth till she felt it tear in her mouth. She could not permit that scream to emerge. All she wanted to do was kneel. She wanted to kneel before her daughter, to kiss her hand and ask for strength. It was strength she wanted, strength sufficient to bear the absence of her daughter and her own loneliness.

In her white gown, Maria descended the stairs. She descended lightly, and her mother, behind the kitchen window, fixed her widely opened eyes upon her daughter. She wanted to absorb that form deep within. She wanted to drink in that beautiful form of her daughter adorned in white, to swallow it, and have it inside as she had once held both her daughter and her soul within her. She held her eyes wide open and fixed her gaze, but then the rain broke. The rain fell in a deluge against the window pane and with both her hands Despinyo wiped away the condensation, but still she could not see. She could only glimpse a completely bright shadow going down the steps, crossing the yard and mounting the horse. Antonis was holding the reins.

"It took you so long, Theochtisti!" Aunt Agni exclaimed.

At the door of the church, she placed her hand on the girl's bowed head.

"It took you so long, dear child! For months you have been sending messages that you would be coming. For months you have appeared in my sleep announcing your arrival."

Harikleio, the ill-tider, turned the corner into the lane.

"Despinyo-o-o-o-o-o-o!" she screamed.

She trotted toward the house with short alarmed steps.

"Sad tidings, my poor woman!" She waved her hands in bleak concern, shouting with glee. Despinyo shivered from head to toe. She wanted to burrow within her house, bolt the door, and cover her ears. She wished to hear nothing but remained on the spot looking at her neighbor with unfocused glance, the way you avert your eyes from an adder in the shimmering light of noon as it rears amidst the dry clods of the field. Magnetized by that voice, the flashing of those eyes, Despinyo froze.

"Mori, Despinyo-o-o-o-o-! That daughter of yours is ruined! She's left that saintly man, deserted Kyr Thymios, without an ounce of pity for her death-scarred spouse! Not a thought for those four poor little orphans! She's abandoned them all, I tell you, to go off to Smyrni with the mustachioed fisherman!"

Despinyo reeled. Sweat broke from all her pores, trickling down her limbs. Drenched, she slumped against the garden wall. The other woman droned on:

"I guessed something was going on, I can tell you. For some time there was all that coming and going of the fisherman with his crates the moment Kyr Thymios left the house. You bet I knew that boded no good. Sure enough, this morning they went off together. She was swept off her feet by his strong arms, his swarthy skin, and charming smile. . ."

Leaning on the wall, Despinyo felt the blood drain from her cheeks. White as milk, she swayed, lost her balance, and collapsed on the verandah tiles. Taken aback, Haricleio stared at Despinyo, the words still boiling in her mouth. For a moment she wavered, wondering what to do. She wanted to help the poor woman, but the words were steaming like foam in her mouth, they were burning on her tongue. She couldn't stand it; she had to release those searing syllables. She stepped off briskly to visit her close friend Louloudio, who lived not far down the lane.

Despinyo dragged herself into the house and pulled herself up onto her bed. She huddled under the covers, hollow and mortified, wishing she could think things through. Scattered images of her children passed before her eyes. Constantis, where was he? Was he really on another continent? What was it Kyra Pelagia, the teacher, had said? "Constantis has gone to another continent where the people are dark complexioned, labor on coffee plantations, and love to sing and dance."

For the life of her Despinyo could not remember the name of the place where Constantis had gone. All she remembered was that he had traveled forty days to go to the country of dark-skinned people. Why he wanted to go she didn't know. And one of her girls had become a fancy woman. She had gone to Smyrni with the tall fisherman. Why had she gone off with him? Why had she not stayed with her husband, Thymios, who had honored her by making her his bride? And Maria? She wasn't Maria any longer. Theochisti was now the name of her daughter, who said she was a bride of Christ. Had all the young men of the village vanished? Had so many handsome fellows of flesh and blood disappeared? The other girl a fancy woman. A street walker in Smyrni. Who would have thought they would bring such dark tidings. Her daughter a whore. And there was Antonios. He had gone to Greece and was sending them letters filled with misery. He couldn't bear the black dirt of the quarry. Was there black dirt in Lavrio, near Cape Sounion? Her boy couldn't stand it and was shedding dark tears. And as for herself, what had she done to have one daughter a prostitute, another covered in black in a nunnery, and two sons in distant lands? What forces had brought it all about? What powers so much greater than mere human beings? "Yet they came from inside me. I bore them ..." she wanted to scream. Maryo came to the side of her bed and touched her comfortingly through the bedspread. Grandmother did not feel her touch.

"Your womb," Maryo said, "like Pandora's box, filled the world. For you there is nothing left but simply to love your offspring. There is nothing else to do and nothing is to blame."

Maryo's soul was full of sadness, her mind with thoughts. Dizzy with so many thoughts, she sighed and fell silent. She felt anguish for this mother who was so fearful, unaware, lonely. She touched her comfortingly through the covers.

"You too have a life of your own," she urged. "Don't miss out! Look to that. You must live and enjoy the gift given to you. Don't dismember your life and parcel it out."

Under the heavy covers, grandmother remained immobile, lost. It was as if she no longer existed. So deeply had she merged with the lives of the others.

Maryo ran swiftly, she knifed through the air as if she were pole vaulting. She forced herself, she strained terrifically in athletic effort. Her muscles taut, knotted, her breast projected, her body light. It was as if she had left the ground and was soaring upward.

Maryo was racing to catch up with time, to reach her mother, and to see how her body had grown. What did the taller girl look like? How had her features changed? How had her thoughts and words progressed? How was her life developing?

One fall morning, a very early morning smelling of rain, Panagiota's father asked,

"Shall we go fishing, kori mou?"

The child's chest swelled with pride to be joining her father. She stepped into the boat. Some distance from shore they threw in their lines and had a good catch. Plenty of big fish were wriggling in the crate. They had come upon a school.

"We're in luck," the father beamed as the little girl jerked her line and pulled out fish after fish.

Panagiota felt pleasure surge through her body, joy in her heart. The time flew by. The sky grew dark, the sea began swell, and the boat drifted on the waves. The two of them were absorbed by their catch; but rising wind and a choppy sea made the father realize his error.

"It's late," he told his daughter, "we've got to go back at once."

Grabbing the oars, he pulled with all his might, but their small boat was borne seaward on the powerful swell. Giannakos's face was dark, darker than the face of the day heavy with surrounding clouds that reached down to the white topped waves. With a small can Panagiota was hastily bailing the water which was mounting the sides of the hull.

"Say a prayer, daughter! Pray for us!"

The father's voice was filled with anguish and the girl who had never said a prayer began to shout:

"Sa-a-a-a-a-a-ve us, Mother of God, sa-a-a-a-a-a-ve us!"

She shouted to the sky so Mother Mary would hear; and then she thought, "Better it be God," and began to cry:

"Come, Lord, sa-a-a-a-a-a-ve us! Bring us quickly to shore, Lord!"

She cried with all her might and imagined that now God would appear and with his little finger nudge the boat toward the shore and ease it up on the beach. But God, she thought, was taking a long time to answer, and she was seized by panic. Darkness fell. Small lights appeared on the distant shore. Inch by inch the water mounted within the hull. Giannakos was terrified.

"He-e-e-e-e-e-e-lp!" he roared, his eyes fixed on the shore.

They did not hear the caique's engine, so loud was the noise of the wind and the waves. But they saw its small lights trembling as it moved through the high sea. The instant they realized they were the lights of a fishingboat, they burst in unison into a cry for help.

Captain Petris heard their call, threw them a line and pulled them into the harbor.

"Hey, Giannako, didn't you see the storm brewing? With your little girl along, you should have been especially careful. The sea doesn't play games; you could have drowned. It was sheer luck I was out this evening and came along when I did!"

Outside his cabin at Litzia, Captain Petris made them herb tea, and they sipped slowly, listening to the Captain who knew the sea:

"You would have drowned. You surely would have been goners if I had not by chance gone out this evening. I was feeling that ache in my leg and knew the barometer was falling, so I hadn't planned to go out. But I ran across my friend Giannos Gialelis, who said the sea bass were biting. So I thought, why not go out for a short run? Let that be a lesson to you, Giannako, the sea takes no mercy on bunglers."

Panagiota, wrapped in a blanket, listened to the fishermen. She was lying down outside the cabin and their talk filled the air. They had switched to raki; and they were swigging glass after glass, jabbering, and laughing. It was all storms, boats going down, and miracles at sea. Of such things they talked and there was no end to it.

Half asleep, Panagiota heard the words and within her marked the phrases and stories which would stay with her. For years she would carry them with her. Before she dropped off to sleep, there was one thought especially that was stamped in her mind: "Nothing is watching over you. Nothing is there to save you. There is only chance. By chance alone you sink or survive." A chill passed over her. She pulled the blanket more tightly around her, covered her head and gritted her teeth. She clamped her teeth so they wouldn't chatter. And there in the cold, in the freezing blackness, she fell into very uneasy sleep.

Maryo ran; she raced to see her mother from up close. To touch her face. To hold her palms against the girl's cheeks the way she did with her children and with her mother when she had become very old and returned to childhood. She had become a child again. A weak, defenseless child on account of the fate which the years held in store for her. Maryo ran to see her mother as a child, or was she forever a child who played the adult?

Panagiota was weeding, and her small face was dripping with sweat under her heavy kerchief. From very early that morning she had been clearing unwanted growth in the fields. She grabbed the thin shoots and pulled with all her might. She wanted to uproot the weeds completely so that they would not again take hold in the soil. As she pulled she felt their strong resistance; refusing to come out by the roots, they broke off at the stem. Their life was sunk deeply in the soil. Her efforts were futile, for with the first watering the weeds would put forth fresh shoots, flower, and once more fill the garden patch.

Sitting back, she shaded her eyes with one hand and saw her mother in the distance under the fig tree at the end of the field. Despinyo had lifted her hand, gesturing to Panagiota. "Come over here for a break and a bite to eat," the gesture said, but Panagiota again bent down, pretending she didn't understand. It was better to pull weeds than have to listen to the stories of ill-fated Panos and Elias. She had heard them over and over again.

Every summer the two men were in the area, and whenever family members appeared in the fields, they would come over to chat. Panos and Elias were inseparable. Panos had lost both his legs from the hips down. It was his misfortune to have jumped into the water to retrieve a crate the very moment that Elias was tossing in a stick of dynamite to stun a school of flounder. The charge landed not a foot from his thighs, and he lost both legs. Only stumps of his thighs remained, enough to provide a hold on Elias's shoulders. Elias was slow-thinking, with just a touch of sense, enough to keep alive. He was endowed, however, with powerful arms and legs. He set his friend on his shoulders and made the round of the villages. Arriving at the square, he would lower his companion into a chair, and Panos would begin to sing. From all the neighborhoods the villagers would gather to listen. Intoxicated by his voice, they would reach deep into their pockets and pull out coins. The women cooked meals for the pair, so that with their stomachs full and their pockets jingling, they would take the road to the next village. Panagiota couldn't stand those 'half men' as she called them.

The field overflowed with melody. In plaintive, liquid tones, Panos sang:

Oh my Garoufalia,
Dost love me true
And cheat me not?

Oh my Vasiliko,
I love thee true
And cheat thee not...

Panagiota abruptly stood up. She shivered as the song brought an image which flowered in her mind and swelled in her heart. It was Maria of the past in the kitchen scouring pots, then drying her hands on her apron. She was leaning her head slightly to the side and singing. On her lips was a slight, barely discernible smile. *Oh my Garoufalia, Dost love me true And cheat me not? Oh my Vasiliko. . .* Tears burst from Panagiota's eyes and streamed down her face. There was Maria right before her eyes in their kitchen, wearing her embroidered apron, in her locks a ribbon which, untied, would let her hair fall glistening on her shoulders, across her face. Her brown, dark brown, hair, swirls on her head, was soft as the wool of their Spring lambs, soft as her voice. Panagiota loved to hear her voice, as she loved to feel her presence near at night in the warmth of the bed. Maria! How bitter, how very bitter was Maria's absence! She never went to visit her at the convent. She didn't want to see her in her black habit. She just waited. Waited for her to return home, return to the world, saying it was all just a game, a joke for their amusement. As if she could go to a convent and take the robes of a nun! Maria was an image. An image which covered the entire surface of her mind and stood totally alive before her.

Her mother was standing close by her side.

"Didn't you see me, Panagiota? Didn't you see me signaling that it was lunch time?"

Panagiota did not turn to look at her mother.

"I've got something to do!" she announced, taking to her heels.

"Where are you going?" the mother urgently called.

Breathless and weary she arrived outside the convent. It was high noon. Her mouth was dust dry and her blouse was soaked with perspiration. The sun struck her mercilessly as she stood hesitating by the great wooden door. She didn't want to pull on the rope which rang the little bell. She feared the countless questions which would be asked by the nun who would open the door. She pulled at the door but it was tightly barred. She ran to the end of the wall and climbed an ancient walnut tree to peer over into the convent grounds. There was the courtyard with flower beds, the white-washed balcony staircase, and, beyond, the hemispherical outdoor oven, the stable, the chicken coop, and, on a little hill, a tree-surrounded chapel. Then she saw the little nun who, staff in hand, was guiding a flock of sheep and goats from the woods toward the stable.

"Maria," Panagiota whispered in a broken voice.

The nun's face beamed as she looked up and caught sight of the girl.

"Why, Panagiota! How you've grown! My little Panagiota! What are you doing here this time of day? Is everything all right at home?" she asked with a troubled close.

Panagiota stared. The sob which would rise in her heart whenever she thought of Maria did not occur. Her eyes rested on this nun whose wide, full-length black habit was tied at the waist with a sash. A faded black head-covering hid half her face and all her hair. Panagiota did not know that woman there before her; she had never seen her in her life. Yet she

149

made Panagiota angry. She felt intense anger churning within her.

"Why are you in this place, Maria?"

"My name is Theochtisti," the nun replied, taken aback.

"What did you come here to do?" the younger sister insisted, her voice sharp with anger.

"Does mother know you're here?"

"Why are you wearing that black sack?"

"I am mourning for the Son of God, our Savior."

"No one is our savior," she shouted with all her might. "No one can save you. Why did you go away and leave me all alone?"

"I wanted to be with God," Maria gently replied.

"Where is God?" the other cried. "This moment! This moment we two are speaking, where is God?"

The other made a gentle arc with her hand.

"God is everywhere. Everywhere. Up there beside you on the wall; down here with me on the convent grounds...".

"And also in our house . . ." Panagiota said.

"Yes, in our house, too."

"Then why didn't you stay with us?"

"Panagiota, dear, though God is everywhere, we must find ways to concentrate on His presence. In our crowded house, in our busy village, I would lose contact, while here. . .".

"Yes, here you are in contact with the chickens, the goats, and the manure! There is manure everywhere! God is nowhere! Nowhere, I tell you! God does not exist. If he did exist, he would have been seen by someone. But no one has ever seen him. They just make up stories. Stories made out of nothing. Nothing! For nothing you left me alone. Completely alone!"

She began to sob. All at once her feelings came to a head and all of her was choked with swelling tears. Her chest was bursting, her eyes and nose brimming and streaming like cataracts. She wept. She wept for Maria. Maria had died; she no longer existed. Her eyes streamed for her lost sister, for their lost moments of shared joys and doubts. Maria was no more. Maybe she had never existed at all. How terrible that thought, for it robbed her of memories.

Swiftly descending the walnut tree, Panagiota at once set off for home, and the other called to her in mournful, troubled tones:

"Don't! Don't talk that way about God! It's blasphemous! And don't cut yourself off from the Lord!"

Theochtisti knelt on the ground and made the sign of the cross.

"Forgive me, Lord," she prayed. "Because of me, sinful thoughts entered Panagiota's heart."

Maryo raced; she thrust her legs and body forward. Her chest cut the air to reach her mother as swiftly as she could. To see the color her hair had taken on. To see her gaze. Why had it become so intense? Maryo raced. She kept coming closer and closer.

Kyra Pelagia, the chubby village schoolteacher came by. She stood by the wall, and seeing the window open, she called to Despinyo. The woman of the house emerged and smiled at the teacher, but Kyra Pelagia did not return the smile.

"Tell me, Despinyo," she said. "What's to become of your daughter Panagiota? Are you going to send her to Smyrni to work as a maid?"

"Lord no!" replied the mother, spitting thrice in her bosom.

"Well, then, send her to school!" said the teacher and angrily continued on her way.

It was October not long before the rainy season. After they harvested the raisin grapes, spread them to dry, and put them in sacks, Panagiota found herself at school. She felt completely alone amidst all the village children who were packed, shoving and shouting, into the single schoolroom. Panagiota withdrew. She shrank far away from the others, loathing contact with anyone. She was deafened by the clamor; and the teacher's screeching voice, harshest of all, pierced her brain. Noiselessly, quietly and gently, Panagiota made her heart a nest, so her soul could slip into hiding. There she huddled and waited for the hours to pass. At recess, she bounded out of the classroom, through the village lanes and out into the farmland. She raced beyond the fields to a dry rocky sea-side hill where she sat down with relief.

Maryo raced to catch up. She dodged through the rocks and threw herself down by Panagiota's side.

Mother and daughter, in reversed time, sat by one another's side. Both of them, winded and exhausted, surveyed the sea spread out before them. Turning to examine Panagiota's face, Maryo was startled. She was deeply frightened by the child's wild gaze. It reminded her so much of the wild gaze which was stamped on that countenance after the passage of many decades of life.

The aged Panagiota was alarmed. She was deeply alarmed by her body, which had ceased to function. Her body was no longer hers. Sluggish, unresponsive, barren, it refused to obey her will. And she, aghast, reacted wildly. It was as if her gaze had become riveted on something unknown to her. Something that terrified her. Everything was a murky whiteness. A white darkness surrounded her. She did not want to face it, but it drew her like a loadstone.

It seemed that now the child was looking at that same white darkness. Her eyes had become wild. A crazy notion seized Maryo. An overwhelming desire to bring the old mother here to this time, to this rocky hill, and to compare her. To see how much alike was the look in their eyes as they were setting out. Both of them were setting out on a journey. The one was taking the road to life. Narrow and dark the path to life, and the child alone. The other was taking the road to death. Narrow and dark the path, and the old woman alone.

That was what Maryo wanted. To bring her aged mother to this time. She willed it with all her might. She concentrated and, with wild fervor, she projected her thought to the old woman. She lifted her out of bed and pulled her with great effort and force, pulled her back to that rocky hill. This was what she wanted! She reached out and put her arms around them. With her right arm she hugged the young girl and with the left the old woman. With love full of hurt she examined the two of them. She studied their gazes. They were lost in the distance. They were staring upon the sea's abyss, and suddenly Maryo felt the ground shift. Like an earthquake, the ground cracked, the rocks broke loose, tumbled seaward, gained momentum, shot downward, and all three women were carried along. They arrived and hung for an instant on the edge of the land, and before they had time to brace themselves they plummeted into the sea. The embrace was broken, and Maryo was alarmed to see the old woman caught in the current. Silently, steadily, it pulled her, and her hollow, awkward body floating on the surface was carried toward the open sea. The open sea, alien, distant, vast, pulled her, dragged her away. Maryo sat in the shallow water without doing a thing. Without raising a finger, she watched the aged Panagiota go off into the distance and disappear into the open sea. She just looked. She didn't even raise her hand to wave goodbye to the old woman who became a black particle in the memory and then vanished entirely.

In panic she looked for the other mother, the child. She saw her sinking. The girl's body sank like a stone, her hair trailing vertically as the water sucked her downward. Her eyes blinked as she strove to orient herself to the surrounding depths. Wet and cold the wall which enclosed her. Masses of water exerted pressure upon her and only her body formed a protective tunnel. Light fell around her. Like rain, beams of light passed through the water diagonally, casting shadows and trembling halos. The light trembled, about to go out as it sank toward the dark depths. The silence was deafening. The girl heard neither her own body nor the life that surrounded her. Fish everywhere. The sea teemed with fish. With amazement she observed how they swam in close formation within their schools. It was as if in unison they had a single life to live. Close to one another and all turned toward the same place, in the same direction, the current pulling them in one sweeping movement. If one fish remained behind, in fear it hurried to reach the school, penetrated within it, and was lost amidst the rest.

She turned her eyes elsewhere. She searched the surrounding rocks, the ocean floor. There she distinguished fish that lived in solitude. Many-colored, scaleless, transparent. In the distance masses of water were blackened by shadows. Large fish were lurking. Solitude. Solitude and heavy silence. The child's feet kicked the ocean floor. She kicked powerfully and shot to the water's surface. When Panagiota emerged she was a tall woman.

As Maryo examined her eyes, she found they had a dark, dense gaze like that of her son. How dark and dense his gaze had become the day he returned home.

Her precious son had told her:

"I've heard tell of King Solomon's treasures. I am going to find them."

Maryo trembled; she was terribly frightened.

"Who needs King Solomon's treasures?" she challenged him.

Yet she understood. Deep inside her she realized it is precisely such quests that give life its greatest value. Her complaint, her sorrow, was that she would lose him. All Maryo asked was time, time to be with him a little longer.

"Who needs King Solomon's treasures!" she challenged him.

But he did not hear her. He kicked the starter of his motorcycle and tore off in a cloud of dust. The young man on the motorcycle roared into the distance and she stood, her hand raised in farewell to his back.

Time passed and he returned. When he returned to the house he was no longer her boy. The one who came back was no longer her child. She leaned her head back to look at him. He had become so tall. How she had to stretch her arms to reach him, to hug him! How broad his back had become. His face: it was not his smooth, soft face that she kissed. It had the rough feel of a beard. She didn't recognize his eyes. He had lost his peaceful eyes. His gaze was dark, dense.

"I found King Solomon's treasures," he announced to her. "I saw them. Now I know."

He was angry. He was angry with her and raged at her like an angry sea. He blamed her; she was at fault, knowing all the things he had seen and never warning him. She had been wrong in hiding these things from him, especially from him. She had never told him the secret of the treasure. Never told him anything about the journey, about the high walls you encountered. She had never uttered a word about the blind turns, the sharp rocks and the cliffs. She had only spoken about light. About calm seas, never about whirlpools.

"I saw and now I know."

His eyes were shooting momentous flames. She, exhausted and empty, didn't know how to tell him, how to explain that the great things in life cannot be told. How could she explain that the great and the significant cannot be framed in words. They do not have shape to be conveyed, nor do they possess typical colors. Each person just perceives them, comprehends them and sketches them, adding the colors he feels. Each person on his own, out of his deepest, obscurest resources—he alone shapes the great and the significant.

"Learn to make your knowledge wisdom," she whispered to him. "*Make your knowledge wisdom!*" she shouted to him.

But he only distanced himself with long strides. He didn't hear her words. All the youth's guts were working at once. His insides were boiling. They raised flames and torrents, and the roar they made covered all other voices. So great was the clamor of his body.

Her mother, a tall woman, gazed toward the village. She was angry. She molded the knowledge that was hers with deep anger and sustained that anger at a high pitch. With fury she proceeded on her way and with fury she survived.

PART THREE

The road was steep. As it left the last lane of the village, it took an abrupt upgrade which led to the village called Stony. The village was eight hundred long strides from Alatsata, and all its houses were old, built of limestone, their walls cracked and crumbling. They were built during the years that the Terrors ravaged the villages in the valley. Wild raiders swept down from the depths of Asia and pillaged. They pillaged people's bodies and possessions.

The Terrors those years were named, and the people fled from the village in the valley to this steep place at the foot of the mountain full of rocks and caves. The dark, damp caves preserved people's lives. They built houses and lived here many years, till the time the wild men forgot their existence. Then the young descended, built houses in the valley below; but here remained the aged Stony men and women. Those who had indelible memories stayed to keep the houses sealed in readiness for the new Terrors to come. Alone and abandoned they stayed, and their children in the valley brought them their ill-borns. They took their ill-borns to Stony village on the steep hillside.

Maryo climbed. She mounted the steep road strewn with stones and potholes, and she drove herself to climb more rapidly. Every so often she stopped and looked up to check her whereabouts. After a brief pause, she took a deep breath and went forward once more. Before sunset, she had to reach the crumbling two-story house whose balcony hung over the road. Each evening, at the time the sun was declining behind the mountain, about to disappear and plunge all into darkness, just before it sank, as it cast a red light over the world with its distant rays, a woman emerged onto that balcony. It was a woman whom time had frozen in her body. She was neither young nor old, she was simply a woman. Tall, with a fierce countenance, large shadowy eyes, and white hair that came down to her waist. Her voice was a rumble of thunder. She emerged onto the balcony at sundown and intoned a liturgy. In a stentorian voice she chanted the Hymn 'To Our Victorious Lady, Commander of our Forces' with so much rage and such fury that her voice resounded throughout the village and beyond, spreading down the mountainside and over the sea, wildly arousing foamy waves across its entire surface.

Maryo had to see this woman from up close. She started out early and hurried along. She wanted to reach Stony village at the time the sun was sinking, at the time that the woman would come out onto the balcony. Climbing strenuously, her sweat ran. Her breath was short and her heart was troubled by the fear she would be too late to catch sight of the woman from up close. She was on time, however. She arrived just before sundown. Waiting under the balcony she noticed that its framework was of cast iron. Strangely, it was the only iron balcony around. It was extremely old, eaten away by rust and heavy winds. Savage seasons had eaten away at it. The road below it was covered with scales of rust. The other balconies were of wood. They too were very old and were riddled by termites.

Her eyes fixed on the woman's balcony, Maryo waited. Time passed, the sun was going down, dusk was falling, but the balcony door remained shut and dark. No one lighted a lamp or candle inside. The windows remained dark, blank, coated with dust and dead insects.

The woman was overdue, long overdue, and Maryo asked herself why she had made the strenuous journey. Why had it really been necessary to come here? She took several steps backward and continued her watch by the balcony. The balcony door as yet remained shut, and Maryo cupped her hands, brought them to her mouth, and shouted upward.

"Kyra Smaragdo-o-o-o-o-o-o-o!"

"O-o-o-o-o-o-o-o!" echoed from the mountainside.

On the surrounding balconies the wooden shutters creaked. They opened, leaned, and threatened to fall from broken hinges. Onto the rotten balcony boards emerged aged women, a hundred years old, crippled, shrouded in tattered black dresses and heavy faded kerchiefs tightly wrapped about the neck. They leaned heavily on knurled canes and the balconies creaked and Maryo feared that moment the rotten beams would separate from the rusty spikes which loosely held them, that the balconies would shake, collapse, part from the wall and fall with a resounding crash to the road below. Everything would disintegrate—the beams, planks, and the old women themselves. Everything would lie shattered at Maryo's feet. The old women trembled. They fixed their blind eyes on Maryo and trembled in rage there on their high balconies.

"Sh-sh-sh-sh-sh-h-h-h-h-h-h!" they commanded.

They held their long bony forefingers to the center of their wrinkled lips.

"Sh-sh-h-h-h."

Their fingernails long, encrusted with dirt, they hissed,
"Quit sh-sh-sh-sh-shouting, damn you."
They hissed like vipers, but Maryo grew obstinate. Again she cupped
her hands and her voice resounded:
"Kyra Smaragdo-o-o-o-o-o!"
"O-o-o-o-o-o-o-o!" came the echo.
The doors below creaked open, young boys, ill-borns with shaved heads,
poured out, followed by old men with round, terrified eyes and fingers held
at the center of their lips.
"Sh-sh-sh-h-h-h-h," they went.
The children had their fingers in their noses and their hands between
their legs. Repulsed, Maryo felt sick to her stomach. Again she got ready to
shout. For the third time she cupped her hands around her mouth, took a
deep breath and prepared to make her voice ring out more fully than before.
She made a great effort, but was interrupted. An old woman, incredibly
old, forgotten by Charon, her aged face no longer stamped by time, appeared
on the highest balcony and cried in a strange, powerful voice:
"Qui-i-i-i-et, you down there! Qui-i-i-i-et! It's wicked to call upon the
dead."
Stunned, Maryo lowered her hands. Her eyes circled the area. The ill-
borns contemptuously thrust their open palms toward her in the sign of the
mouja, slapping the one on the back of the other hand, sneering together in
chorus:
"Na-a-a! Na-a-a! Na-a-a!"
They thrust their spread palms.
"It's wicked to call upon the dead! Na-a-a! Na-a-a! Na-a-a!"
Maryo was terrified. She was truly terrified; she expected that any
moment Kyra Smaragdo's narrow window would open and from within
would emerge the tall skeleton of the woman, bits of flesh showing through
her tattered clothing, the flesh eaten away and stuck loosely here and there
on the bones, her hair fallen from her scalp, a few hard white tufts on her
shoulders and chest, a few strands remaining on her head; her mouth would
open to show the set of teeth screwed to the jaw, and the rows of teeth
would part to release the chant. Maryo's hair stood on end and her eyes
filled with the horror of the image. Turning on her heel, she fled.
It was late at night when she finally got out of Stony village. They
called them the Terrors, and Kyra Smaragdo, that ageless old woman, they
named the Savage One, the Wrath of Mankind.

"Villagers! Villagers! Hear this news!"

The town crier's voice cut like steel. Everyone froze. They cocked their ears to catch every syllable, every word, every implication. Dark, heavy, unsure, the days passed one after another. A vast upheaval had begun at a great distance on another continent, beyond their sea, but echoes of unrest, like waves of flame racing across dried fields, swept toward the village.

"Hear this news, one and all!"

Everyone froze on the spot, breathlessly awaiting what was to follow.

"Everyone must gather at Aghios Panteleimonas church. Go there today before vespers. The mayor wishes to speak to you. Let no one be absent. The mayor's message is deeply urgent. Everyone must be there! Villagers... villagers!"

The town crier had begun very early in the morning, and everyone knew at once that the news was bad. The tone of his voice, sharp, metallic, pierced their memory; and the winds of war, which were nesting within them, rushed into their minds. Their bodies trembled and their hearts grew faint.

"What do they want from us? The savages are on the rise once again, damn them!" Giannakos swore under his breath.

"May it all somehow come to good!" Despinyo crossed herself.

She gazed at the icon of Aghios Panteleimonas. Her legs and arms felt weak.

"Ach! When did they ever call a meeting for something good?" Panagiota snapped. "They're up to no good. They are scheming again."

"Hush, Panagiota, hush!" Despinyo begged.

In the afternoon, long before vespers, the villagers gathered at the church. They filled the sanctuary, the churchyard, the square, and the neighboring lanes. When Despinyo saw the expression on the face of the school teacher, Kyra Pelagia, she was terrified. There was a smile on the teacher's lips. It was a frozen grimace, and her chubby body was rigid. Her feigned calm shook Despinyo.

"They're going to tell us lies again," Panagiota said loudly so everyone could hear.

"Do they ever do anything else?" added a woman long familiar with torment and suffering. "All they ever do is fill us with lies!"

"They've been doing it forever and they lap it up!" Panagiota added.

The village elders had gathered in a corner of the sanctuary and were speaking in low voices.

"Panagiota, get as close to them as you can and listen to what they're saying," her mother urged.

She gave her daughter a shove.

"They're scheming again. . ." the daughter replied without obeying. "They're scheming how to line their pockets. They never get enough!"

Her mother sighed. What a problem Panagiota was. She embarrassed her mother. If people heard, what would they think and say? Her daughter was always so angry!

Father Vagellis went to the pulpit and raised his hands in prayer toward the icon of the Pantocrator in the dome.

Panagiota moved from the spot where she was standing and hid behind a column. She wished to see neither the Pantocrator, who had the savage eyes of a primordial man, nor the fat hands of the priest-devil, as she called him. Her mother was biting down on her mantilla. The priest's trembling hands made her heart sink.

The priest stepped down from the pulpit, and the mayor took his place. He was dressed in his Sunday best, a white shirt and black trousers. His son, who was studying at the university in Greece, had brought the trousers as a gift. He was among the first in the village to replace his knickers with trousers, as had the doctor and the school teacher Kyra Pelagias's husband.

"Dear fellow villagers, I have invited you here to say but a few crucial things. Conditions necessitate that we temporarily leave the village. It will be only for a few days. For a maximum of three weeks to a month, we all must go away to Greece. You must not be alarmed. Think of this as merely lost time. For a few weeks your lives will be disrupted. The authorities in Smyrni and the Polis have determined this. They know best."

"They know shit," Giannakos muttered.

Panagiota grinned. That was why she loved her father so much. He knew what was going on in the world.

"Take clothing and a few necessities for three weeks," the mayor continued. "Leave plenty of food for the animals in their stalls. Lock up your houses and as if you were simply going away on vacation."

A black mass, the congregation poured out into the streets, breaking into continuous waves of comment:

"Why leave when we could simply secure ourselves in our homes? What will happen to the animals if it's more than three weeks or a month? . . . I won't budge! You won't catch me abandoning all my worldly possessions! . . . Where they are taking us! We are surrounded by armed enemies!"

"Villagers. . . Villagers . . .".

Every morning for a week the town crier passed through the streets.

"No one is to remain the village. Lock your houses up tight and go to Chesme or Agrilia. From there boats will take you to Pireus or Thessaloniki."

"Villagers. . . Villagers. . . You will see Greece, our motherland."

The still water of the sea was thick; the ship crossed it with difficulty and slowly approached the port city. Dusk fell softly and before they tied up in the harbor dense darkness had closed in. A motionless dark mass, the refugees waited on the ship's deck. They waited for dawn to break to see the city to which they had been brought. They had finally arrived, and dressed in their best clothes they were eager to see Greece. Hanging over the ship's rail at dusk, they had made out in the distance the green touches of trees, the red tiles of roofs, and white lines of roads, but before they had time for a fuller view darkness fell. They huddled together on the deck, resigned to waiting another night.

In the morning, at the raw break of dawn, the people began to move. Like a tidal wave they swept forward and poured fiercely into the city, overflowing her bounds, drowning her. The town opened and stretched out her arms. Spreading in all directions, beyond meadows and rolling hills, she strained farther and farther to receive the newcomers, till the bounds of her body broke. Many refugees were arriving, and even more were already there. They flooded and burst the wide roads and the narrow lanes. Soldiers, too, from around the globe were gathering here.

The city was belabored by the weight of the human mass. Choked, she bore the weight with great difficulty. The refugees' thoughts were intense, their desires many. Their anxieties radiated from every pore. The city buzzed with talk, inquiries, and the sound that hovers in the breathing of exhausted sleeping bodies. At night the city's streets and the lanes flashed the gleaming eyes of predators—packs of wolves, the soldiers lurked.

Thessaloniki quaked. She trembled and shook with the fear that war provokes in people's hearts. The darkness of war had seized Europe. It was bleak and terrible, and. the people called this the First World War. It reached the borders of the city, it penetrated the borders of their lives. Suffering was in the air. The threat came from all sides. From the sea it came as enemy war ships. From the sky it came as metal birds made by people's hands. They were called "Zepplins," and they carried bombs. Suffering was everywhere. Traps were ubiquitous.

NOSTOS

As refugees Greeks from Asia Minor arrived in Thessaloniki. It was the first purge of 1916. They were given tents. Rains came and creeks were formed around the tents; rivers poured through them. Muddy water soaked their clothes and cracked their bones.

The three weeks passed. They built tin shacks and made do for a time. Then Vardaris blew with rage; with incredible fury the wind tore off the roof from above their heads and slammed the walls to the ground. Months passed. Crammed into schools, churches, abandoned houses, they waited for the fury to pass, for the blessed time to come when they would return to their homes. In their pockets they gripped the keys to their paternal houses. They clasped the keys like talismans. The first year passed, and the second. The third year was coming and still they were wasting away in an alien land.

Despinyo was crying. She was sobbing and biting on her scarf.
"Who can sweeten the bitter life my daughters lead?"
She tore her scarf to tatters as she looked upon her comely daughters. Their bodies were blooming boughs, fragrant buds, but their hearts were unrooted, desiccated. They walked with lowered heads, reining in their youthful passions, their fragrance erased.
"Who can erase the shame of the refugee from my son's minds?" Giannakos asked.
He wept and cursed over the fate of his young sons.
The local people came; they chose strong male bodies for heavy work. They gave them merely enough bread for subsistence. Sicknesses came and harried the weakened bodies. Epidemics spread, death triumphed. Yet the women went on working. They bore the young in tents, in shacks, in crowded houses. They even gave birth in the streets.
"We will survive!" they insisted. "We will return to our homes; we will regain our sacred ground!"

Far in the depth of Africa, in the thick, dark forests, there is a small country filled with wild animals. It is called Guinea and it is a treacherous place. Its lakes are like small seas. With water colored green by the heavy vegetation, they are rife with crocodiles. Still as logs in the water, the crocodiles lie in wait for the people living there. They nourish themselves on their thin bodies. But the natives are not afraid of these reptiles. They know their territories and generally avoid them. What makes them tremble in fear, is a minuscule organism, invisible to the eye, that breeds in dirty, stagnant water. The tribesmen come naked, barefoot, to bathe or clean a cut. Then the tiny invader enters the body; it finds a vein, is nourished by the blood, and becomes a long worm. Inhabiting the blood, it extends beyond a meter in length, and if it reaches the heart, the host dies. If it remains in the leg, the host is crippled There are many crippled people among the inhabitants and many more who die. The parasite is called "the Guinea worm."

The city's borders shrank. Her resources were diminished. The worm of fear fell amidst her populace. Their hate grew large. The face of the enemy appeared. It was their fellowman.

"You parasites from Turkey, get out of our city!"

"You selfish Greeks, exploiters, you are drinking our blood!"

"You lazy good-for-nothings! Eat our garbage and be glad you're alive!"

"We are from Ionia, an ancient, proud race."

"Your mothers are madams, your wives and daughters whores, and you are thieves and crooks!"

"You Greeks are pimps and bums. You itch for easy profit!"

Maryo's shuddered. She shivered and despaired. She feared that the worm of prejudice had gone beyond a meter in length.

A young woman climbed the school steps, paused at the entrance, proceeded hesitantly down the corridor, and stopped by some children playing on the floor. Her thin dress stretched to cover her overflowing flesh. Her eyes and mouth were heavily made up. Her hair was short, dyed red, and done in a permanent. She spoke in a trembling voice:

"Children," she asked. "Do you know a Kyra Despinyo ?"

One of the children pointed to the room on the right.

"Panagiota-a-a-a-a!" he yelled; "someone wants your mother."

Panagiota opened the door. Staring at the woman, her eyes grew wider and wider as surprise turned to shock.

"Mana," she said softly as she turned back into the classroom, "Aggerou is outside."

Despinyo leaped to her feet, and her eyes gaped with horror.

"No-o-o-o-o-o!" she screamed. "No one goes out of this room! No one shall see her! Let no one dare open this door!" She pressed her back against the door, trembling. She was shaking from head to toe, and Panagiota gazed at her in amazement. She was deeply shocked by her mother's features.

"Mana, let me by."

She took her gently by the shoulder and went to pass.

"I want to ask Aggerou something. There is something I need to know."

"No-o-o-o-o!" the other woman screeched. "Whoever says one word, whoever lays eyes on her, has my curse on her head!"

The daughter's eyes flashed in anger and rage. She violently pushed her mother out of the way.

"Neither blessings nor curses touch us any longer. Haven't you learned even that?" she sneered.

Panagiota stepped into the corridor, but Aggerou had vanished. Panagiota hurried along the road to the White Tower, and there, a block ahead, she saw her sister. Her body was a beacon. She still had that lively walk; her body swung dance-like, though it was puffy beneath the cheap, tight dress. Behind her, half a dozen service men joked coarsely with her.

Panagiota ran to catch up, and approaching, observed Aggerou more closely. It seemed that her sister's flesh was indented where men put their hands. Panagiota slumped to the top of a low wall lining the road. She felt she would faint from horror. Leaning on the stones, she watched her sister as she moved off into the distance. The soldiers were chuckling and pinching Aggerou. She too was laughing, coyly giggling as they persisted; and looking on, Panagiota gazed within that body, imagining Aggerou's insides. Aggerou's uterus was like thin gauze eaten away and torn at the edges, riddled with holes where the desires of men had dripped, as they had dripped throughout the stomach cavity, contaminating the intestines, the liver, the kidneys.

"They are rotting her! They are rotting her!" she cried.

Honored Parents and Beloved Brothers and Sisters,

May the Virgin be with you and bless you. I have learned your news and am pleased that with the help of Almighty God you are well and have returned to the homeland. I ask for your prayers that with the Grace of the Almighty we may continue our blessed work here for the benefit of the Church, for the spiritual growth of the order, and the welfare of all. We work to give thanks to the God of Love, our Creator and the Maker of the cosmos seen and unseen. We strive to apply His blessed commandments, that our earthly lives may be holy, perfect, peaceful, blameless, and we pray that God may judge us worthy of eternal life for which he created and prepared us.

CRIST

Mother, come to Aghia Skepi as soon as you can. It is three years since I have seen you. I have missed you so very much. May you have health and blessings in Christ,

Your daughter,
Theochtisti

The breeze of the homeland blew. It danced around their bodies. Their bosoms swelled, their hearts exulted, their eyes filled with tears. Their vision did not rest on their vandalized, looted houses. Their gaze surveyed the homeland and their lungs inhaled her air.

Scattered groups of refugee families returned to the blessed land. They knelt, caressed the soil, and pressed it to their faces and lips. They knelt to knead the ground. They soaked it with sweat and blood; the time of harvest came and the earth repaid them.

***

Seated on the ledge of the moudi with a note pad in his hand, Giannakos recorded sack after sack of produce from the fields. In the evening everyone got together to eat and drink raki. All the kinfolk were there: Giannakos's and Despinyo's brothers and sisters, their sons and daughters. The celebrating went on after each day's work. The men drank, sipping raki they had made themselves, with their own fermented grapes. They drank and told stories from the old days, from long ago. They spoke of all the things that took place in the homeland, here on this soil, in these houses.

Where was Greece? What went on those past three years in Greece, in Thessaloniki, nobody cared to remember. How sweet life is, sweet and delightful! And how short, how very short! They knew how quickly it was flying by. Swift as a sip of raki slipped to the stomach, time sped; it evaded grasping fingers and palms, but loved ones touched one another, and the warmth of the body entered the heart with sweet words and carefree laughter. The moudi overflowed, dusk fell, night passed, midnight arrived, and they were still here by one another's sides remembering old times, reliving them, drinking, and laughing.

"Time to say good-night!" Despinyo urged. "Looks like we've had another endless 'Armenian Party' tonight."

Among them, Maryo shared the laughter and pleasures of her kinsmen. She forgot what was to come; it slipped her mind and she enjoyed the moment itself. "Everything in life is an interlude. But this interlude, with these high spirits, is the best of all!" she gaily told herself. She was heard by no one, but she spiritedly affirmed, "Gather the energies of joy; that alone increases life!" She touched her kinsmen, caressed them, especially her mother, laughing continuously the way they laughed.

In the morning, very early, just as the sun took the dawn by the hand for a walk around the village, everyone arose, first of all Giannakos.

"Hey, Lord!" he shouted boisterously. "Tell me where you've got the earth's handle. Tell me where it is, so I can grab onto it and fling the globe around!"

With more than enough joy to spare, Giannakos's heart overflowed.

Panagiota held her friend's hand. She felt her friend's hand tremble as she looked fondly at Antonis. Panagiota laughed.

"Mori, send your father. Send him this Sunday, mori! I know Antonis loves you too!"

The girl blushed deeply and lowered her head, but Panagiota insisted: "Come on! We'll be sisters!"

The girls' hearts burst with laughter.

After church, early on Sunday, Philio's father arrived. Dressed in his good suit, he sat on the edge of his chair addressing Giannakos.

"A fine lad, Antonis!" he told him.

"Your Philio is a jewel!" the other replied, and they shook hands.

There was a big grin on Antonios's face and there were tears in Philio's eyes as the great preparations began. The marriage would take place the following Sunday.

"In rich happiness spare no expense!" boomed Giannakos. "Nothing but the best." They bought lamps, filled them with oil, lighted the house, the verandah, the lanes; and heaped trays of food arrived continuously. Day after day the women baked as the village looked on with approval. Antonis's wedding and the following celebration were spendid indeed. The musicians played with great gusto, the wine flowed, pistol shots cracked in the air to salute the newlyweds, and Despinyo trembled.

"We can do without this rowdiness," she warned. "There are a lot of Turks just outside the village."

The youths laughed and kept loading their pistols. All smiles, Antonios laid his hand on Philio's knee. He felt a thrill in his fingertips and excitement in his breast. Laughing and toasting the couple, Panagiota got up to dance, and Maryo clapped her hands in rhythmic accompaniment. How overjoyed Maryo was, how delighted to see her mother as a girl on this splendid occasion.

Twenty-two years old, slim and blooming, she danced the balo.

There is a hill in Alatsata,
Its name is Karantai.
Alatsatanians of the Upper Village,
You call it Karantai.

Her hands raised, her head slightly inclined to the shoulder, her body swayed to the strains of the balo, and Tsortsis, opposite her, drew her attention with his own swaying. Maryo watched Panagiota's eyes sparkle and her emotions rise as she tried not to turn toward the young man who was dancing with her, as if he was not there, as if she was dancing alone. She seemed to ignore Tsortsis but threw glances at him out of the corner of her eye. Her tongue moistened her dry lips, and Maryo knew her mother's heart was aglow. Following the tempo, Maryo kept her gaze on Panagiota, who inclined her head slightly and sang.

"There is a hill in Alatsata," sang Panagiota's blood: that hill which was theirs, most deeply theirs, with neighboring meadows and deep green, richly fertile fields; and they were the landowners, their granaries loaded to the brim, their roads and lanes fully lighted. And Panagiota knew all those who walked there day and night; she feared nothing, for her father was rich; she never had to be a maid in a great mansion, munching her vittles alone in the kitchen; she never had to be anyone's servant, cleaning filthy underwear. Hers was a family with possessions, and the lane in front of their house was safe; she has never been lost in wide dark streets; has never been pawed, violated, shoved against a wall with sharp stones that cut her back. Never has a rough skinned soldier of some distant place pulled something repulsive out of his pants and emptied it on her white dress, her soft, silk dress which she made with her own hands, whose material she bought with savings, got the pattern and sewed herself, put on; and going for a stroll stayed out a bit late in the dark streets of Thessaloniki, and that soldier, that huge man. . . she could kill him with her own hands. She felt nauseated by all the swaying to the strains of the balo and all the wine she had drunk and all the food she had eaten. She left Tsortsis as he tried to catch her eye with his broad smile. She went out into the yard behind the chicken coop, bent over as low as she could, and threw up the baked lamb, cheese pastry, tidbits, and wine. She emptied herself and only the bitterness of the memory remained. That was lodged in her tender insides.

Tsortsis danced the balo and laughed. He was excited, for this girl was giving him the eye as if to egg him on. He felt his strong frame tremble. He yearned for her, wanted her for his woman. He felt like going right now to her brother Antonios, bending over and whispering this in his ear. He danced; he danced the zeimpekiko. His hands became an eagle's wings; he looked upon the ground with disdain and slapped it with his palm. He soared upward, his body sliced and imprinted the air. Again he touched the earth softly on the tips of his toes; he bent his knees and stroked the ground with the back of his hand, a small caress, and then flew into the air and there up high inclined his head to the right, lifting his bent leg somewhat to touch before he turned his body in space.

Maryo was shaken. She was deeply shocked seeing the young man in this position with his breath cut short. She alone, among all the others, who are clapping with the dance, shuddered, seeing what was coming, what was going to happen as this motion occurred. Tsortsis inclined his head slightly and raised his foot. His hand ready to reach to the back, his breath was cut by pain, his face took on a grimace of agony, as his hand reached to his back pocket where he had a bottle. There the enemy man struck, he shattered the water bottle Tsortsis had for the long march to Smyrni. It broke into splinters, driven into his flesh, and he bent his leg, he reached back to stroke the place the pain was killing him. His breath was cut short. "Ach! ach!" Maryo wanted to scream, and she felt a crazed impulse. She would go find the young Turkish soldier, who was from Anatolia too and knew the zeimpekiko, knew the body's movements; and she would bring the young Turkish fellow here, to this very place, to see this youth the moment before he would become his enemy—this moment as he danced at his friend's wedding, and he would dance and the Turkish fellow would clap along, for he knew the dance's movements; and Maryo wanted to see: would he then strike Tsortsis with his rifle butt, would he strike him in the back trouser pocket and pull the trigger when the officer shouted 'Fire!' there in the ravine outside Smyrni? And Maryo searched, she wildly searched among the ranks to find that soldier to bring him to the dance, but she could not find that enemy infantryman; she could not single him out, so great had the numbers of the enemy become.

There was a great hullabaloo. The streets and lanes filled with the sound of happy voices. The children came running. They were bursting with joy, babbling together with their rosy-cheeked young mothers, who were chubby after repeated child-bearing but still youthful, running along with their kerchiefs tied around the face so as not to show the delight that overflowed from their glowing flesh. They were all running behind the head shepherd. He, with his great, turned-up mustache and his clarinet under his arm, paid them no heed. With long strides, he arrived at the wedding feast. The villagers were crammed on the verandah, in the rooms, in the kitchen. Crowding the hallway, they overflowed into the garden and the lane, waiting to listen. The player took his instrument from under his arm and rested the reed on his lower lip. The tone penetrated the gathering, pierced hearts, evoked awed silence. Everyone felt their breath taken away, their feelings electrified, as inhibitions gave way to erotic flow; hearts were lifted up, sorrows dissolved, memories multiplied, spirits united, souls embraced, and all became one.

Maryo was dazzled, overwhelmingly moved; never had she heard such sounds. The shepherd gently kissed his instrument; with trembling touch he stroked it, and it responded. Its tones cast enchantment. Maryo turned her eyes upon the musician to observe him closely, but the man no longer showed behind his instrument; he had become one with the instrument he was playing. The man had disappeared and only his music existed. That alone! Maryo wondered about the player as he would walk in that dark file into the ravine outside Smyrni, to be riddled with bullets. Here at the wedding feast, the bold player had vanished; the man did not exist, there was only the fecund overflow of nature through the fingers that caressed the clarinet's tones into life.

Uncle Stavris cleared his throat and shifted in his seat. He spoke as if his soul was in his mouth. He had a dark look; his face was clouded and his hands shook

"We will not abandon our homes again; we will never become refugees again!" He spoke with deliberation. "We will stay in our homes, prepared for the worst from the Turks. When the storm comes, we will hide in the attic and wait for the peak of the hurricane. After that we will come out and submit to servitude."

"I will never submit to the Turks!" Uncle Sideris jumped up. "I would rather submit to Greeks."

"Have you already forgotten them, Sideri?"

The sarcastic voice electrified memories, and the bodies quivered.

"Is this a time for such memories?" Despinyo challenged.

"Which of you is willing to be a refugee once more?" Uncle Stavris demanded angrily.

Heavy silence fell over the company. They were dazed by horrid thoughts.

"I, too, say we stay," declared Uncle Nikolos.

"Flee for your lives!" thundered Constantis. "The Terror is upon us! A great Terror will fall on our village! Fear nothing more than an army in retreat or the pursuing forces!"

His voice thundered. He had just come from the front lines, and atrocities were fresh in his mind.

"I will stay!"

"Me, too!"

"I will not set foot on foreign streets again!" asserted Panagiota.

"Nor will we!" agreed Aunt Marigi's daughters in unison.

Their bodies grew heavy. Heavily, darkly, they buried their fears beneath their decisions and returned with dragging steps to their homes. The decision was made: they would remain in their homeland though the war had been lost. Despinyo went about her work in the kitchen: gathering dishes, washing, straightening up the rooms. She took the lighted lamp, went into the garden, cared for the animals, went into the storeroom and sat down at the loom. Passing the yarn through the strings, she moved the shuttle back and forth. Maryo was jarred awake and went to sit by Despinyo's side.

"How are things with you, dear Giagia?"

The woman continued to weave and Maryo watched her sorrowfully.

"Everything could end here, so you would never become a grandmother," Maryo said. "Nothing would remain but suffering. The great suffering of family disaster. That could destroy you completely. Tell me, Giagia dear, if you can see and hear me: What did you experience in your life? What did the world give you? You were only a stepping stone on which others tread to move into the future." Maryo sadly nodded her head. "I, in any case, will not be a mere stepping stone. I want to live!"

Maryo was angry.

"I will be a stepping stone for no one. No one will tread on me!" she said out loud.

She felt pain throughout her body, particularly in her left breast, as if everyone had stepped precisely there. Grandmother's hands flitted across the loom. Swiftly and skillfully she threaded the colorful yarn and brought the shuttle knocking from side to side. The sounds became musical measures that lulled both of them. It was then, as their eyelids drooped, that they heard the woman's sigh.

Dressed entirely in black, she was a woman getting on in years and harried by spiritual torment. She appeared, sat down between Despinyo and her future granddaughter, and began to weave. She brought the shuttle back and forth, knocking on either side, but now the rhythm had changed; it was not the musical beat that had lulled them. It was harsh, threatening. Dry, abrupt, monotonous, it struck "Bam! Bam!Bam!Bam!" as the woman continuously sighed. Despinyo shot to her feet. She crossed herself, grabbed the lamp placed beside the loom, and rushed out into the yard. There she leaned over the lamp flue and blew out the flame.

Daylight had already come. With her heart in her mouth, Despinyo entered the middle room where her daughters were sleeping.

"Get up at once!" she urged. "Get ready right away; we are going to Chios, to the convent."

Sleep in their eyes, the girls were angry with their mother.

"What are you talking about, mana!"

But Despinyo had no more words left in her. She ran from the house and rushed up the lane to the window of her sister's house.

"Marigi, mori Marigi! Wake up your daughters! We are going to Aghia Skepi. The Tsetes are coming! The Tsetes are coming, I tell you! The Mother of God herself told me!"

A wave of fear swept up and down the lane, and many villagers were shaken in the depths of their sleep. As if bitten by scorpions, they felt their spirits go numb, their bodies ache. The sun arose and seemed to radiate its morning splendor, but its beams fell on ravaged lanes where the Tsetes were slaughtering the townspeople.

I have come here. I have returned to this point in time and here I will forever return. Maryo stops by a wall where she sees Sophaki in her yard. She is seventeen—her parents' pride and joy. Her father's severed head lies pitched into a corner of the yard by some flower pots. Sophaki is lying on the rocky ground—on top of her a heavy, repulsive man. He is moving with little moans, and her mother is lying beside her; her head against her daughter's shoulder, her lips pressed to her ear, she is whispering, hastily, as if drunkenly, and her voice sounds like an old, a very old, lament. "No-o-o-o-o, don't be dismayed, little soul—nothing is happening, all these things never happened, they never took place. It's a dream—a nightmare. It will pass—it will dissolve. Horrid nightmares always vanish, my precious one. It is a dream, like life, and it will pass." The heavy man goes away giving his place to another who looks like a mouse. He has been waiting for some time, trembling—holding his thing in his hand. The mother resumes. "No-o-o-o, my little soul, it never happened. Never. Never." Her voice beats on and on like a muffled drum.

Maryo backs away. She goes to a corner of the wall and vomits. The vessels of her mouth burst, releasing blood and pus—so much bitterness has swelled within her. She hastens to flee, to save the pupils of her eyes from these scenes. She presses her palms over her ears to protect her ear drums from the savage cries of triumph which erupt from the victors' mouths as they top the women. She rushes to leave the village, to smell no longer the blood of slaughter. At the Well of the Virgin there is an uproar. Wild-haired women are screaming lamentations, mourning that they have not had time to hurl themselves into the well and drown. The well is filled up and the bodies at the top are thrashing and the women outside are scrambling to pull them aside to make a place and fall in, as the blaspheming victors arrive on horseback to seize their prey; and Maryo rushes to distance herself from the spot, plunges into overgrown fields, briars stretch themselves in her way, tear at her legs, trails of blood fill her shoes, her feet slip, she discards her shoes, and bleeding, barefoot, she dashes away from this landscape of hell.

The shouts fade. Only the echoes remain that have lodged in her ears. Still she runs. Silence falls over the meadows, which are illuminated by a bright moon. From her mouth Maryo's breath comes in panting grunts, till her pace slows. Walking slowly now—very slowly, she surrenders herself to the gentle embrace of nature. Her way lighted by the radiant moon, the path glistens ahead, meandering among blossoming trees whose branches spread in the night like the light arms of children, and the trees, the plants, grow in the night far from human abode.

Maryo walked, following the path, and she heard the crickets' chorus, the baying of dogs, and the distant howls of jackals. She walked to reach her time, and the sweet call of a whippoorwill suddenly fell on her ears. Its vibrant refrain demanded a response and another whippoorwill answered. Sweet, poignant, her notes pierced Maryo's heart, and from those holes the bitterness poured out just as the salt poured from her eyes. The streams flowed and flowed for a long time, emptying, too, the heaviness from her body. Maryo was refreshed—she heard the whippoorwill's clear call, and her soul was revived.

The one whippoorwill sang:
>Oo-hoo oo-hoo oo-hoo
>Mourne ne more, abandon rue—
>Tyme an unrulie Boy hee be,
>His Moder hight Forgetfulnesse,
>his Fader clepped Deethe,
>and alle oure worldlie torments be
>onlie noisome games that hee
>plaieth and plaieth continuallie—
>oo-hoo oo-hoo oo-hoo
>sorrow ne more, banish rue. . .

And the other whipporwill sang in the distance:
>oo-hoo oo-hoo oo-hoo
>sorrow ne more, banish rue—
>Tyme hee be a Sorcerer,
>Alle thinges in his power,
>The worlde be his magick sacke
>Fro which he draweth straight
>War, dishonour, paine, and rape,
>Anguish, shame, and everie lacke,
>and fro that sacke, I telle thee true,
>he plucketh joys and pleasures, too—
>oo-hoo oo-hoo oo-hoo
>mourne ne more, abandon rue. . .

Maryo took the road to reach her time. Her legs moved rapidly but her body stood still. The hills passed her by—the trees, the crossroads, the voices, the moonlight. These all passed her and she remained immobile, feeling her body emptying out, her flesh gradually departing, and her skeleton beginning to wear down, to turn to dust, to fall on the path of time. Only her soul remained. Only that existed—within a totally radiant, deserted, totally illuminated meadow.

Maryo departed on foot. On foot she took untrodden byways. She didn't want to cross paths with anyone. She was ashamed to look suffering humanity in the face. She traveled only during dark, wild, nights. On moonlit nights she hid in damp caves and hollow trees. Years passed. The shame dripped into the channels of forgetfulness and then she wished and sought again human company. She arrived at a village. It was named Aghia Eleni and there Maryo approached. There was a large crowd awaiting the festival. A throng gawked at those who were preparing in spirit to walk barefoot on burning coals. They were called the Anastenarides and neither food nor water touched their lips during the period of preparation. They were reverently holding icons, old icons stained by time and charred around the edges by many fires of pillaging. They held the icons reverently in their arms with infinite care as if they were holding sickly children; and every so often they bent and kissed the faces, hands, bodies of those saints. The lyra insistently warbled the wild tones of life. The drum beat to the rhythm of blood which tried to break out and was suddenly blocked by natural dams, turned back, and again surged to find an outlet. This was the blood of those celebrants who threw their heads down toward the burnt earth and then back up to heaven and bent with closed eyes to inhale the smoke that spread from the white and yellow candles, the intoxicating herbs, myrrh, and incense. These touched unbearably their memories of trying times.

They were Anatolians. As refugees they had come from the depths of Asia. They had departed with tears and lamentation, scourged by the cruelest of human beings from their stone houses set amidst rocks and boulders. They left frenzied, taking with them only those icons of saints—and fire. They enclosed the fire deep within their bodies and brought it forth annually at this festival. It was their inheritance. Scarlet silk kerchiefs waved in the air, played like flames above their heads, and the soles of their feet, hard, etched, deeply scored, struck the ground. They were ecstatic in the movement of lament.

A man approached whose body was hard and whose face was

weathered. In his hand he held a keen butcher's knife. They called him Holy One. He was the first among the villagers. He led the dancing celebrants around a young, five-month old, coal-black bull who had no memories of gleaming knives but simply shied, attempting with little jerks to break the rope or slip the noose from around its neck. The Holy One raised the blade; he lifted it high and it gleamed. Just for an instant it glittered in the air and fell. It struck the unsuspecting beast which felt the swift cut that severed the nerve holding its young body erect. With a barely audible grunt of pain the bull collapsed heavily to the ground. The lyra's tempo increased, the drum beat wildly, the hard steel slit the artery, the blood sprang and flowed, encountered no block, poured out, and was blackened by soil and muddy water but still gleamed in the flames of the pyre. The burning coals glittered, ready to receive the feet of those Anatolians.

Maryo hurried on her way. She pressed forward in time to reach her mother and her father in their home. Weary to the bone, she searched among the small refugee homes in that Athens neighborhood. They were all small houses built of stones and mortar, with tin roofs. The streets were narrow, damp from wash water thrown out through the door. Around each house was a small yard filled with flowers.

Gentle fragrances wafted through the garden of the heart. Maryo was moved as her eyes fell upon the sky-blue shutters, the dark blue door. There was the house in which she would be born. Now she was arriving with a withered countenance, a face drained, worn by experience. Her hair was dry, white, and thinning. Her body was gaunt, skeleton-like, hollow. The veins in her legs were swollen; her heels were cracked and crusted with dried blood.

Her hands trembling, she opened the gate and haltingly entered the yard. Immediately she saw the boy, who was not quite two years of age. He was barefoot and wore only a pair of baggy shorts sewn by his mother. He was playing on the ground with a little shovel.

"Giorgaki," Maryo whispered, beginning to cry. "I got your letter. Your words were dipped in chocolate. People's words should be sweet like that, but even sweeter their acts."

She touched his little head, the curly black hair.

She saw her mother, and with sobs shaking her breast she moved toward her. She sat down beside her by the wall on a cement block, one of many lying near the house. Panagiota was sitting on a ledge by the wall sewing. The cloth she was stitching fell over her knees onto the rag throw-rug placed neatly beneath her feet. Her dynamic youthful figure bent alertly over the tempo of her skillful needle. Maryo leaned back against the wall, her head resting on her mother's shoulder. Her tears fell in cataracts.

"I've come, mother," she said between sobs. "I've come, mother, and brought you the secret, the thing you want to learn."

The woman jumped to her feet.

"How hot it is today!" she exclaimed.

She spoke to the child and then wiped her face, neck and arms with a damp washcloth. She flapped her short sleeves to cool her underarms and a sweet fragrance of youthful womanhood passed through the garden. Asimakis appeared at the gate. With head lowered and a little smile, he gently opened, entering the yard.

"Tell me how you and Asimakis got together in Athens," Maryo asked, settling back against the wall. Some of the stones were sharp and she shifted to find a more comfortable position. "And tell me about your wedding," she said, and waited.

Asimakis stood in front of a large full-length mirror. He was pleased. The uniform looked sharp. The dark blue jacket had eight gilt buttons and shoulder boards were trimmed with light blue and white. The trousers were also trimmed with stripes of blue and white. They were custom tailored for him. It was the first time he had tailored trousers and they suited him; they had a handsome male flair. Asimakis preened himself before the mirror in the hotel lobby. He experimented with his hat, testing the angle that he wanted. Finally he placed it so an unruly lock of hair fell casually above his forehead. He smiled. He liked the glow his face took on when he smiled. He knew how his play of expression could convey melancholy, thoughtfulness, carefree joy. He stroked his mustache. It was the sort he liked, a thin black line above the lip. It looked fine. He arranged his jacket, checked the buttons, settled it on his shoulders, adjusted his collar, and with deep satisfaction went out through the door. It was time to go on duty. He stood with easy alertness by the hotel entrance, his hands clasped behind his back, waiting for guests to appear. When one did, he would step quickly to open the door, bow slightly, touch his hand to the bill of his hat and say warmly:

"Bon soir, madame; bon soir, monsieur."

Asimakis knew French. He learned the language in France at the time of the first expulsion. In 1916 at Chios harbor, separated from his sister and mother, he boarded a ship for Marseilles instead of Pireus. Only fifteen, he found himself in a place where everyone spoke a foreign tongue. They found him a job in a cigarette factory. The job was great; he could smoke all the cigarettes he wanted, he had a mattress to sleep on in a warm corner of the factory, he ate in the cafeteria, and they gave him pocket money. The girls, the young woman workers, patted his hair and said, "Mon dieu, mon dieu, Greko!" Asimakis was pleased; he especially liked the girls, but the pleasant interlude was interrupted. Greece made war against Turkey and he was inspired to volunteer. He went straight to the front and fought all the way to Ankara. His commander was known as "Today's Leonidas," the finest commander of them all, and Asimakis himself received two crosses, two medals for bravery; for he knew no fear. Many things took place, a great many things, and finally he ended up hurrying back to Smyrni. It was then that he felt afraid; frightened by ugly incidents he had witnessed during the retreat, he rushed to find his mother and sister. Anxious and exhausted, he finally came upon them in Chios and put them on the ship for Pireus.

Life was fine, after all; it was long and filled with so many experiences. Asimakis felt this as he stood alertly, eyes shining, at the hotel entrance.

"Bon soir, madamoisellitses!" he bowed with a sweep of his hat.

He bowed low, almost touching the pavement. Passing by him on the street outside the hotel were young seamstresses, girls from the home country, on their way to Ermou Street where they would purchase their thread, buttons and buckles. All of them were headed that way, walking briskly, almost trotting, their heads held high, not looking at Asimakis, pretending not to know him.

"Panagiotitsa!" he whispered to one among them. "You are the one for me!"

Hurrying more quickly down the incline, the girls shouted to him from a distance, breaking up with laughter:

"Bon soir, monsieur, bon soir!"

"Marry him, Panagiota! He's such a good looking guy!" laughed Malama, Aunt Marigi's elder daughter.

"You won't catch me marrying that harlequin," Panagiota said, shrugging her shoulders in disdain and sneaking a glance to check Asimakis's good looks.

"Marry him, Panagiota. You know how prosperous his family was. His father was a big merchant," Giannakos urged, resenting his daughter's reluctance.

Giannakos had been bed-ridden for three years. When the royal stables were being restored, foremen had come to the refugee neighborhoods to hire laborers. Giannakos worked tearing down walls. He took the job because he was lonely. His life's companion, Despinyo, had died of grief.

"Don't be foolish, woman," he had told her, repeating the saying, "There's no way to mourn a slew of deaths."

But she had taken the calamity deeply to heart. Every morning she would take out Antonis's wedding suit, lay it on the bed, and collapse into sobs.

"How could they have killed you, my son? How could they have done it? How could they do that to you, my darling, my little soul?"

Crying from dawn to dusk sapped the mother's life; Despinyo died and Giannakos took work as a day laborer. A wall collapsed on his back, breaking his spine.

"They paralyzed you, father, for a bite of bread!" Panagiota's eyes darted with a rage that threatened to sear the whole world, but the thing they seared most was Asimakis's heart.

"Marry him, marry him, my daughter! He's one of us from the homeland. You know what they say: 'Take a shoe of your own, even though it may be patched.'"

"I'll take the dirty patched shoe, father," Panagiota said at the end of the summer, and everyone roared with laughter.

A great fuss broke out the evening after the wedding. Liapis was seen giving Lenaki, Kyra Penelope's daughter, a kiss, and her relatives took offense, raising an argument. Garoufalo, her husband and children, said it was uncivilized to behave that way over a little kiss. Theochtisti, wearing her fine new robes, said that the power of love brings reconciliation and Liapis should marry Lenaki. Nikolos, who had just arrived from foreign parts, laughed, saying the matter was trivial and not to be taken seriously. Constantis, dressed in his old monk's cassock and knurled by his struggle against his own nature, commented that there were many problems in the world to discuss. What happened this evening was not worth a moment's notice.

Watching Asimakis, Maryo's heart ached for the young man. She ached for Asimakis as she had when he was a very old man. Asimakis hesitantly pushed open the outside gate and threw hidden glances in Panagiota's direction. He seemed to be afraid, this man with medals for courage, broad shoulders, and handsome thin mustache. This man with a body that danced to life's tempo.

"How beautiful life is! What a beautiful bitch she is!" he had exclaimed to Maryo, even after passing the age of eighty.

He entered the yard, came up to the boy, and stroked his hair. The child looked up and smiled.

"You're late, you scum!" Panagiota barked. Her eyes were shooting sparks. "I've been waiting for you since three." She made a grimace of disgust. "And if he hadn't come at all, what would it have mattered," she thought.

Without a word of reply the man went into the kitchen. On the table he found a covered plate. The dish was cold—potatoes baked in tomato sauce. It was an unappetizing meal, and to be eaten alone, always alone! He shoved the plate away, spilling the sauce on the table cloth. He stepped into the yard, slamming the door.

"You can go to hell!" he yelled viciously.

"Go there yourself, and don't come back!" she answered.

Rising, she rushed to the gate to catch him there, so he would be sure to hear:

"Harlequin!" she taunted. "You harlequin!"

The child's face showed he was on the brink of tears. Panagiota took him in her arms.

"Don't fret, my little pasha," she told him tenderly, covering his face with kisses.

Panagiota's dearest friend, Anna appeared at the gate.

"I see that your man beat a hasty retreat," she commented. "Cheer up," she added. "Put on your nice dress. Let's go to the Zappeion for the Varieties."

With eager steps, smiles, and a thousand signs of delight, they took their little children by the hand and strolled to the city's center. In front of the Olympic Stadium they passed the ravine of a narrow old riverbed which marked the boundary of their neighborhood. On one side were the refugees, on the other the long-time residents of Athens, among whom were the hacks who wrote the cheap satirical songs. The catchy, malicious lyrics they wrote for the Variety shows set audiences roaring with laughter. Above all they laughed at the female impersonators who played women from Smyrni.

"Let people laugh; it does us no harm," Giannakos said repeatedly. "Greece was our haven—thank God. With no place to go our throats would have been slit. The Turks would have butchered us. Look what happened to the Armenians."

At the Zappeion audiences laughed till tears came to their eyes. The humor was endless, but one woman from Smyrni was offended. There in the Variety theater, by the refreshment stand, she rose to her feet and spoke out.

"What do you think you are, you stupid, dirty Athenians! You should see what we had in Smyrni! Our houses would put yours to shame!"

She went to sit down but was struck by another thought. Gesturing for emphasis she added:

"Why, you poor miserable beggars, we even had mirrors in the outhouse; we could see our asses on the can!"

The audience roared and bellowed with laughter. Dark flames shot from Panagiota's eyes.

"Let's get out of here!" she told Anna.

The two of them grabbed their children by the hands and dragged them out of the park.

When they crossed the ravine by the Stadium and reached their own territory, they took their children in their arms and proceeded.

"We did have a lot, didn't we, Panagiota?" Anna's voice was broken, sad. "We had not only homes and possessions, but fields and livestock!"

"We had as many fields as our hands could till and such harvests that we never rose hungry from the table." Panagiota's voice was firm and clear. "But what we had in greatest abundance was life itself. Life generously offered everything it had. What we have lived is not the stuff of silly songs and jests. And even the sympathy some people show is out of place. For we immersed ourselves in life itself, we broke its limits, we touched its essence. Life denied us nothing. It opened wide its wellsprings and saturated us to the bone."

They walked briskly, virtually running with their children in their arms. The veins in their legs were taut blue streams and their sweat beads, silver beads on foreheads and arms. They affectionately touched their children's faces and bare chests, pouring tenderness into their sweet bodies.

Darkness fell upon the refugee homes. The neighborhood grew silent. Maryo made herself comfortable on the stone ledge in her parents' yard. She lay on her side, curled up into a ball. Her thin legs, blackened by much travel, touched her chin. Wrapping her arms around her legs, she tucked in her head. She stayed in that position waiting.

Panagiota came into the yard with little Giorgaki in her arms. Entering the house, still holding the child, she lighted a lamp and placed it on the table. Maryo heard her bathing the child, feeding him, putting on his pajamas, and nestling him in the cradle:

Come, sweet sleep, take my boy-y-y-y-y
Rock and lull my tiny boy-y-y-y-y
Rock him here, rock him there-re-re-re
In the town and everywhere-re-re-r-re . . .

The sweet voice evoked the rustling of leaves in deep woods, and Maryo traveled; she traveled into memories of those times when Panagiota held her in her arms and rocked her. What a gentle breeze, that distant memory! Her eyelids closed and she felt herself sinking gently and softly. Sinking into sleep.

She was travelling way up high. Oh so high. She was riding a cloud and looking down. Splendid the globe, in colors dipped. The deep blue of the sea, the green of the foliage and that shy silver glinting on the leaves of olive trees. Red bands stood out, the color of newly ploughed earth. There ahead, very far below, the cosmos appeared. It spread out; it poured vastly and inclined; it inclined, dropping away below to return on the other side and come back to meet her, to unite with her and begin to turn once more from the beginning.

It took her breath away. Infinity frightened her. She lifted her hand and sought the tender warm hand of her husband. Together they set off on the journey upon a little white cloud they called their own. The surface where they walked was soft. Like deep snow before it hardens, it sucked in their legs and they sank; as if dancing in slow motion, they lifted their legs with infinite care, placing one foot ahead of the other.

Maryo was disturbed by sweet emotions. From there up high, she saw her life being traced. It was a straight line made with many colorful images. The scenes were like a reel of film that was being projected the moment a silence was falling. It fell like a bright river that enclosed everything. An explosion followed. A great explosion with no sound at all. Without breaking the silence. Everything was blown into the air like fireworks; the images of her life shot upward in bright red particles. Then they began to fall slowly, to fall and to dissolve, and Maryo was frightened, afraid that everything would be erased, would no longer exist as if it had never been. As if it never had come into being at all. She was seized by anguish; she trembled from head to foot, and holding on to her husband, she watched the particles continuing to fall, not dissolving, as if they were the small pieces of a child's puzzle falling beside one another, adhering, forming a colored image, an image which was circular.

A splendid circular image entered the pupils of her eyes. It flared for an instant and then went out. It went out before she had time to see it well, so as to put it into words. It vanished before she could say what it was. Some tints of color, only tints of color, remained in the pupils of her eyes.

The chamomile flower. The black-eyed Susan.
The velvet-petalled scarlet poppy.
The anemone rooted in the rocks.
The turtle bustling along, busily pulling her shell.
The snail laying down her slow silver trail.
And a child, a small naked child.

Asimakis walked slowly. With weary steps he approached the gate. He saw the faint light thrown by the lamp. It was turned down low. The sense of Panagiota washed over him; his love for her became a knot in his throat. He stepped into the yard and the aroma of flowers caressed him. The little yard was full of blooming flowers. The ledge of the garden wall was lined with pots of basil.

Inside the house his sight was filled with colors. Everywhere there were embroideries done by Panagiota. In the kitchen, by the table, there was a small bath trough filled with water, with a pail nearby for rinsing. His body began to tremble, his heart to overflow. He instantly began to undress, throwing his hat toward a chair. He missed and it landed upside down on the floor. He tossed off his jacket, trousers, shoes, underwear, and stepped into the trough. The water overflowed onto the kitchen floor and was greedily absorbed by the packed ground. Asimakis studiously soaped his body, rinsed off, dried himself, and thus naked approached the bed.

Panagiota was wearing her white nightgown, the bosom embroidered with flowerets. He gently lifted the sheet. The woman's body moved in response, turning face-up in the center of the bed. The woman opened. Her body was earth dampened by recent spring rain. Strong and tender the embrace of the man.

Maryo was jolted. She was jolted and began to shake. A hot dart pierced the cell containing her. Maryo, a tiny egg in velvet sheaths, broke open. The cell of life was liberated. It rushed to emerge but lodged in natural walls. It split. It broke with explosions and united with collisions. With pain and striving Maryo took shape; her body became. She became within the strong elastic cave of her mother's womb.

Time, a cloudy galloping white horse, fashioned her body and when time had finished, when it completed shaping her, a tender breeze arose.

A single breath blew and created her soul.

Glossary

Aghios Panteleimonas: Saint's name suggesting "the all-pitying one."

Aghia Skepi: The name of this convent suggests protection ('a holy roof')

Agni: the name suggests purity.

Anastenarides: an actual group of religious fire-walkers whose name suggests the word *sigh*.

amanes: a type of melancholy Turkish song adopted by the Greeks of Asia Minor.

askousoum: Turkish word meaning bravo.

Asimakis: The name recalls the word for silver.

barba: colloquial for *uncle*.

Chesme: Asia Minor port opposite the island of Chios.

December demonstrations: The government's response to political demonstrations was a factor in bringing on the Greek Civil War, 1945-49.

Despinyo: variation of the name Despina, which refers to the Virgin Mary; cf. *despozo* (to reign)

Erotokritos and Aretousa: hero and heroine of the Cretan epic poem of the 16th century.

Garoufalia and Vasiliko: carnation and basil; also suggestive of personal names.

Giagia: prounounced ya-ya; grandmother.

hanoumissa: harem girl.

kale: my good man/woman.

kori mou: my daughter.

koumbaros: best man.

kyr/kyra: colloquial for mr./ms.

Liapis: nickname for Elias.

lyra: a small Cretan stringed instrument.

madamoisellitses: formation of a Greek diminutive plural with the French word.

magali: a bucket of coals used for heating a room.

Malama: the name susggests *golden*.

mana: mother.

Maryo: Mar-YO; variation of the name Maria.

mori: Mor-EE; a term that can be used either derisively or affectionately.

moudi: the family's word for verandah.

mouja: a gesture of derision, considered crude, often accompanied by the syllable *na*.

mouse oil: new-born mice are preserved in oil which is used as a cure-all.

nostos: Homeric word referring to longing for home; cf. *nostalgia*.

Panagiota: the name refers to the Virgin Mary, the *Panagia,* 'the all-holy one'.

Pantocrator: the almighty.

papou: grandfather.

Phtychaki or Phtychio: nickname for Ephtychia, meaning happiness.

"Praise for the sea, who shall say"; from *The Builders* by Giorgos Heimonas.

polis: city. 'The polis' refers to Constantinopolis; the Turkish, Istanbul, derives from the Greek, '*eis tin polis*' (in or to the city).

Sideris: The name refers to *sidero* (steel).

Theochisti: The name means "formed by God."

Tsetes: The *Tsetes* were particularly savage irregular Turkish troops.

Vardaris: the north wind.

yeh mou: my son.

The Author and the Translator

Despina Lala-Crist was born in Athens of parents who were refugees from Asia Minor. She came to the United States to study literature, history and psychology (at the University of Charleston, West Virgina), married her college teacher, Robert Crist, became the mother of two children, and for two decades has been engaged in writing children's stories, fiction and criticism.

"My life has been deeply rewarding. From early childhood, my memories have been filled with human striving and passion. As evening descended on our neighborhood of little houses built by refugees from Asia Minor, I would be awed by stories of life in the home country on the Anatolian coast—endless tales, imaginary and real, charged with the directness of history and the vitality of the spoken word. With the coming of war and occupation of Athens, life in our needy neighborhood was further burdened by starvation and terror, but the courage and bonding of my people were profoundly inspiring.

College study in the United States was my realized post-war dream. Entranced by immersion in the insights and magic of literature and psychology, advanced studies took us to the University of Chicago during the years of quest and learning in the 1960's. Our two children further expanded our world, as did teaching in Elizabeth, New Jersey, where my black students (all girls) gave me more than I could ever learn from books.

As teachers and writers (Robert is on the faculty of literature and literary translation at the University of Athens) going to and fro our Greek and American homes, we have experienced the countless joys of two cultures. The fecundity of human feelings, the divine magic of existence, is the fabric of our life and work, as expressed in Nostos and—it is hoped—in the translation."